DARK MOON WALKING

A DAN CONNOR MYSTERY

DARK MOON
Walking

R.J. McMILLEN

TouchWood
Editions

TouchWood Editions
touchwoodeditions.com

LIBRARY AND ARCHIVES CANADA CATALOGUING IN PUBLICATION
McMillen, R.J., 1945–, author
Dark moon walking / R.J. McMillen.

(A Dan Connor mystery)
Issued in print and electronic formats.
ISBN 978-1-77151-066-0

I. Title.

PS8625.M56D37 2014   C813'.6   C2013-905985-7

Editor: Linda Richards
Proofreader: Vivian Sinclair
Design: Pete Kohut
Cover image: Kayak: plherrera, istockphoto.com

 Canadian Patrimoine Heritage canadien Canada Council Conseil des Arts for the Arts du Canada BRITISH COLUMBIA ARTS COUNCIL

We gratefully acknowledge the financial support for our publishing activities
from the Government of Canada through the Canada Book Fund, Canada
Council for the Arts, and the province of British Columbia through the
British Columbia Arts Council and the Book Publishing Tax Credit.

The interior pages of this book have been printed on 30% post-consumer
recycled paper, processed chlorine free, and printed with vegetable-based inks.

1 2 3 4 5 18 17 16 15 14

PRINTED IN CANADA

For Bud.

► ONE ◄

► He didn't know what woke him, but it might not have been much. Sleep no longer came easily to Dan Connor. It was over a year since he had lost Susan and still he found himself waking in the night, listening for the quiet sound of her breathing. Sometimes it was just the weight of the silence that disturbed his nights, the overwhelming sense of *absence*. But not this time. This had been something external: a sound, a movement too gentle to intrude upon his consciousness but enough to alert senses minutely attuned to wind and weather and ocean. Something.

The boat rocked gently as he pushed open the hatch and climbed onto the deck. A fine rain filled the air with mist and clung to the dark branches of the trees. Wind riffs chased across the water and above the shore, while cedars shivered against the night sky. Dan's eyes carefully scanned the shadows, measuring the angles and distance from shore, making sure that *Dreamspeaker* had not dragged her anchor.

Dan was a big man, maybe two inches over six feet tall, with a solid frame and the deceptively lean body of a martial arts practitioner. Sun and sea had turned dark hair light and light skin dark. The job had added a narrow scar that slanted down across his cheek. Loss had added the lines around his eyes and mouth.

He moved forward along the deck, bare feet silent on the damp wood, and ran his fingers along the anchor rope as it curved over the drum of the winch and ran out to the bow roller. It was smooth and taut, and he could feel the faint vibration made by the anchor chain as it moved gently over the gravel bottom. Above him, the masthead light burned steadily. He leaned over the railing and looked astern to check on the dinghy. It floated quietly at the end of its line, bobbing a few feet off the stern.

A sudden gust of wind, this one stronger than the others, swung the boat toward the shore and Dan straightened, glancing up at the sky. It was September, still a little early for the violent winds that came raging down the mountains with the winter and gave Storm Bay its name, but perhaps it was time to think about moving. He wondered if that was what had wakened him. In his sixteen years on the police force, he had learned to listen to his intuitions. If he had been back in Victoria, over four hundred miles to the south, he would have gone on instant alert, checking and rechecking everything and everybody around him to identify what had attracted his attention. But here? Here, except for the ruins of the old Namu cannery, there were only trees and water.

He gave a slight nod, the movement dislodging the moisture that clung to his hair and sending a chill down his back. It was time to go. He would spend the remaining hours before dawn plotting a slow course back down south. He was ready for the familiar noise and bustle of the city, and the reality was that no matter how much he had gained in terms of self-acceptance and quietude of soul these last few months aboard the boat, winter would be more enjoyable with the comforts of the marina.

Truth be told, he was looking forward to being back in civilization. Just thinking about catching up with Mike and the guys from the squad brought a smile to his face. Amazing what four months alone on the ocean could do. He had barely spoken a word to them in the weeks and months before he left, and here he was, eager to see them all again. He could already imagine the yarns they would have to tell him, full of cynicism and the black humor that came with the job.

He slid the hatch back and felt a wave of warm, dry air rising out of the cabin. As he stepped over the sill onto the steep steps of the companionway, he froze, heart racing and adrenalin surging as a piercing scream reverberated through the night. Seconds later it was joined by another, and Dan cautiously exhaled. Mink. The damn things were everywhere, searching the rocky shoreline, fighting for food and for territory. That was one of the few things he wouldn't miss.

He leaned on the hatch, allowing his eyes to lazily follow the track of the moon on the water out toward the open ocean. Suddenly his gaze sharpened. Out beyond the rocky cliffs of the headland, the pattern of waves changed. The random movement of the water stirred up by the restless gusts had taken on a smooth herringbone shape that was unmistakable. It was a wake. Sometime in the last few minutes a boat had passed. It should have been clearly visible, its running lights demanding his attention, yet he had not seen it. Even more disturbing, he had not heard it. With a wake of that size, it had to be a large vessel traveling at a high rate of speed, yet he had been totally unaware of its presence.

Frowning, Dan slid quietly down the companionway and sat at the navigation station. Beside him the radio sat silent, a glowing red light confirming that it was set to receive. He reached out and turned the volume up, but he heard only static. He turned on the radar, knowing it was too late for it to show the passing vessel but wanting to confirm the familiar contours of the bay.

He wasn't sure why he felt so uneasy. Even at this time of the year, there were occasionally other boats. Perhaps it was a fishboat, although the season had ended long ago and they seldom moved at night. But why would anyone be running dark? And he was sure the vessel had been dark: he would have seen the lights otherwise. Even more puzzling was why he had heard no engine sound. A quirk of the wind? It seemed unlikely, as there were no whitecaps, no sign of any disturbance on the water except for that arrowing wake.

Another burst of static from the radio interrupted his thoughts and he strained to hear. Reception was poor in Storm Bay, the steep mountains and high cliffs blocking most of the signals, but the night often improved it. He could faintly hear a voice. It wasn't clear enough to make out the meaning, but one word was unmistakable. "*Dreamspeaker.*"

▶ His name was Walker. It was not the name his mother had given him, but it was the only one he answered to now. Early on in his career on the streets, they had called him "Ghost." It had suited his talent for slipping in and out of buildings unseen and unheard. Later, some wit had added "Walker" in a nod to his Native ancestry. It had amused him for a while. Ghost Walker. Like a character in a book one of his several stepfathers had liked to read. Finally, like him, the name had gotten pared down. Now it was just Walker, although it no longer suited him. Not since he had fallen from a roof after a robbery went wrong and broken both legs so badly that the doctors told him he might never walk again. Not since he had spent over three months on the physio ward, forcing protesting muscles to move, willing stiff joints to bend, and fighting the urge to scream. Not since he had spent three long years in jail. Now he spent most of his time on the water, paddling through the narrow channels that his ancestors had called home. Odd how priorities could change.

Other things were changing too. He had never had much time for people, knowing only too well the pain they could inflict. Even as a child, he had preferred to keep himself aloof, learning early that the less he was noticed, the fewer beatings he would receive. Now he found himself dropping in more often to check on the few folks who had found their way to this remote tangle of islands and rocks and bays that clung to the rugged central coast of British Columbia.

Oddballs and loners for the most part, but good company all the same. He had even paddled over to the old lodge on Spider Island a couple of times in the last month just to make sure the girl was okay.

He shook his head as he thought of it. Didn't seem right to leave a young girl alone all summer, a city girl at that, but she seemed happy enough, filling up a stack of notebooks with stuff about kelp and sea otters and herring roe and who knows what else.

He glanced up at the sky, checking the time by the height of the sun. He could use the last of the ebb to reach the bay, see if the girl was still there, and then catch the flood to take him home well before dark. She would want to know about the otters he had found, and if he was honest with himself, he would appreciate the company.

He pushed aside the dark hemlock branches that drooped down over the water and let the canoe slide gently out into the current. Summer was almost over, and despite the fact that it was barely past noon, it was dim and cool here on the lee of the island. The falling tide had exposed a patch of jagged black rocks, and Walker deftly steered out past them into deeper water. The sharp smell of iodine assaulted his nostrils as his paddle caught in a mass of undulating seaweed and then the slender boat picked up speed as it moved out into the channel.

By two o'clock he had covered more than nine miles and Shoal Bay slowly opened up in front of him. It formed an almost perfect circle, its shore fringed with a sloping gravel beach. The land rose steeply at each of the points and then dipped down to form a wide valley in the center, where the trees had been cleared to make an open meadow. In the middle of the meadow sat the lodge, an old wooden building with graying walls, empty doorways, and windows that stared blindly out over a rickety deck. Years ago, it had welcomed fishermen and miners and, occasionally, an adventurous sailor returning from a voyage to some remote inlet, but it had been abandoned long ago.

A narrow, weed-strewn path led from the deck down to a wharf. Blackened pilings, each clothed with orange sea anemones and purple sea stars, marched in a gentle curve out into the deep water at the center of the bay. A metal ladder attached to the end of the wharf led down to a float where an old wooden fishboat bobbed gently alongside. The words *Island Girl* were stenciled across her flat stern in faded and peeling yellow paint. The drum and net that had once hung there had been replaced with two davits that now held a bright-blue dinghy, and the cabin had been extended aft to make a small salon. A tattered flag fluttered lazily from the masthead, and Walker could see in through an open door to the empty wheelhouse. No smoke came from the stack, and the deck chair that sat out on the float surrounded by crab and shrimp traps was unoccupied. The only sign of life was an occasional burst of static and the oddly distorted cadence of a voice emanating from a marine radio.

Walker maneuvered the canoe up to the float, wrapped a line around the rail that ran along its edge, and used his arms and torso to pull himself up. On the water, in the boat, he looked to be a big and powerful man in his mid- to late thirties, his arms and shoulders wide, his brown skin smooth and taut over healthy muscle, his body moving easily as he pushed through the water. On the shore, he aged ten years and lost several inches. His body bent and twisted to one side as his damaged legs worked to balance his weight, and he dragged one foot at an odd angle. Pain sharpened his features and gave his dark eyes a hard, flat stare that made those few people who hadn't already turned away, either from his ancestry or his injury, suddenly drop their gaze in discomfort.

But not the girl. That had surprised him when he'd first met her. She was not a refugee from society like the other outcasts and misfits hidden in the coves and beaches of these remote islands: old Toothless Tom, who shared his tiny cabin with his "voices"; Big Annie with her rusty old boat full of cats and her harsh screams; Frankie Magee, who would curse you one minute and start crying the next. She was simply a girl doing a job, conducting research for some government agency.

She was young, maybe late twenties or early thirties, and her name was Claire. She had offered that up to him along with a strong handshake and a wide smile of greeting that had not wavered for a second as he lifted himself out of the canoe and hobbled awkwardly toward her. He found himself smiling as he thought of it. That greeting had been a gift, completely unexpected, and it had somehow established a tenuous link with a world he had thought closed to him forever.

He knew that Claire would hear him long before he reached the boat; it would be impossible for her not to, considering the racket he was making dragging himself along the wooden float. When he saw her appear on deck, he realized that she had been working down in the hold. He could see pieces of some kind of packing material sticking out of her straight, blond hair and her cheeks were smudged with dirt. She was dressed in a pair of faded blue jeans and a too-large flannel shirt that hung almost to her knees, and she was holding a coil of bright-yellow nylon rope.

"Walker! What a lovely surprise." Her smile of pleasure both warmed and welcomed him. "Want some coffee?" She didn't wait for an answer. "Hang on. I'll go and get it. Why don't you sit down?"

She dropped the rope back into the hold, pointed to a large wooden crate that sat on the float, and disappeared into the cabin. A minute later she was back, carrying two large, steaming mugs, which she placed carefully on the cap rail before jumping down to join him.

"Your timing is perfect." She grinned at him as she kicked a crab trap out of the way and dragged over the deck chair. "It's fresh. I just made it."

An easy silence fell and as Walker sipped his coffee he noted with pleasure that she had remembered his preference for sugar.

"I didn't expect to see you for another week or two," she said. "I was talking to Annie yesterday and she said you had gone out to Labouchere to fish."

He nodded agreement. "Yeah. I planned on doing that, but I caught a bunch of pinks off Owl Island so I came back in to smoke them."

It was a long speech for him. He had always been a man of few words and his isolated life had reduced them further. He lifted his face to sniff the breeze. "Wind is changing. Gonna rain soon." He looked back along the wharf, frowning a little. "Where's the kayak?" he asked.

She smiled and tilted her head toward the fishboat. The kayak had been the subject of their only disagreement. Walker had been horrified when he found her paddling home one night just after dark. She had appeared both amused and charmed by his paternal concern and had made light of it, but he had been deadly serious. He loved the ocean in all its moods, but he never took it lightly. The abrupt lecture he had given her spoke volumes about the depth of his knowledge of tides, currents, and weather and was more than he would ever have shared in regular conversation.

"It's up on the deck," she said. "I wanted to get a coat of epoxy on it before I grind the bottom off completely, hauling it up on these beaches. I won't be needing it for the next week or so anyway. My boss is coming up. He'll probably want to go up to the big pass, so we can use his boat. Or take the dinghy."

He nodded, relieved that she wouldn't be using the kayak. Like his canoe, it was safe and reliable in skilled hands, but, also like the canoe, it did not leave much room for error. He was perfectly comfortable taking his own risks, but he did not like the thought of Claire out alone on the ocean. Seemed crazy when he thought about it: worrying about some white girl he barely knew, but there it was. He shook his head. Must be getting old.

"Better take your camera and lots of notebooks too." His face twisted into a rare smile as he saw quick understanding brighten her eyes. "Saw maybe three, four families of otters there last week. Couple of young ones and a baby," he continued.

"Really!" There was no mistaking her excitement.

She jumped up and started for the boat, glancing back at him as she climbed over the coaming and onto the deck. "If I get the chart, can you show me exactly where you saw them?"

▶ The sun slipping behind the trees, throwing the float into shadow, finally broke up their afternoon. Walker scanned the sky before looking down at the water lapping against the float. Huge clouds massing to the west had taken on an ominous purple hue that foretold a storm. The current had changed a good two hours ago, and it was starting to flood hard. He found it difficult to believe how quickly time could pass talking about nothing, but it was definitely time to leave.

He twisted slowly to his feet. "Gotta go," he said. "The currents are running pretty strong right now. It'll be full moon in a couple of days."

She nodded and rose to walk with him down the float, waiting comfortably while he maneuvered his body awkwardly down onto the wooden boards and then into the restless canoe. It wasn't until he had let go of the tie-up line and pushed off that he remembered. He dug his paddle into the water and turned the bow back toward her.

"Did you see a big fancy boat anywhere round here in the last few days?" he asked. "Maybe seventy, eighty feet and all black. Black plastic and smoked glass."

"Black? Sure it's not a tug or something?"

He smiled. "It's no workboat. All sleek and shiny—and quiet."

She shook her head. "Nope. It's been really quiet here. Not even a fishboat. Why?"

He shrugged, twisting his paddle in the water to keep the canoe steady. "No reason. Just seemed strange." He gazed out across the water, remembering the odd feeling of unease he had felt when he had seen it. "Couldn't see anybody on it. No lights. No noise. Nothing."

His paddle swept backward in a strong, smooth sweep that sent the tiny boat surging ahead and he raised his arm in a brief salute.

"Who knows? Gonna blow hard tonight. Be safe."

She waved an acknowledgment and started back along the dock. From the look of the sky, the storm was building fast.

▶   It arrived just after midnight, sweeping in from the west and covering the islands and inlets and fjords and bays with a black curtain of rain. On the ocean, it whipped the waves into a frenzy of foam. On the shore, the trees writhed and twisted and the rich, petrichor scent of wet earth gradually replaced the sharp smell of ozone that accompanied the lightning. Above it all, the thunder rolled and boomed and the wind screamed in a fierce and awful symphony.

In a tiny cove, both protected and hidden by an offshore islet of jagged rock and stunted trees, Walker sat quietly inside his cabin. Earlier, he had built a small cooking fire and now he lit a woven rope of sweetgrass and wild sage. He waved the twisting spiral of smoke over his body and inhaled the aromatic scent. The rain was a welcome gift. It would nourish the earth and fill the creek, and its rhythm echoed with the pulse of his blood. He closed his eyes and joined his voice to its steady beat. The power of his chant filled the air around him.

It was hours later when his drifting spirit was recalled by a disturbance he could not identify. He stood up and moved to the open door, looking out toward the ocean. There was something out there that he could not identify but it felt . . . wrong. Perhaps even evil. A shiver ran down his spine and he turned back to the fire, closing the door behind him.

▶ THREE ◀

▶ The rising sound of the wind and the increasing slap of waves against the hull woke Claire from a restless sleep and drew her up to the wheelhouse of *Island Girl*. The barometer had fallen sharply and the wind was already gusting to thirty knots. She knew that if it kept veering, she'd be in for a rough night. For a moment she listened to the creak and groan of the hull as the timbers worked and strained, sensing the movement as the boat bucked against the lines that held her to the float.

She had her father to thank for both her boating knowledge and her sea sense. He had instilled in her the lore of the ocean as he steered his fishboat from one school of salmon to the next, holding her in front of him at the wheel, telling her stories, passing on his love of the sea as he hauled the net. By the time she started university, the rhythms and moods of the ocean had become almost second nature. Sea temperature, the movement of fish, wave patterns, tides, weather, navigation—it had all seeped into her pores over the years so that even now, after a degree in marine biology and two years of mostly desk work at the Pacific Maritime Research Centre, she couldn't imagine being far away from the water for long. Like the sea life she studied, she needed it to live.

She should have known that earlier. Much earlier. Before she met Garrett. Before she let herself fall in love with him and follow him first to Ottawa and then to Dallas as his career blossomed and hers languished. Before she had wasted three years of her life trying to force herself into a mold that she could never fit. Before her discomfort and frustration and misery drove her to ask him for a divorce.

She should have known long before she married him, when he first started hinting that she sell her boat. And maybe somewhere deep down she had, because the boat was the one thing she had held on to.

She had her father to thank for the boat too. *Island Girl* had been the last boat her father had owned and his final gift to her. She had moved aboard when she returned from Dallas, finding solace in the familiar spaces and routines, letting herself be soothed by the chuckle of water past the hull. Even when she decided to return to university, she stayed aboard, commuting from marina to campus by kayak whenever the weather allowed, hauling the sleek little vessel across the wide expanse of sand that hugged the base of the cliffs at Point Grey, below the sprawling campus of the University of British Columbia. She quickly came to know most of the students, food vendors, palm readers, and psychics who hung out there and was secure in the knowledge that she could leave the boat under their watchful eyes while she climbed the four hundred and seventy-three steps that led up to the university and her classes.

A peal of thunder pulled her back to the present and she quickly shrugged on her rain gear and stepped out onto the deck. Braced against the storm, she worked her way carefully along the cap rail, testing knots for tightness, checking cleats and gunwales for roughness, sliding her fingers down each line to check for wear. The rain worked its way past the collar of her raincoat to trickle in a cold stream down her neck, but she ignored it, intent on the task at hand. When she had satisfied herself that everything was in good shape, she stepped down onto the dock and repeated the process there.

She was almost finished when some sound, some change in the timbre of the wind, some alteration in the pattern of the waves, disrupted her concentration. It was so faint, she was not sure she had heard it. She strained her senses to locate the source, but there was only the wind and the rain.

The next two mornings brought more of the same weather, although the color of the sea and sky slowly changed from black to gray: heaving gray sea, brooding gray sky, and a sinuous curtain of silver-gray rain. The wind howled from the southeast, knocking the tops off the waves and hurling the spray into streaks of white foam.

It took three days for the storm to ease enough to reveal the familiar contours of the land. By noon on the third day, the rain had become a fine mist and a pale sun appeared. The forest was wet and dripping, the leaves shining with a metallic glint as they flickered in the wind, the green of the undergrowth newly bright. Overhead, small white gulls wheeled in the sky, screaming a challenge to the elements.

Claire pulled on a jacket and stepped out onto the deck, glad to be able to get outside and stretch her legs. She flexed her shoulders and inhaled the clean rain-washed air as she took in the sparkling world that surrounded her. Jumping down to the float, she checked the lines that tethered *Island Girl*. Three days of twisting and pulling had done little damage, but she retied them anyway, sliding protective sections of rubber hose into place where the rope passed over the scuppers. Satisfied that all was well, she wandered slowly up the wharf and followed the path to the old lodge.

Close beside it, just past the edge of the meadow and running right across the island from Shoal Bay in the north to an unnamed rocky indentation on the southern shore, was a shallow depression. Although dry most of the time, for a few days each month when the moon was near full, the tides rose high enough to fill it with water, turning it into a channel that cut the island in two. Little more than knee-deep, it was perfect for the kayak and she had used it several times for easy access to the waters lying south of Spider Island and the protected reefs and outcroppings that could be found there. Right now, with both the full moon and the storm surge working together, the channel was deeper than she had ever seen it.

She glanced up at the sun. There was plenty of daylight left and the other side of the island would be protected from the wind. Even if she didn't make it back before the sea retreated and turned the channel back to a dry gulley, she could leave the kayak pulled up into the rocks on the south shore and go back for it the next day.

It was midafternoon when Claire emerged on the other side of Spider Island. Without the wind, the day was pleasantly warm and she lost track of time as she paddled through schools of darting silver herring. Although she would have liked to spend the entire afternoon doing nothing else but drifting with the current, neither her conscience nor habits ingrained by both her father and years of study and research would let her. She had already lost three days to the storm. She couldn't afford to waste another one if she was to fulfill the terms of her contract. Easing the kayak up to one of the shallower reefs, she peered down through the clear water at the spiny red urchins and sunflower sea stars that clustered in the dark crevices of the rocks. Soon she had her sampling net out and was filling her notebook with detailed notes.

Daylight was fading and the tide had ebbed by the time she got back to shore. Since the channel had long since reverted to a dry gully, she dragged the kayak high up into the rocks and tied it securely to a tree. The tides would stay high for at least a couple of days. Tomorrow or the day after, she would return and paddle it back. She was returning later than she had planned, but the clouds had cleared and the moon was already up, bright and full, lighting her way. It would be an easy walk back to the lodge. In a couple of hours, she would be back on board *Island Girl*.

▶ The smell of cigarette smoke stopped her as she emerged from the forest and started into the meadow. That and the creak of a board as someone moved on the deck of the old lodge. It was so completely out of place, so unexpected, that she froze in place before instinct made her step back into the trees, where the darkness was suddenly comforting. Her eyes scanned the moonlit clearing ahead of her and roamed the familiar shape of the bay, searching for some explanation. She found it as they reached the dock: an unfamiliar and ghostly shape loomed up into the night sky, dwarfing *Island Girl*.

She could just make out the outline of a large yacht, but it was like looking at a negative image instead of a print: the hull was so dark it merged into the night, a deeper shade of black. Two radar antennae were mounted high above the bridge, moonlight glinting off the turning arms, and a dim trail of bubbles foamed at the stern where an exhaust was disturbing the water, but there were no other signs of life. Only the moon, reflecting off the black hull, gave the vessel form and definition.

Looking at it, Claire recalled Walker's question. This had to be the boat he had asked about, and his description was apt. It was strange. Eerily so, although she couldn't pinpoint exactly why.

Shrugging off her initial shock, she mentally chided herself for letting her foolish imagination run away with her. It was the darkness that made the yacht seem strange, its black hull melting into the night. That and the surprise of finding it there so unexpectedly. And of course whoever it was on the deck of the lodge had to have come from the ship. She herself often wandered up in the evening to sit and look out at the bay glittering under the dark canopy of stars. It was only natural that others would too. She would go and introduce herself. It would be nice to spend an evening in conversation after a summer of relative isolation, maybe share a coffee.

As she started forward, the deck boards creaked again and she heard what sounded like a chair scraping against wood. Then a harsh voice pierced the night, the words carrying clearly on the cool air. "She ain't coming back tonight. It's too late."

The voice hung there, alien and surreal, floating on the night air. Once again Claire found herself inching back into the shadows of the forest. A chill of fear shivered across her skin and crept down her spine. Her pulse raced and she felt her hands clench into claws. She dug her fingernails into her thighs as she crouched, waiting to hear some response. But there was only the thundering of her heart and a silence that hung heavily over everything. That too seemed wrong. There must be at least two people there. And who were they talking about? Her? Surely not. They didn't know her.

Movement caught her eye, and a dim figure appeared at the edge of the deck. Even in the darkness, she could see that it was a man. He was tall and slim, but she couldn't make out any details except for his hair. It was cut very short and it was so white, it caught the moonlight and glowed against the black sky. He stood there for a moment before slowly turning toward where she stood, hidden in the trees. As he moved, the same moonlight glinted off the metallic object he cradled in his arms, and a surge of fear stole her breath. It was unmistakably a rifle.

Time slowed to a standstill. She could hear the sound of her heart beating so loudly she was sure the man would hear it. A minute or maybe a lifetime later, the reply she had been waiting for reached her.

"Fernandez does not like loose ends. He said to make sure she can't talk and that's what we're going to do."

She didn't know how long she stood frozen in the shadows, but gradually the awareness that she had to move seeped into her consciousness. Slowly, placing each foot with exquisite care, she inched backward farther into the darkness of the trees. When the lodge was no longer visible and she was completely enveloped by the forest, she turned and crept back along the trail toward her kayak. It had been a pleasant, joyful walk on the previous occasions she had used it. It had seemed so easy and welcoming, but now it became the most difficult journey of her life.

An owl swept overhead, its outstretched wings pale and silent in the gloom, and she covered her mouth and fought back a scream as she cowered under a tree. The normal sounds of the night, familiar sounds she had heard over and over again since childhood—the quiet rustling of leaves, the scurry of small animals chasing through the leaf litter, the click of branches swaying in the night breeze, the whisper of roosting birds—all brought fear and terrified her. Her heart raced and her breathing seemed unnaturally loud. Brush tore at her clothes as she passed. Twice she tripped over unseen roots. Returning to the kayak took most of the night.

By the time she emerged again on the other side of the island, the first glimmer of dawn lay on the water, touching the waves with a faint gilding of gold. The start of a new day. Normally she found it exhilarating, but today it only added to her fear as she felt the cloak of darkness slip away. Exhausted, her body cold and clammy and aching with every step, she clambered awkwardly up the rocks and slid into the familiar confines of the kayak. She was dirty and tired, so tired that she could no longer think straight. She needed to rest. Slowly her head dropped forward onto the paddle that lay across the cockpit coaming in front of her.

► F O U R ◄

► Walker used the storm as a gift. He rose early, stripped off his shorts, and hobbled outside into the rain. The heavy drops stung his shoulders, forming rivulets that ran down his body and pooled at his feet. Normally he bathed in the creek, but this was different; a cleansing rather than a cleaning. It cleared and focused his mind, made him feel more alive. It joined him with the creatures and spirits that inhabited the land with him. It heightened his senses and calmed his soul. Allowed him to hear the voice of *Dzunukwa*, the wild woman of the forest, carried on the wind that moaned through the cedars.

He spread his arms and tilted his face up to the sky, relishing a feeling of well-being. For perhaps the first time in his life, he felt at peace with himself. This was not an easy life, but it was a good one and it suited him just fine.

The people had embraced him when he returned to his village. They knew his story, had seen it played out a thousand times as the legacy of loss created by the white man spread its diseased tendrils through the nations and tribes and clans. They had mourned his pain and celebrated his spirit. The elders taught him well. They shared their knowledge, gave him back his name and his clan, taught him new skills, honored his being, gave wings to new dreams. But it still wasn't enough. He needed a purpose, a place, a role to play in life.

He was helping two of his uncles shape a canoe, carefully adzing the wood to tease the boat out of the tree, when he'd first met Percy.

Percy had been his salvation. Percy, with his simple philosophy and deceptively complex program, had taught him how to live again.

Breathing deep, Walker shook the rain from his hair and headed back to his cabin. He would spend the next few days doing chores: sort and store his food cache, make new fishing gear, repair the net he had made from strips of cedar bark. Then, when the storm had cleared, he would head out again in search of the fish that would see him through the winter.

The salmon that graced the crest of his clan, his *'na'mima*, had always been generous and gave themselves to him freely. Perhaps he would take some back to the village, give some to his grandmother and to old Joe. He hadn't been back since spring, and it would be good to see his people again. He could stop off at Percy's camp on the way. It would take him several days and more to get back, and the storms were already starting. He would need to go soon.

Two days later, shortly after sunrise, with both the wind and the rain still slanting noisily into the cove, Walker lifted his head from the net he was working on. He was not sure, but he thought he had heard a new sound. Not quite a sound, but more a change in the tone of the storm. He closed his eyes and reached his senses out into the swirling air, but nothing reverberated. Still, he thought there had been something.

He pushed open the door and walked outside, but there was only the steady hiss of the rain as it beat on the saturated ground, the angry howl of the wind in the trees, and the roar of the waves crashing on the rocks. He would have to wait till it cleared to load his gear into the canoe, and he could not launch until the water had calmed, but he was filled with a sudden sense of urgency. He had heard two ravens call at dawn and it had sounded like a message.

The cabin was a sanctuary of warmth and quiet, filled with the smell of cedar. Walker picked up the net from where he had dropped it on the floor and spread it out over his knees. Maybe it was nothing. Two days spent in the gloom of the cabin, surrounded by the noise of the storm, was enough to make anyone restless.

It was to be yet another day before the waves diminished and the storm surge released its grip on the cove, but by the morning of the fourth day he was out on the water before the sun had risen.

▶ The boat hung suspended between sea and sky, the gray wood of the hull blending with the silver surface of the ocean and the soft gray gleam of morning light. She lay tilted on her side, the starboard rail and part of the cabin underwater. An eerie silence wrapped the bay. The morning chatter of birds, the soft rise of fish, the gentle drone of insects, even the sound of dew dripping from the branches, was stilled.

Walker edged the canoe closer to the wreck, sliding slowly past the bow. The knot in his gut grew tighter as he approached the stern. He already knew what he was going to see. Over the past few days, he had experienced a growing sense of unease. He had felt it first when he saw the black ship, but he had dismissed it as some lingering association with his old world. It had returned during the storm, when he had sensed rather than heard or seen some disturbance. He had dismissed that too. He should have known better. If he had learned anything out here, it was to trust his instincts.

The canoe bumped gently against the curve of the hull, and he reached out a hand to touch it. It looked undamaged, although that made no sense. If it had run aground in the storm, it would have hit the rocky bottom many times before coming to rest. Even if it had settled farther out and been lifted in by the tide, it should show the scars of its passage.

Slowly, heart pounding, he drifted toward the stern. The name was partially submerged, but it didn't matter. The letters were clearly visible. In faded yellow paint they spelled out the words *Island Girl*.

As the tide fell, Walker slid out of the canoe and worked his way around the hull, half swimming and half walking. He ignored the cold that puckered his skin and sent stabbing shafts of pain down his legs. He peered in portholes and checked fittings. He saw that the kettle had fallen off the stove and was floating in the water that covered the cabin sole. It was the only thing out of place. The switches on the electronics panel were all off. The anchor was winched tight to the bow, with the brake set. The life buoy was clamped firmly in its fitting.

None of it made sense. Claire would have had the engine running and the switches on if she had been fighting the storm. And if she was losing the battle, she would have tried to anchor. Unless she had not been aboard and the boat had come adrift from the dock. He glanced down to where the mooring lines floated in the water, undulating like seaweed in the waves. Maybe that was it. But where was the dinghy? And the kayak?

He pushed the canoe to shore, slipped behind a fringe of branches, and slid up on the rocky beach. He needed time to think, to absorb whatever information the boat could give him. As he clambered out over the rocks, one of his questions was quickly answered. Behind a mound of jumbled logs and flotsam, a small, bright-blue boat lay wedged tightly under an overhang, a gaping hole in its bottom. He had found the dinghy. Claire was not in it.

Much later, he let the canoe drift back out into the current and turned it toward the pass. He would take the long route to Shoal Bay. It would take him past the coves where Claire and *Island Girl* might have been seen if she had headed up to the big pass. It would also let him arrive after dark, and some instinct told him that might be a good thing.

By dusk he had covered more than twenty miles. He was tired and hungry, even though Annie had shared her meal of oysters with him when he had stopped to talk to her, and Old Tom had given him a handful of dried berries. He had told them that Claire was missing but not that he had found her boat. He didn't know why he had withheld that information. At first he told himself that he didn't want to frighten them. There was truth in that, but it wasn't the whole reason. That was something more personal. More raw. His grandmother would have said that his spirit was linked with Claire's. That perhaps held more truth, although he did not understand how that could be.

He had never really believed in the world of totems and spirits he had been born into, never called on the powers his membership in the Salmon and Raven clans gave him. Yet he knew the meaning that that world held for his people. Knew the beliefs that sustained them. He had seen the ceremonies, heard the stories, even danced the dances, but he had been too cynical, too hungry, too restless to listen. Now he wished he had. Now he wished he could turn into a raven and fly.

None of the water folk had seen anything of Claire, but he knew they would search for her. He had wanted to warn them to be careful but didn't know how to put into words what was only a gut feeling. Instead, he pointed them north and east, reserving the southwest for himself. There was something happening that had nothing to do with the storm. He could feel it. It was man-made and it was evil and somehow it involved the black ship.

Long after the sun had set he rounded the point of Benjamin Island, across the channel from Shoal Bay. He kept close to shore, steering the canoe gently among the rocks. Even before Shoal Bay opened up, he could see movement on the water. Three small boats moved back and forth, the narrow beams of spotlights focused on the water ahead of their bows. The sound of voices occasionally reached him above the sound of the motors, but he could not make out the words. Above it all, he could hear the rattle of chains and the harsh sound of metal striking metal. The sounds were punctuated by loud splashes.

Slowly he edged the canoe forward, using the rocks to propel himself so that the splash of his paddle would not draw attention. The black ship lay alongside the wharf. It was no longer silent. Bright lights lit the deck, where several men were maneuvering some kind of metallic cylinder over the railing using one of the davit cranes. As each dinghy approached, the crane swung a cylinder out and lowered it gently to the waiting boat. Two men in the dinghy then carefully settled the metal tube into some kind of device set near the bow before releasing the crane hook and heading over to the east shore of the bay, where they disappeared from view behind the point. The process was repeated for the next dinghy. And the next. Supervising it all was a man with hair so pale it seemed to be alight with its own luminescence.

▶ Walker stayed motionless against the rocks. It was almost midnight when the activity in the bay ceased and the three dinghies were winched back aboard. An hour later the black ship was quiet again. Still Walker remained. He felt the current slow and then reverse, gently tugging him backward. Several times he thought about moving, but the occasional glow of a cigarette tip high up on the western point of the bay held him. Finally, his patience was rewarded as the thin beam of a flashlight pierced the darkness, moving slowly back down toward the ship.

Cautiously, he let the canoe float free, guiding it gently with his hands until he felt safe enough to dig the paddle into the water. Grimacing as the muscles in his shoulders protested, he steered back toward the bays he had visited earlier. He was exhausted. He had been on or in the water for almost eighteen hours, and he had long ago lost most of the feeling in his legs. Mind you, that was probably a good thing, he thought grimly, as a shaft of pain shot through his hip. The rest of him hurt more than enough to make up for it. Not that it mattered. There was the girl to find, and his gut told him that there was very little time to find her.

▶ Annie's boat rocked gently in the shallows, lifting slowly with the waves. Its dark hull loomed a solid black against the night sky, forbidding and silent. Walker hesitated for a moment before reaching out and rapping the hull with his paddle. Annie was quick with her shotgun, and he had no desire to test either her accuracy or her temper. He craned his head back to look up at the railing as he rapped a second time, a little harder.

"Annie! Annie, it's Walker."

He waited a couple of minutes and was about to try again when her harsh voice screamed down at him.

"What the hell do you want?" she yelled as she leaned out over the rail. "It ain't even light yet!"

He heard the sound of metal scraping against metal and caught the glint of a barrel sliding down toward him.

"Come on out where I can see you," she rasped. "You ain't Walker. He was here yesterday."

"It's me, Annie." He slid out cautiously from under the curve of the hull. "I need your help."

"Walker? That you?"

He couldn't make out her expression, but he thought she might have relaxed her grip on the shotgun.

"Goddamn it. You scared the shit out of me. What the hell are you doing here in the middle of the fuckin' night?" She peered down at him for a few more seconds, then moved away from the rail. He heard her clumping heavily along the deck as she headed toward the bow. She was muttering as she went, and then came the sound of a door slamming. A light appeared in the cabin.

It took Walker a long time to get out of the canoe. He had moved around to the beach behind the boat, but he was so cold and stiff he wasn't sure if he would ever get his legs moving. Finally he managed to twist himself upright using a rusty ladder that hung down the side of the hull. Staggering over the rough ground, he slowly made his way over to the narrow boards that formed a path up from the shore to the deck. He used his hands to pull himself up them.

Inside the cabin, Annie was bent over a cast-iron stove, angrily stirring the embers with a poker. She kept her back to him, pointedly ignoring him as he slid awkwardly past two large black cats and onto the bench of the dinette.

He leaned his head back tiredly against the cabin wall and closed his eyes. "Thank you," he rasped, his voice sounding as rusty as the rest of him felt.

There was no response, but he heard the sound of the kettle sliding across the grate and water being poured. Minutes later a cup landed on the table in front him and the smell of coffee filled his nostrils.

"Find her?" Annie's voice was still harsh, but underneath he could hear her concern. She too had grown fond of the girl over the summer.

He pushed himself up and shook his head. "Nope. Found her boat though."

Annie's gaze sharpened. "Where?"

"Over in Half Moon Cove."

He heard her sharply inhaled breath, but she didn't speak. He turned to look blindly out the dark window.

"Lying in five feet of water." His voice roughened with sudden anger. "Looks like someone towed it there and sank it." He looked back at Annie, his dark eyes burning with a flat, black fury. "The dinghy's there too, thrown up on the rocks. They holed that too."

"Holed it?" Her weathered face took on a look of complete puzzlement. "What the hell are you talking about? You crazy or something?"

She turned away from him to poke more wood into the stove, then reached over to pick up one of the cats. It nuzzled into her neck, purring loudly as she gently stroked its back.

He watched her, drawn by the tenderness he saw in the action. She was a big woman, perhaps six feet tall, with rough, calloused hands and feet that were perpetually stuffed into caulk logger's boots. He had never seen her in anything but a torn flannel shirt and stained work pants held up by red suspenders. Now she was wrapped in a threadbare robe, the hem of a flannel nightgown brushing the toes of a pair of worn fleece slippers. The long iron-gray hair she usually wore in a braid hung in wisps over her shoulders, giving her a look of vulnerability he had never noticed before.

"Why the hell would anyone put a hole in it?" she continued, staring at him as she tried to make sense of his words and obviously failing. It was a rhetorical question, and they sat in silence as they both considered the implications.

"So where's the girl?" she asked finally. "She get blown ashore or what?"

He shook his head, still staring out into the darkness. "No. I don't know what happened, but the boat was sunk deliberately. I think maybe Claire got away in the kayak. It's not there."

Silence fell again. There was nothing to say.

▶ It was Walker who woke first. The warmth of the cabin had wrapped around him, relaxing tired muscles and bringing a deep and dreamless sleep, but the first pale hint of daylight brought him instantly alert. He was alone. Annie had covered him with a blanket before returning to her bed. He could hear her steady snoring coming from the forward cabin.

He pushed himself upright and looked around. He had only been inside Annie's boat a couple of times before, and he remembered his amazement the first time he saw it. It was certainly not what he had expected. The outside matched the woman who owned it: large and rough. The inside was an entirely different matter. Simple padded benches surrounded a wooden table, a cast-iron stove gleamed against the bulkhead, and a heavy black kettle issued a welcoming wisp of steam. China cups swung from hooks below the cupboards. Colorful prints filled the open spaces on the walls, most of them scenes of thatched cottages and gardens, and the oiled wood floor was covered with a scattering of faded rugs. It wasn't opulent, but it was neat and clean.

Even more surprising were a small refrigerator he found humming softly in the galley and the speakers that were almost hidden behind shelves of books in the salon. As his eyes took it all in he came to the understanding that this was a home, warm and comfortable and well cared for. By the time he had reached the bridge and seen the gleaming array of instruments sitting on the wide ledge in front of the windshield, his face had taken on the bemused expression of a child at a magic show. Annie had laughed at his look of amazement.

"Bit more than you expected?" she had cackled loudly as she proudly showed him the generator that kept the batteries charged.

Now he stood up and moved forward to the wheelhouse. The dial on the radio glowed green and the power light blinked reassuringly. He picked up the microphone, feeling awkward and uncomfortable with it in his hand. It was a reminder of another life, an alien technology he had thought he would never need again. He didn't want to use it. It was the one link he had to the man he had once hated. The man who had put him in jail. The man who had helped give him his life back. The man who might be able to help him find the girl.

He pressed the switch. "*Dreamspeaker. Dreamspeaker. Dreamspeaker.* Walker calling."

▶ FIVE ◀

▶ The black ship floated gently at anchor at the head of a small inlet, her name, *Snow Queen*, inscribed in pale charcoal-gray script across her stern. Someone, Harry couldn't remember who, had come up with it as a joke, but Harry had liked it.

On deck, Javier Fernandez sat quietly, his lean frame draped easily over an upholstered teak chaise. It was not the kind of quiet that Harry Coombs liked. He had seen Fernandez like this before and two men had died in the fury that erupted when the quiet ended. He did not want that to happen here. Not only would he be one of the ones in the line of fire, but if he survived the tempest, he would have bodies to dispose of and a boat to clean. Neither was easy.

Harry glanced down at his empty glass and gestured to the man behind the bar. If this had been his regular crew, he would not have needed to ask, but Fernandez had insisted that his own men staff the yacht and Harry had reluctantly agreed. Only Harry's captain remained aboard, and Harry shuddered to think what it would have been like had he also been replaced.

Harry Coombs was sixty-five, shorter and heavier than he liked to pretend, with the engaging look of an aging leprechaun. His florid cheeks and unruly shock of black hair had served him well and, combined with brilliant blue eyes and an impish smile, had helped him amass a fortune exporting used heavy equipment to war-ravaged countries in Asia and Africa. When the iron curtain fell, Harry easily switched to buying and selling other things: surplus tanks, rocket launchers, and machine guns were followed by bombs, land mines, and all kinds of electronic devices. There was never a shortage of either sellers or buyers, and while trade in weapons was frowned upon by authorities at home, it was still legal if you followed all the rules. Harry didn't, but he paid his lawyers enough to ensure that it looked as if he did. Other things he had more recently added to his inventory were even less acceptable. The occasional shipment of opium or heroin. Carefully wrapped bricks of hashish. Blocks of pressed marijuana. Boxes of oddly colored pills. Even occasional passengers who used only a first name and had no papers to identify them. Harry was not fussy as long as it paid well.

Fernandez was his best customer. He provided an endless supply of goods of one kind or another, all of them packaged in such a way as to pass inspection and all of them complete with documentation that eased the task of the carefully nurtured and amply rewarded customs officials at the destination.

The barman finally arrived with his drink and slid it carelessly across the table, ignoring the two empty glasses already there. Both belonged to Harry; Fernandez had yet to touch his brandy, although his long slim fingers tapped slowly and rhythmically on the snifter.

"It's not going to be a problem." Harry spoke into the silence. "She'll come back and find her boat gone and figure it went adrift in the storm."

The figure across from him remained silent, and Harry's unease grew. "We need to move," he continued. "If we're seen here, it will look odd. There's nothing here, no reason to be here. We're supposed to be taking a quick trip along the coast to test the new engines and show you the wondrous sights." He laughed at his own wit as he let his glance wander around the gloomy bay that surrounded them.

Still Fernandez remained silent, and Harry finally stood up and wandered back to the wheelhouse.

▶ Fernandez followed his passage with half-closed eyes, his fingers maintaining their hypnotic rhythm on his glass. Harry was fast becoming a nuisance. He had good instincts where his business was concerned, but he was becoming too fond of the rewards. In a year or two he would simply be another aging playboy, uncaring and incautious, totally immersed in living the high life. That trait served Fernandez well right now, but once this was over, Harry would have to go. In any case, he was wrong about the girl, although he was right about moving. It was time.

Their passage up here had been carefully plotted to appear casual: a business associate taking a break on board a friend's yacht. Fernandez had flown in early in order to ensure their departure appeared leisurely. There had been a couple of lunches at which Harry introduced him as a business colleague. Dinner with a group of lawyers and accountants. A night at the theater with an investment banker and his wife, who had sported a stunning display of jewelry and spent the evening alternately stroking her husband's coat sleeve and looking at Fernandez from under her false eyelashes. They had even hosted a party aboard the yacht the evening before their departure, lavishly catered and attended by an eclectic mix of neighboring yacht owners and the artistic types that Harry loved to mingle with.

They loaded crates of food and wine, which delivery boys placed on waiting palettes to be winched aboard. Fishing rods, encased in graphite tubes, were delivered by a UPS truck. New electronic gear, sealed in original cardboard boxes, arrived in a black van emblazoned with the name of a marine electronics company and were carried aboard by two tradesmen dressed in shirts embroidered with the company logo.

Alex and Gunter came aboard separately. Harry greeted each of them warmly and publicly and later took them all on a tour of the harbor in the big runabout that now hung on davits above the top deck. A van brought a mountain of luggage and disgorged it onto the dock. Four more of Fernandez's men, all wearing the navy-blue shorts and monogrammed T-shirt that Harry provided to his crew, carried it aboard and stowed it in the cabins. Meanwhile, Harry and Fernandez wandered the decks with binoculars and cameras or relaxed on the aft deck, drinks in hand.

They left on schedule and without a hitch. Fernandez had expected none. The goods had arrived weeks before, each shipped separately in small, carefully hidden containers. They had been received, repackaged, and carefully placed in the cartons and crates that had been delivered and loaded on board *Snow Queen*. Fuses coiled in fishing rods. Timers stowed inside electronics. Explosives inserted into cereal boxes. Small canisters of gas mixed in with the kitchen supplies.

If there was going to be a problem, it would have been at customs when the items first arrived, not now, when they were simply being loaded aboard a yacht at a marina.

Everything had gone like clockwork . . . until now. They had to find the girl. They only had three days until the team arrived in Shoal Bay and they could not be delayed. The schedule was too tight. The first of the targets would arrive in Vancouver eight days from now. Two days after that they would all meet in the new convention center, and by then the weapons had to be assembled, the team trained and given their instructions and each of them put in place.

Silently he cursed Alex. Sinking the boat had been stupid. They should have waited for the girl to return and taken care of her before setting the boat adrift. If they had timed it right, the boat would have drifted out with the wind and current before it sank and the emergency radio beacon would have focused attention far away from Shoal Bay. As it was, they had to hope that no one would come across the wreck and set off an alarm. At least Alex had been smart enough to remove the beacon before he sank the boat, but they still needed the girl—or at least her corpse. A search for a possible survivor would threaten everything.

The sound of an outboard motor caught Fernandez's attention and briefly stilled his tapping finger. He turned his head to glance at the barman and gave a faint inclination of his head. Minutes later he was joined on deck by two men, both wearing jeans and orange Floater coats.

Gunter Rachmann, blond hair cut short and blue eyes hidden behind dark glasses, dragged over a chair and sat down. His companion, a short, dark-skinned, dark-eyed man known only as Trip, remained standing.

"Nothing." The dark man shook his head in disgust.

Fernandez turned his head and let his stare rest on Trip's face. Trip shuffled his feet but did not flinch.

"We searched the whole island. There ain't no sign of her."

Fernandez moved his flat gaze to Gunter. The man remained silent for a few minutes, then spoke in careful, clipped words that held the trace of an accent.

"We have picked up no other boats on the radar, either here or on the dinghy. We have heard no other engines. There has been only a little local radio traffic." He paused, then continued. "I think she has a small boat. Maybe a canoe or a kayak. There is some new paint on the float. Not much. Not regular paint. Maybe some kind of fiberglass coating. It forms a rough outline."

"That's nuts," Trip interjected. "Why would she take a toy boat out in a storm? We arrived the day the storm quit and she wasn't there then." He shrugged. "Anyway, the paint ain't that new."

Fernandez ignored him, keeping his eyes fixed on the blond German.

"The paint is new," Gunter reiterated. "And it is yellow. Her boat was old and it had no new paint. The dinghy was blue." He shrugged. "I think she has a small boat."

"Well, if she went out in a toy boat she's probably dead by now," Trip snorted. "The last two days have been good, and she ain't back!"

The German still did not show any expression. "She could perhaps be with someone else. There are surely people who live around here somewhere." He gave what might have been a shrug. "Or perhaps she is stranded, her 'toy boat,' as you call it, damaged or sunk."

"So who cares?" Trip snorted derisively. "If she's stranded, she'll end up dead!"

"Enough!" The single word from Fernandez was enough to silence both men. "Get Alex and Marty."

Trip left and returned minutes later with two other men.

Fernandez stood and beckoned to Harry, who was watching them from the wheelhouse, then turned back to address the men now gathered around him, keeping his voice low.

"Take the Whaler and the inflatable, two men per boat. Take fishing gear in case you meet up with anyone. It will give you a good cover. I want every beach and inlet searched. If you find cabins or boats, check them out. Make up a story. Say you are looking for the owner of the boat. Maybe say you are worried about her. Act friendly. But find the girl." His eyes briefly met Gunter's. "And lose her."

He turned to greet Harry. "Time to move, my friend."

► SIX ◄

► Annie had the kettle boiling when Walker returned to the galley. "So?"

"I called a guy I know." Walker knew he would have to tell Annie the whole story. She would not welcome a stranger into the bay, let alone allow him onto her boat.

"When I was a kid . . ." He stopped, not sure how to begin. "A while back, ten, twelve years ago, I got into trouble." He hesitated again, then forced himself to continue. "I was down in the city. Got to drinking. Got into drugs." He looked across at her, his face twisted with remembered pain. "I needed money, so I broke into a house. Stole some stuff." He gave a bitter laugh. "Guess I was good at it. Didn't get caught."

He paused to sip at his tea, his eyes staring unseeingly across the cabin. The words came a little easier now. "Did that for a long time. Houses, then a couple of stores. Got so it seemed easy. Got a reputation, I guess. The guys called me 'The Ghost.'"

He looked back at Annie, searching for a reaction, but she sat calmly, her expression unchanged.

"Couple of guys asked me to help them rob a bank. Said it would be easy. Had it all planned out." He shrugged his shoulders. "I was on the roof when the cops came. Tried to run but fell off instead. Ended up in the hospital, both legs busted."

He stopped and looked down at his twisted legs, vividly remembering the pain and the long weeks in physio. Annie remained quiet.

"This cop. He kept coming in to see me. Had all these questions. Who else was there? What other stuff had I done? All that. Wouldn't leave me alone. Every day, it seemed like. Same goddamn questions. Over and over. Made me mad." He shook his head. "Finally told him to fuck off, but it didn't make any difference."

He pulled himself back to the present. "Pretty ugly story, huh?"

Annie shrugged easily. "I've heard worse—and a lot of them don't end up as good as you."

He stared at her. That wasn't the reaction he had expected.

"So what happened when you got out of hospital?"

He shrugged. "Went to jail. Same cop—his name was Dan—came to court. Told the jury the whole fucking story. Knew a hell of a lot more than I'd told him. Ended up doing three years."

They sat in silence for a while, both lost in their own thoughts. Finally Annie reached out and poured them both another cup of tea.

"So it was the cop you called?"

"Yeah. Crazy, huh? But you know what? He came to see me in jail a few times. Not for more questions, just to see how I was doing. Gave me a couple of names, people to see when I got out." He gave an odd, twisted smile. "I thought I hated that bastard, but he was the only one came to see me. He was even there the day I got out. Drove me to a shelter and wished me luck!"

Annie nodded. "So you stayed in touch."

"Nope." He shook his head. "I left town. Went back home. Never saw him again till about three months ago. I was over at the floating store and this boat comes in. Nice boat. Wood. Converted fish packer but a real good job. This guy jumps off and comes into the store and it's him. Couldn't believe it at first. It was weird. I didn't know whether to talk to him or not. Hell, it's been eight years now. But he recognized me too. Asked how I was making out. Said he was going to be spending the summer up around here and if I ever felt like it to call him on the radio." He shrugged.

"So he's coming?"

"Yeah. Guess he's already heading back south. Said he would be here later today." He looked across at her. "I didn't tell him what's happened. Didn't want anyone listening in."

Annie thought about that for a moment. "Guess that was smart," she answered slowly.

▶ *Dreamspeaker* entered the bay at midafternoon, slowly nosing past the rocks that marked the entrance. Walker and Annie had been hauling crab traps on the foredeck and they stood and watched as she dropped anchor and backed down on her chain. It wasn't till the anchor was set and the boat was sitting quietly, bow to the wind, that they saw Dan step out on deck.

Annie grunted. "Knows what he's doing," she said.

Walker smiled. Coming from her, that was a huge compliment. "It would be easier if he came over here," he said.

She shrugged and turned back to the crab traps. He knew the gesture was the only acknowledgment he was likely to get. He moved down the side deck and beckoned to Dan as he stepped out of the wheelhouse and looked across the water at him. Walker hoped the simple invitation would be accepted. The boats were too far apart to be able to shout a greeting, and he didn't want to use the radio unless it was absolutely necessary.

He needn't have worried. Within minutes *Dreamspeaker*'s dinghy was being pulled up to the swim grid that hung off her stern. As he watched Dan row toward Annie's boat, Walker's feelings alternated between a strange kind of dread and an odd excitement, tension humming through him like a plucked guitar string. A brief greeting at a dock was one thing. That had felt strange enough. But reaching out to this man after eight years and inviting him onto Annie's boat was entirely another. Was he crazy? Had he made a mistake? If he had wasted this day, it was Claire who might pay the price.

▶ If Dan had any of the same qualms, he didn't show it, greeting Walker with an easy handshake and the small talk of an old acquaintance. The apprehension and nervousness Walker had been feeling began to disappear, and he soon found himself responding in the same vein. After a few minutes the two men moved into the cabin and sat down.

"Nice boat," Dan said as he looked around. "This where you live?"

Walker inclined his head toward the bow, where Anne was still busying herself with the traps. "Nope. Belongs to Annie."

"Huh. So you're just visiting? Where's home these days?"

"Got a place over east of here."

Dan nodded. "Over east" could mean any one of a couple of hundred islands or several inlets that slashed their way deep into the mountainous shores of British Columbia. With over six thousand islands scattered along its shore, the western coast of the province was renowned for its tiny, far-flung communities and hidden coves, many of which harbored loners or losers or one of the new wave of hippies trying to survive off the land. It was a major headache for administrators and a nightmare for the coast guard and the marine police. "Over east" told him nothing, but he remembered Walker well enough to know that "over east" was the best he was going to get.

"You got the summer off?"

Walker's question caught Dan off-guard. He hadn't really addressed any of the issues that had brought him out here, hadn't given a thought about his own situation. Certainly hadn't talked about it with anyone. Even when he had seen Walker on the dock over there at the floating store and recognized him from years before, he had been operating on auto-pilot. He supposed the shrink the chief had wanted him to see would call it self-denial. He thought it was more likely self-preservation: thinking about what had brought him here meant remembering how he had found Susan that day, remembering how he had ignored the tips he had received, remembering how he had missed the warning signs of stalking. Those memories brought a pain that was simply too much to bear. But here he was, and Walker had obviously assumed he was still on the force, and that demanded some sort of explanation.

"Ahhh, no. Not exactly. I quit the force. Took retirement."

The words sounded odd to his ears, as if someone else had spoken them, and he realized it was the first time he had said them out loud. Hearing them float across the cabin was disorienting, almost schizophrenic, as if he had somehow stepped out of his body and was looking back at it. He had been a cop for so long, the job had seeped into his soul. It had become his identity. It was who he was—or, at least, who he had been. Who the hell was he now? He suddenly remembered the words of a poem Susan had read to him. What was the name of it? "The Hollow Men," that was it. By some guy called Eliot. He remembered her voice as she read the last lines to him, something about the world ending not with a bang, but a whimper. She had been whispering, almost, and the words had taken on an eerie quality that twisted in the air between them. Hearing them had given him an odd feeling, but he had laughed it off, teased her for selecting such a dreary piece for her students. Now they seemed like the perfect accompaniment for his life.

He fought down a wave of loss and loneliness and looked across at Walker. For the first time since he handed in his badge, Dan felt a conscious pull of regret—was it regret?—for his decision to quit the force. Another kind of loss. Or maybe it was just the uncomfortable feeling of being asked for help and knowing that he had only himself to offer and no resources to fall back on.

"Why? You in trouble?"

▶ Dan's statement that he had left the police force caught Walker by surprise, and as he watched the play of emotions on Dan's face, he realized he had never thought of him as a man, only as a cop. And he had been a good one, as Walker knew only too well. A good man too, even if their association had been a difficult one. Something had happened that had changed the course of Dan's life. Some kind of loss or trouble.

Trouble. That had been the story of Walker's life the last time they met, but now, as he heard Dan's question, he smiled as he shook his head. "Nope. Not me. But maybe someone else. A friend."

He felt an odd tingle run through his brain as he said the word. He hadn't called anyone a friend for a long time. Maybe never.

Annie chose that moment to join them. She acknowledged Dan

with a brief grunt, ignored his outstretched hand, and slid heavily onto the bench across from him, her eyes fixed on Walker. "You tell him?"

"Not yet." He turned back to Dan, who was looking quizzically from one to the other. "I thought maybe you might be able to help find her."

"Her? Huh. Well, I'm certainly willing to do what I can, but it's going to be just me. Like I said, I'm off the force." He lifted his hands, palms up. "So tell me about it."

The conversation moved to *Island Girl* and the black ship. Dan listened quietly as Walker told him how he had met Claire and explained what little he knew about what had happened. And it was that quietness, that willingness to listen, that convinced Walker he had done the right thing. Until that moment, he had not been sure. Even so, once he was finished, he waited for the questions that he was sure would come. He was not used to putting so much into words. Spoken out loud his reasoning sounded flimsy, even to his own ears. Surely someone like Dan, trained as a cop to follow fact and logic rather than instinct and hunch, would dismiss it as crazy. The ramblings of a crazy Aboriginal ex-con who spent too much time alone.

He didn't.

"So you think this girl escaped in the kayak?"

Walker nodded.

"Any thoughts on where she might go?"

"I've been thinking about that," Walker replied. "She might have gone to the other side of the island she's on—Spider Island, it's called on the charts."

He described the channel and how it filled during spring tides. He and Claire had talked about how easy it made it for her to use her kayak to visit the southern side of the island.

Dan nodded. "Makes sense. Worth a look, anyway." He checked his watch. "Want to run over there in the dinghy? I can put the motor on and we can be there and back before dark."

Walker nodded and felt some of the tension drain out of him.

For the first time in two days, he felt a small surge of optimism. He pushed himself up from the table and followed Dan toward the door. The sound of an approaching outboard engine stopped him before he got there.

It slowed to an idle, and although he couldn't see the boat, Walker watched and listened as Dan, out on deck, lifted a hand in greeting.

"Hi," Dan called. "You folks are a long way from anywhere. Help you with something?"

Walker could barely hear the reply, but as the words registered, he felt his body stiffen.

"We came to visit a friend, but she is not on her boat," said the unfamiliar voice. "It is over in Shoal Bay. We wondered if you might have seen her?" The accent was oddly clipped and the words precise.

Walker started to warn Dan against replying, but Dan's voice stopped him.

"Sorry. Can't help you. Just stopped here for the night on my way back south, but let me check with the captain." He stepped back into the cabin. "Looks like we are not the only ones looking for the girl," he said quietly to Walker. "You see enough of anyone at Shoal Bay to be able to recognize either of these two?"

Walker shook his head. "Couldn't see anything. Too dark."

Dan nodded. "Wait till I'm back outside, then both of you take a good look. They won't be able to see you through the porthole, but you both need to be able to recognize them if you see them again." He moved back out to the deck.

Walker leaned over the table and peered out at the big inflatable floating just feet away. The two men in it both had their eyes hidden by dark glasses, but he could sense them checking out every inch of Annie's boat. One had long, dark hair and a heavy build. The other was tall and slim with short hair so white it seemed to glow.

Dan's voice drifted back to the cabin. "Nope. Hasn't been anyone here for weeks. Is there a problem?"

The reply was almost drowned out by the rising pitch of the outboard. "No. She is probably just out exploring. We will go back and wait."

Walker straightened and was about to move when the outboard quieted again.

"That is a nice canoe. Do you like to use it here?"

"It's not mine. My friend uses it to paddle around a bit."

The outboard sped up again, and its whine diminished as the men left the bay.

Dan stepped back inside. "I think our plans have just changed."

► SEVEN ◄

► For the first time in a week, the morning sun burst through the clouds and set the water dancing. Gliding past the familiar shoreline, Walker felt a growing anger replacing the dread of the past two days. This was his land. *Gigame' Kana'l,* the Creator, had chosen this place for his people. Thunderbird ruled these skies. *U'melth,* the Raven, had placed the sun and the moon here, and Raven had given them the salmon, the namesake of his clan and sustainer of his village.

The People, his people, had lived here, fished these waters, walked these beaches, for thousands of years. Like them, he had come to love and respect this world. He knew every bay, every cove and every inlet, not only by its shape and depth, but by its scent and the rhythm of its swells. He knew what lived there and where it lived. He knew the pattern of the seasons and the surge of the tides.

There were mornings when the tendrils of mist rising from the water wrapped around him and almost stole his breath with their soft caress. When the frolicking play of a family of river otters held him rapt and spellbound. When the wheeling flight of a flock of gulls, pure white against a hard blue sky, made his heart sing.

There were evenings when the canopy of stars, brilliant against the black depth of the night, shone so brightly that it frosted the trees with silver light and lit the ground around him.

There were days when the orcas leaped from the ocean, huge and magnificent, water sheeting from their smooth, muscular bodies, and his world stilled in awe.

Like his ancestors, and like the creatures he shared this land with, he too killed, but only for food, and he wasted nothing. He had learned long ago, on the harsh asphalt streets of the city, that violence was never an answer. And this was violence. Of that he was completely sure.

Claire shared his world and shared his appreciation of it. A white girl from a different culture, she had effortlessly gained his respect with her warmth and her work and her simple lifestyle. Her values echoed his own and those of his people. She had given him the gift of her friendship when few others would have considered it. He would not turn away from her now.

Whether or not Claire was still alive, he had to find her. He had to find out who was doing this. He had to find out why. Most of all, he had to get his world back into balance and restore the harmony that was both his sanctuary and his birthright.

He had left Dan and Annie last night, slipping away into the darkness. They all agreed that he should be the one to continue the search for Claire. She would not be likely to respond to a stranger in a strange boat, and Walker had an intimate knowledge of the waters and currents and hidden coves of this crowded archipelago that no chart or GPS could possibly duplicate. Dan would check out the black ship for himself. He could easily plot a course that would take *Dreamspeaker* past Shoal Bay and, because he had already been seen and had spoken with the two men in the inflatable, his presence should not raise an alarm.

Dan had given Walker a hand-held marine radio he said was tuned to some restricted duplex channel, saying it was a hangover from his time on the force and was only accessible to the police and from the single-sideband radio he had on board *Dreamspeaker*. Walker didn't know anything about radios, but he liked the idea that he and Dan could use it to talk without risk of being overheard, while Dan had said he liked the idea that Walker could call for help if needed. At the same time, Dan cautioned him against using it unless it was really important. If the marine police were near enough to hear it, they would not be pleased, and they would ask some hard questions about how Walker had come to have it. Dan said he figured he could come up with a story that would cover his ass, but he would rather he didn't have to. Walker understood his caution but wondered again about the pain he had seen on Dan's face when he talked about his former career.

He found himself relieved to know that Dan was no longer on the force. He had not been entirely comfortable with the idea of the police coming in, but he knew he could not take on the black ship alone. Plus, he had figured he could disappear once Claire had been found. Now he didn't have to worry about it. Dan was just a friend who would try to keep an eye on the black ship and could help out if needed. And although it felt strange, Walker had to admit he felt good about having a friend, someone to talk to and call on.

Now he let the rhythm of the waves work their magic on his spirit. He had not slept. Once dusk had stolen the last of the light and the horizon had merged the ocean with the sky, he'd angled his canoe out into the current and let it carry him toward his destination. As the sun rose higher, he moved in closer to shore and started to chant in time with his paddle.

Ahead of him a fish jumped, breaking the surface of the water. As he watched, an image of *Sisiutl*, the three-headed sea serpent, formed in the waves. Walker remembered the carved cedar mask that hung on the wall in his mother's house. That *Sisiutl* was painted in intricate patterns of red, green, and black. This *Sisiutl* was formed from ripples of silver water, but it was still *Sisiutl*. The legends said the serpent had once transformed himself into an invincible war canoe to help an ancestor. Perhaps he had come to help again. Walker hoped so. One glance from the serpent could turn an adversary into stone.

▶ Dan hauled anchor before dawn. The moon was low, its pale light illuminating the faint mist that rose off the water to float like layers of gauze above it. He wanted to reach Shoal Bay just before sunrise, when there was barely enough light to see. Experience told him that was the best time to catch people unaware. It was also the best time as far as the explanation he had come up with went. If he was really heading back south as he had told the two men at Annie's boat, he would certainly start out early.

He debated trying to call Mike but decided against it. Even if he could reach him via the satellite phone, his ex-partner wouldn't be able to do much. Without hard facts, he would find it impossible to convince the brass to send anyone up. Dan was no longer a member of the force—he had quit more than six months ago. That wasn't a long time, but it was long enough to make him an outsider, and any information he provided would be suspect. He didn't doubt Walker's story, but there were too few details. Maybe once he had seen the black ship for himself he would have something more.

He slowed the engines long before he reached Shoal Bay, staying well out in mid-channel. It was important that nothing seem unusual, although simply being seen was not really a concern. He set the radar to close range and switched on the recorder. It would not give him enough detail to positively identify the black ship again later, but it would help.

As soon as he passed the eastern point of the bay, he knew all his efforts were wasted. The wharf was empty. The black ship had left. Shoal Bay was deserted.

Dan swung the wheel over hard. He had no idea if or when the black ship would return, and there were still the men in the inflatable to worry about, but he could always say he just wanted to see if they had found their friend. Besides, this was an opportunity to check out the sounds Walker had heard. From the description he had given, the small boats had been going from the ship to the shore. They had to have been unloading something.

He turned *Dreamspeaker* so she was bow out and tied her to the wharf. If he hurried, he could use the dinghy to explore the shore before the sun rose high enough to steal the shadows from the bay. That gave him at least a small sense of security.

The tide was low, exposing the gravel beach. He cruised slowly along it, from the head of the bay to the outer point, but saw nothing out of place. Then he reversed his course and tried again a few feet farther out but with the same result. It didn't make sense. He needed to talk to Walker again. Try to figure out what he was doing wrong.

The first rays of the sun were hitting the water as he turned back toward *Dreamspeaker*. They reflected off a row of small black buoys that floated just below the surface. No wonder he had not seen them. He let the dinghy drift up to them and peered down through the clear water. At the base of each tether was something dark. Maybe a metal box or cylinder. He reached down and cautiously tugged at one of the buoys. Whatever was down there was too heavy to be easily lifted. He was going to need help.

► EIGHT ◄

► Claire huddled under a tree as the shore emerged from night. A leaf, mottled gold and brown, drifted down to settle on her shoulder. Summer was over and the chill of fall was in the air. It had been three days now. Three days and three nights. She had no food left. The few cookies and handful of dried fruit had long since been eaten, although she had twice managed to refill her water bottle. She was hungry, she was tired, she was cold, and she was trapped. She was also lost.

She had spent the first day hiding in the rocks, too frightened to stray far from her kayak. Twice she had heard the sound of an outboard. The first time it had come in slowly, moving very close to shore. Like a child trying to will the bogeyman away, she had closed her eyes. Even after the sound of the motor had faded, she did not move until the agony of cramped muscles forced her to.

The second time was late the same afternoon. She had crept up into the trees when she heard it. This time the boat was moving fast and its wash slammed onto the shore, dislodging rocks and driftwood. She had only caught a quick glimpse of the occupants, but that was enough. There could not be another man with hair that white. Her stomach heaved as a cold claw of fear gripped it. The fear was so intense it brought bile to her throat, and she fought off a wave of nausea. This could not be happening. She felt disoriented, alone in a strange world that no longer made sense. She crawled back into the rocks and huddled there until darkness fell again. Then she made her way back to the kayak.

Early the next morning, long before the sun was up, her body aching and her brain numb, she forced herself to lift the kayak from its hiding place. It was impossible not to make noise and she winced at each sound, but she could not stay there any longer.

Once on the water, she headed southeast. In the dark, she couldn't distinguish detail or judge how fast the current was pushing her, but by the time the sun rose she was in a tangle of tiny islets.

She had to get off the water before it got fully light. The first opportunity was a narrow gap between some rocks. It was barely wide enough to allow the kayak through, but at least it gave her some protection. Ahead was a bare hump of surf-washed rock where a single contorted tree clung to life. Exhausted, she clambered up to the flattest point and lay down. Surely they would never find her here.

They didn't. But she heard them, the sound of the outboard motor swelling and fading as they searched, and the sick fear stayed with her. She ate the last of her food and rationed her water knowing there was no more to be found here. The rain the storm had dumped had long since drained off and there was only a thin layer of drying seaweed and a few barnacles beneath her. She would have to move again, but with the dinghy still searching, that was impossible until dark. She had never felt more alone and vulnerable. Nothing in her life—not her education or her work—had prepared her for anything like this. She knew she had to get the fear under control and start thinking rationally but had no idea where to start.

She heard the motor again about an hour after sunset. And then again two hours after that. Surely they would not search all night. She pressed herself against the damp rock and willed herself into stillness.

Unbelievably, she slept, but it was a brief sleep filled with nightmarish images, and she woke sweating and cold. In the darkest hours of early morning, her head throbbing, her body sore, and her belly empty, she slid back down to the kayak, squeezed it back through the narrow gap, and felt the tiny boat turn into the current. There was a darker smudge against the darkness ahead. If she could reach it, and if there were trees and soil, perhaps there would also be a creek. Not that she had a choice. This was the way the current ran, and she did not have the energy to fight it. Besides, she needed the speed it would give her. If she was caught out in open water when the men came again, there would be no need for water. Or for anything else.

Four hours later the tiny boat slid up onto a narrow ledge. Summoning her last dregs of energy, she dragged it up into a cluster of trees and stumbled toward a shallow cleft where she hoped and prayed rainwater might have collected. When she saw the tiny pool fringed by a green ring of moss and fern, she collapsed beside it and wept.

By noon, she had managed to claw her way up a small rise that gave her a view to the east. Instead of the channel she had hoped for, where she might be able to attract help, there were only more islands. And in among them, in a small bay almost hidden from view, was a black ship.

▶ The day had barely started when Dan left Shoal Bay. Once again he debated calling Mike but decided against it. There were still too many unanswered questions. Too many loose ends.

He checked his charts and picked a tiny indentation on the coast of an island a few miles south of Spider Island and Shoal Bay. It would be close enough for Walker to reach and too small for something the size of the black ship to anchor. Walker did not carry charts, but Dan was confident he could give him clear enough directions when they were needed.

He thought about Walker as he steered *Dreamspeaker* through the labyrinth of islands and passes. He realized that he admired the man. Admired what he had done with his life. Not the early stuff. Not the B&Es. There was nothing to admire there, but it wasn't important: he was just a kid lost in the city. There were hundreds of them, maybe thousands, but few managed to turn their lives around the way Walker had done. He was different. Dan had sensed it then. Saw it now. There was an inner core. A steel thread that ran through him. A knowledge and awareness of himself and an acceptance of who and what he was. That knowledge had grown into a belief that sustained him.

Dan tried to imagine the kind of courage it would have taken to go from convicted thief to the quiet, confident man he had just met. Perhaps the admiration he felt came from the belief that he could not have done it himself. Hell, he could barely function now, and it was more than a year since he had lost Susan.

Even as he thought of it, he felt the familiar shaft of grief. She had been his anchor. No matter what his day had brought, he had known she would be there at the end of it. He had clung to that knowledge in the midst of the worst times, when nothing seemed to make sense and the sound of gunfire and racing engines and screaming almost overwhelmed his sanity.

He had always enjoyed his work on the force, first on the street and then as a detective, but when the opportunity to move into the anti-terrorist squad appeared, he didn't hesitate. He savored the challenge of out-thinking his opponents, enjoyed the thrill of the chase, delighted in the adrenalin rush it provided. Truth be told, he loved the danger. It was a natural high that had been addicting. Riding the edge, nerves taut, blood pumping, feeling the thrill. Then coming down with the rest of the guys over a few cold ones. Or more than a few. Then he met Susan.

She had been twenty-eight, three years younger than him. A teacher working at a school for the deaf. She had come to the station to help question a witness, a profoundly deaf boy who used sign language to communicate. She was small and dark, her black hair pulled back in a failed effort to control an unruly mass of curls. He was attracted to her looks, but it was her personality that entranced him: a mix of intense energy and languid grace. She was vivacious, outgoing, and confident, but she channeled it all into a gentle warmth that immediately put the boy—and everyone else—at ease.

He phoned her the next day and asked her out for coffee. The day after that it was dinner. Within a week he was spending every possible minute with her. Three weeks later he was a fixture in her house, and two months after that, they were married.

She sold her apartment and they bought a house together. Suddenly he found himself spending all his time off painting and sanding, working on projects he had never bothered with before. Together they searched second-hand stores for furniture. On those rare summer afternoons when he wasn't working, they would sit in the garden, relaxing in the shade of a huge crab-apple tree. He was happy. Content in a way he had never known and never expected. He had the best of both worlds.

Not once did he imagine that any part of the job could reach her. Not once did he consider that the violence he sparred with every day could touch her. Until it did. And then it was too late.

He tried to survive it. He told himself that she would want him to continue working. He could even hear her voice telling him it was not his fault. That he was one of the good guys. That his job was important. But none of it worked. After eight months of trying, he put in his resignation.

He had already sold the house. He couldn't go back to it. He couldn't stand the thought of opening the door. Even to turn the corner to the street brought back memories of the evening he had found her sprawled across the table, her white dress dark with blood. He'd spent the months after her death crashing in hotels or sleeping in his car. He drank too much and ate too little. He avoided friends and colleagues alike.

It was Mike who had finally pulled him out of it. He had found Dan in a pub one night and taken him back to his apartment. The next morning he had fed him breakfast and driven him down to a marina. He knew Dan's love of the ocean. Knew much of his childhood had been spent on a fishing boat. Knew that a boat might be something that could give Dan back a sense of purpose. Maybe even give him a reason to live again.

Even sitting neglected at the dock, the boat they found was perfect. She had wide decks, a high bow, and a graceful sheer. A conversion from fish packer to pleasure boat was more than half finished, and it had added bronze ports below deck, a wide teak cap rail, and an extended cabin. And there was even a faded For Sale sign tacked on her hull.

Despite his depression, Dan could not resist her. He and Susan had dreamed of sailing down the coast to Mexico. This boat would have been perfect. He bought her that same day, and two days later he moved the few belongings he still owned aboard. Mike checked in on him every few days, brought food, and stocked the galley. On days off, he brought some of the other guys from the squad to help with the work.

Dan threw himself into finishing the conversion. He used the money he got from the house to equip her the way he wanted. Only thirty-seven, his sixteen years on the force had given him a small pension. That, plus his savings, would be enough to live on. The rest he put into the boat.

Eleven weeks after he bought her, he carefully painted her new name on both her bow and stern. Two days after that, he let go the lines and pointed *Dreamspeaker* north.

A wave smacked the bow, and Dan shook off the memories that threatened to engulf him. Now was not the time for reminiscence. There was work to do. A missing girl who was being hunted by gunmen. Sunken containers to check out. A strange boat to investigate. He shook his head at the irony. He had given up police work, but here he was, doing it again—and at the request of an ex-con!

He steered *Dreamspeaker* into the tiny cove using the depth sounder and GPS as well as the chart to guide him. There was not enough room to swing at anchor, so he took a stern line ashore and tied it to a tree. Even if a wind came up, he was protected by a hook of land that almost closed the entrance. In fact, if the black ship passed right outside the cove, there was a good chance its crew wouldn't notice him. As soon as the boat settled her bow into the wind, he headed for the bridge and the radio.

Walker answered his call immediately. "She was here. I found her trail."

Dan breathed a sigh of relief. So the girl had not been on her boat when it sank. She had gotten away. But if Walker could find her trail, maybe others could too.

"How easily? You think the guys in the dinghy could find it?"

"Probably not. It's just scratches on the rocks and some crushed barnacles and stuff."

"You sure it was her?" Dan regretted the question as soon as he asked it. Of course Walker would be sure.

"Yeah."

Dan shook his head as he considered the amount of knowledge wrapped up in those simple answers. "Any idea when she left? If she's out on the water, she'll be pretty easy to spot."

"She left at low tide. That was the middle of the night. Maybe two o'clock in the morning. The current would push her southeast."

Dan pulled the chart toward him. "Where are you now?"

"Still here. Gotta wait for the next low."

"You see those guys in the dinghy?"

"Nope. Heard it a couple of times though."

Dan nodded to himself. That was good. It meant they hadn't found her yet. But they were still searching, and he didn't like Walker being out on the water alone in daylight any more than the girl.

"You might want to keep to the dark hours too."

"Yeah." There might have been a hint of amusement in Walker's voice.

Dan ended the call. He knew Walker would be cautious, but there was something going on with the black ship that spoke of a level of planning and sophistication he had not seen for a long time. Something that could easily overwhelm simple survival skills.

He reached over and lifted the satellite phone from its cradle. It was time to talk to Mike. He just hoped he had enough to convince him.

Rosemary, Mike's secretary, answered. She was a fixture in the department, had worked for Mike for longer than the sixteen years Dan had known him, and he had never seen her flustered, but he thought she sounded flustered now. "Dan! Good to hear from you. Where are you?"

"I'm on the boat. Still up north. What's up?"

"Oh, nothing really. Same old stuff. Short of staff. Too many meetings. Too much happening. Not enough time." She laughed. "I guess I don't have to tell you. It's not like it's anything new. Are you looking for Mike?"

"Yeah. Is he there?"

"No. He's over in Vancouver—in yet another meeting! Lately he's been spending more time there than he does here in Victoria. This damn UN thing is taking up all his time, and everyone else's too. And then there's the concert . . . Sorry, I'm ranting. He won't be back here until tomorrow at the earliest. Is there a problem? Can I give him a message?"

"No. No. It's fine. Just checking in. I'll be back down in a couple of weeks anyway."

No use worrying her. Maybe by tomorrow he would have a better idea of what was happening.

► NINE ◄

► Three days later Walker still hadn't found her. He was following his instincts and the current, searching for the faint trail she had left. Like Claire, he was traveling mostly at night, using the soft, purple light of dusk and dawn to check shorelines and search the rocks. Several times he heard an outboard, although it never came close. Still, it was enough to tell him they had not given up. Enough to keep him cautious.

On the evening of the third day, the sun low on the horizon and streaking the cloud bank with liquid fire, he reached an island well to the east of Darby Channel. The telltale signs started halfway up the bank, just below the high-tide line. They were partially covered, as they had been made when the water was at its highest point and a later high, lower than the first, had washed over the lower ones.

He pushed the canoe into shallow water and struggled out. There was no place he could hide it, but it sat low in the water and the dark hull would be hard to see with the daylight fading.

Earlier in the day he had found a handful of salmonberries the raccoons had left, and he had put them into a small deer-hide bag along with some dried salmon from his food stash. He thought about eating them now but decided against it. It would take him a while to clamber up the bank, and he would have to use the stunted trees that twisted out of the rock to pull himself up. Better to save the food till he reached the top. He didn't think Claire was still there. The signs were a couple of days old, and it was hard to tell if the most recent led in or out of the water, but he hoped that from the highest point he would be able to get a wider view of the islands that lay still farther to the east. That was the direction she was traveling, and it would give him a better idea of where she might have gone.

It was slow going, but finally, he reached the summit. An out-cropping of rock blocked out the south, but otherwise the view was clear. A scattering of small islands lay both east and north, none of them more than half a mile wide and almost all of them low. Beyond them the rugged shore of the mainland heaved up in steep tiers to the jagged peaks of the Coast Mountains. Could Claire have made it that far? It didn't seem likely. The nearest point was probably two days away by kayak, and the currents here would be against her at night.

And even if she had, there was no place to land. Once past the islands, the inlet became a fjord: steep cliffs dropping straight down into a deep underwater trench. But the islands didn't look promising either. None of them was big enough to provide decent shelter, and he doubted that any of them would have water.

He sat down and let his mind slow. He thought that perhaps he had always had the ability to sense the presence of another person—it was probably what had made him so successful at break and enter back in the city all those years ago, but he hadn't really been conscious of it then. It was only after he had come back to the village, had spent all those evenings talking with the elders, absorbing the culture and the lore he had previously disdained, that he had thought about and embraced it.

The elders told him that it was as if the lines of the universe bent a little around each living thing—and that he had the gift of reading that disturbance. At first, he had scoffed at the idea: he certainly hadn't read the cops arriving at the bank too well, had he? But deep within himself, he sensed the truth of what they were saying, and secretly he was pleased. He had had few if any gifts of a practical kind given to him in his short life, and he was honored to think that the Creator might have chosen one for him. Proud that the elders recognized it in him. He started working to develop it, finding quiet, hidden places and sitting for hours, eyes closed, reaching out with ears and nose and skin and fingertips and, finally, with his spirit. He didn't know how long it had taken for awareness to move into his conscious mind and he couldn't have explained how it worked. He just knew it did. Now he closed his eyes and reached out into the gloom. Claire was still out there: he could feel her. But where was she?

Suddenly, his eyes snapped open, and he peered down at the rocks below him. They were hidden in deep shadow, their outlines dark, blurred by a couple of twisted trees and broken by crevices, but as he let his gaze slide slowly along the contours, he saw that there was something there. Just the faintest hint of movement disturbed the stillness. A deeper shade of black. It might be a raccoon, or even an otter, but he didn't think so. It was too big, too still, and the location was wrong. It felt human.

He glanced down to the shore below. There was no boat there, no kayak, no dinghy, and there was no way to get up that steep cliff from the water anyway. Whoever was there—if it was someone and not something—had to have come around the island from the other side, scrambling over the rocks. Had she—or he—heard him? He had made no attempt to silence his approach, and he was very aware of how much noise he had made. Was it fear that was causing the stillness or simply a desire for concealment? Was it Claire or was it one of the men searching for her?

He twisted himself up and moved about twenty feet to the left, hoping to get a better view from the side, maybe catch an outline against the rock face. He tried to keep quiet, but he thought that any sounds he was making would be blocked and reflected by the angles and planes of the cliff. Carefully, he lowered himself to the ground and peered over the edge. And there, silhouetted against the fading sky, he saw the girl. She was slumped against the trunk of a stunted spruce tree that twisted out of the rock, facing the ocean.

If she had heard him, she had made no attempt to move, and she was not looking up to see who or what was above her. In fact, she was sitting absolutely still, tension written in the taut, clenched lines of her body, her gaze apparently focused on the waters that lay in front of her. He could sense fear, smell it drifting up to him on the dark breeze, and he searched for a way to get her attention without startling her. He couldn't be certain there was not someone else there, someone she was watching, so calling to her was out of the question.

He picked up a handful of pebbles, small and few enough to sound natural when they fell but sufficient to create a sound, and let them slide down the rocks. When she didn't respond, he did it again. And again. Finally, it caught her attention. Her head snapped around and she slowly looked up, her face a pale oval in the deepening gloom.

"Walker!"

There was more feeling packed into that single word than he had heard in many years, and the depth of his response stunned him. He had expected her reaction. He had not expected his own.

The surge of emotion brought with it a wave of memories that almost overwhelmed his senses: woodsmoke and laughter; the sour smell of eulachon grease; the sheen of dancing bodies; hot sweat mixed with cedar; the insistent beat of a drum. They were so intense, so vivid, he forgot where he was for a moment, forgot the girl, forgot the black ship. The tick of a falling twig brought him back, and the sudden transition was disorienting. Disturbed and off-balance, he fought for calm. He could revisit the memories later. He needed to focus on the present.

A smile glimmered on Claire's face, allowing him to read both her pleasure and relief at his arrival, but it was so brief, he thought it must be tempered with something else. Perhaps she was just cold and tired. She had made no attempt to stand, and now she turned and looked back out at the ocean, tension still written in the tightness that gripped her body. For a moment he worried that she was hurt, but he would have seen the signs if that were the case. Quickly he scanned the area again. Was there someone else there? Had his noisy scrabble alerted the men who were searching for her?

She glanced back up at him, the smile gone, then turned back toward the ocean. Crawling forward, he let his gaze follow the dark shape of her raised arm, out past the pale hand and pointing finger. There, almost hidden in the night shadows that wrapped the maze of islets, was a tiny gleam of light. It flickered as the breeze stirred the trees, and heavy branches blocked his view, but as he stared through the fading light, he realized he could just make out the dark outline of a large boat. Almost certainly the black ship.

His breath caught in his throat, and his voice was barely a whisper as he called down to her. "How long's it been there?"

Her shrug was a barely discernible movement of shadowy darkness, but he heard it in her voice. "I got here last night—well, early this morning, I guess. I noticed it just after it got light."

"Have you seen the dinghy?"

She nodded. "Two of them. Two people in each one. They left together this morning, but then they split up. One came back this afternoon, but it left again." She glanced back at him, eyes dark against pallid skin. "And I heard an outboard yesterday too. At another island. Three or four times. And the day before as well."

"Yeah. Me too." He looked down at her, feeling her fear grow again. "Hungry?"

She stared up at him for a long moment and then the outline of her body relaxed onto the rock. "Oh, God! I'm starving. Have you got anything?"

He reached back and took the bag off his belt, holding it out over the edge so she could see it. "How does smoked salmon and fresh berries sound?" he asked. "You'll have to come up here, though. I don't think I can get down there."

"Okay, but it'll take me a while. I have to go round to the other side to get off the ledge."

Walker wasn't sure he liked the idea of her clambering around the cliff. "It's pretty dark. You gonna be all right?"

"I'll be fine. I'll take it slow. It's not as bad as it looks from up there. Besides, there'll be more light on the other side. The sun hasn't been down that long."

▶ It was almost half an hour before she appeared beside him. For a while he had listened to the small sounds she made as she moved slowly along the ledge, but soon they had stopped and he'd sat listening to the silence and watching the flicker of the light through the trees.

"Walker!" she said again as she slid to the ground beside him. "It is so, so good to see you."

He smiled and opened the bag, reaching in to pull out a piece of salmon. He handed it to her, his smile widening as she snatched it and crammed it into her mouth.

"Oh, that's so good!" She spoke around a mouthful. "I was ready to chew the bark off the trees!"

He looked up the oddly twisted trunk that grew beside him. It was shedding its bark, jigsaw pieces of reddish brown wood flaking off to reveal the pale green cambium layer underneath. "Nah." He smiled. "Not a good idea. It looks pretty, but it would taste terrible."

He turned back to find her staring at him, her eyes huge. "How can we be joking? They want to kill me!"

"How do you know? What happened?"

She turned to look across to where the ship's light danced in the darkness. When she answered, her voice was again tight with fear.

▶ "There has to be a reason they're hunting her," Dan said.

Walker and Dan were talking on the radio, and even though Dan's voice was distorted, Walker could hear in it an odd, distant quality, a change in cadence that he recognized. He pictured Dan staring off into space, his eyes unfocused, as he leaned across the bridge. Ten years ago, when Walker had first met him across a scratched metal table in a cold and featureless interrogation room, Walker had mistaken that distant look for arrogance, had called him an "arrogant white bastard." He had been wrong. It was Dan's way of relaxing his mind so he could let it run free, sorting through the details, connecting the dots, noting the gaps in the story, trying to put it all together.

"You sure she didn't see anything?"

"Nope. Came back from kayaking and they were waiting for her with guns," Walker replied.

"Huh. Gotta be something big. Drugs, most likely. Those containers could hold a lot of coke or heroin. That kind of money would make it worth going to a lot of trouble to get rid of her."

The radios fell silent as the two men considered the possibilities of the events that had occurred. Walker looked across at Claire, curled up on a bed of ferns beside him, her face slack in the depth of sleep. A faint hiss of static emanated from the speaker as he stared up into the dark bowl of the sky and watched the stars wheel overhead. It felt strange to be talking to Dan as an equal, stranger still to feel a sense of kinship, but it also felt right and natural, and he realized that he was enjoying it.

The radio came to life again. "Thing I can't figure out is why the hell they would sink it all, then hang around." Dan sounded like he was mostly talking to himself, and Walker figured he didn't expect an answer, so he didn't offer one.

"Any chance you can stay where you are for the night?" Dan's voice had become strained. "I can't get hold of Mike till tomorrow, but I'm going to see if he can get the guys in the marine division to send one of their boats up here to take a look. I'll have to use the satellite radio to call him, so I need to be here, and it would be good if we knew whether the black ship was still anchored over there."

Walker heard the rushed words and understood that Dan was talking too much in an effort to deal with the discomfort he felt at making such an outrageous request. He smiled as he listened to the awkward pause that followed, remembering his own discomfort years ago sitting across from this man in that dingy interrogation room. It wasn't just the situation that had changed; their roles had been reversed.

Dan spoke again. "I'm not sure it's a good idea to bring the dinghy over there now either. Sound carries really well at night, and it could be a problem if they hear us."

Walker looked around the rocky knoll they were sitting on and nodded to himself. He and Claire had talked about moving again, getting away from the black ship under cover of night, but it might be safer to stay where they were. He could find enough food for them both and Dan was within reach if they needed him. Plus, he knew Dan was right in thinking it would be good to have someone watching the black ship and keeping an eye on dinghy traffic.

"You still at Shoal Bay?" He needed to be absolutely sure Dan was close enough to be able to reach them quickly. It was the least he could offer Claire as reassurance.

"No. I'm in a cove on the north side of Midsummer Island. I'm pretty well out of sight. If Mike can get the marine guys to come, they'll probably come down from the north, through Wells Passage. Maybe anchor up in Kingcome somewhere and send in a couple of guys in one of the inflatables to take a look."

"We might need you here if the guys from the black ship come sniffing."

"I'll keep the radio beside me, and the outboard is already mounted. Tell me again exactly where you are."

Walker listened to the sound of paper rustling as Dan hauled a chart out and followed the route he gave him. He wondered about the kind of strings Dan would have to pull to get the marine division to divert one of its big catamarans to come and check things out. He knew from talk back in the village that the division was stretched pretty thin, with only thirty cops spread between four boats, patrolling an area that was about six hundred miles long as the crow flies and stretched from Vancouver in the south to Stewart, on the Alaska–British Columbia border, in the north. And if that wasn't tough enough, the deep, twisting inlets and over forty thousand islands that formed the complicated coastline of the land his people had called home ever since the ancestors had arrived made the actual distance closer to seventeen thousand miles.

Whatever Dan said—or promised—would have to be pretty spectacular, and Walker was pretty sure that if he did manage to pull it off, there would be some form of payment extracted from him when he returned to his home down south. But Dan didn't seem to be bothered by the possibility and Walker guessed it would simply be something the ex-cop would deal with when the time came. For now, he just sounded glad for any help he could get.

"Okay. The radio is on and the dinghy is in the water and ready to go. I'll call you as soon as I get through to Mike. I don't need to wait for the marine guys to get here. If they come, they'll do their own thing. They won't need me to help them out. I'll just give them the information and tell them where to look. And you call me if it even looks like someone is coming your way."

"Okay. How long will the batteries last in this thing?"

"They're good for at least a couple of days with the spares I gave you. I'll be there long before that."

Walker turned the radio to standby and put it back into the bag that hung from his belt. He would have to move the canoe before it got light, but that would wake Claire and it could wait for a few hours. He settled himself more comfortably against the tree and closed his eyes.

▶ The Great Bear constellation hung far to the west when he nudged Claire awake and slid down the bank. Another hour and the first pale fronds of dawn would stain the horizon. Enough time to find a hiding place for the canoe and something to eat. A fish would be easy, but he could not risk a fire, and no fire meant that most of the roots and bulbs he could collect were also off the menu. He had seen a sea cucumber and a few sea urchins clinging to the rocks, but he doubted he could reach them unless he dove for them, which meant a long, hard scrabble back up. That left the oysters and mussels that were clinging to the rocks, and there were plenty of those. Plus, he could see kelp floats undulating just off the shore and they would be easy to pull. There was dulse too, and rice-root lilies in the clearings between the trees, as well as ripe berries on the wild lily of the valley that grew in the shadows. They wouldn't go hungry.

▶ "Walker!" Her voice was low. "There's another boat coming!"

The urgency in her voice jarred him. He had been so busy thinking about starting to collect food for their meal that he had not heard her approach. Earlier, they had decided to split up, each finding a spot with a good view of the black ship but on opposite sides of the island. That way, if either of them spotted one of the dinghies returning, or anything else, for that matter, he or she could alert the other. It was a good plan, but it required patience, and he had allowed himself to be diverted while he got caught up in planning their meal.

"A boat or a dinghy?" He pulled himself to his feet.

"A boat. Looks like a crew boat or a water taxi or something. It's fast. I think it's going to the black ship."

He sent her back ahead of him, knowing he would slow her down. "Keep your head down."

She gave him a quick smile. He knew she hated being in sight of the black ship, but when he had suggested staying there, she had immediately understood the reason. Now perhaps it was paying off.

By the time Walker caught up with her, he could see that it did look like a crew boat with its aluminum hull and narrow decks. The new boat was throttling back, the bow wave moving forward as the hull settled deeper into the water. The roar of big diesels dropped to a rich purr as it slid easily up to the side of the black ship. Two men came out of the cabin and reached out to grab the bumpers that were already hanging from the railings. The newcomer had obviously been expected.

Walker and Claire lay and watched as a steady stream of men emerged from the new arrival and stepped onto the deck of the black ship. They clustered together for a few minutes and then there was a brief flash of movement in the cockpit as someone came out and called them in and they all moved aft and disappeared. The black ship lay quiet yet again. After watching for a few minutes, Walker pulled out the tiny radio once more. He needed to let Dan know that something was going on.

► TEN ◄

► Javier Fernandez checked his men again. He had to admit, Harry's idea to dress them as loggers and put them in a crew boat was brilliant. It provided the perfect cover. Who would question seven loggers heading back from camp?

Gunter and Trip had been searching for three days and had come up empty. Likely the girl had drowned or was holed up somewhere. Either way, they were not going to find her in time. So far it appeared no one was checking on her absence. That could change at any time, but at least with the crew boat, the danger of discovery was not so high.

He glanced up at the wheelhouse, where Harry stood watch. Fernandez had told him to call Gunter and Trip and the other two back an hour ago, and they should be arriving anytime now. They were already a day behind schedule. They had lost hours of daylight and the few left would not give them enough time to retrieve all the canisters safely. With the girl still missing, he could not risk *Snow Queen* being seen in Shoal Bay. It would raise too many questions and put the whole operation at risk. They would have to rely on the crew boat, and it did not have winches and lights. That meant they could not work at night. They would have to haul the last of the canisters in the morning and it would take the rest of the day to assemble and test the equipment. That left less than two days to rehearse the attack. It was tight, but it was doable.

▶ Almost two hours after it arrived, Claire and Walker watched the crew boat leave again. They were too far away to see any of the men who had gone aboard it in detail, but there had been a lot of them. They had also seen the two dinghies return, and the four men in them had joined the others. The dinghies were both still floating off the stern of the black ship.

"It's heading your way," Walker told Dan. The roar of the crew boat's engines had faded enough to allow him to speak at a reasonable volume, although the wake was still pounding along the shore.

"Damn. We need to know if they're going to Shoal Bay," Dan replied. "I got hold of Mike and he's going to pass everything we've got so far on to the marine division. He can't promise they'll act on it, but he thinks they will at least call me."

He snorted. The sound transmitted through the radio as an explosive burst of static.

"Knowing Mike, that means he's probably going to really put the screws to them, but it may take a while and until I hear from them, I'd rather not stray too far from the radio unless I have to."

Walker grimaced as he heard the words, knowing what was coming and feeling the twist of guilt in his gut as he thought about what he would have to ask Claire to do.

"Look," Dan continued, "I know it's asking a lot from both of you, much more than I damn well should, but do you think you might be okay there for a while longer?"

Walker glanced over at Claire. She had lost some of the tension he had seen when he'd first found her, and while she wasn't completely back to being the confident girl he knew from Shoal Bay, she was much more alert. "Think you could handle another night here?" he asked.

A shadow crossed her face, but she quickly masked it. "You fixing supper?" she asked.

He smiled. "Sea cucumber coming up." Then he said to Dan, "Yeah. No problem."

▶ The call Dan was waiting for came less than an hour later. The police boat was under the command of a sergeant by the name of

Carl Hargreaves. Dan had never met him, but he knew him by reputation; the marine-division guys who had worked with him said he was a hard-ass, but good at his job. Hargreaves didn't sound happy about talking to a civilian, and Dan quickly realized that he wouldn't welcome too much in the way of input or suggestions. Dan would have to be careful with what he said and even more with how he said it. On the other hand, Dan had information that Hargreaves needed.

"The thing is, they couldn't see who was in it," Dan said as he told Hargreaves about the crew boat leaving the black ship. "They're too far away. But it looks as if it's headed in this direction. If you come here, you need to stay out of sight."

"Yes," Hargreaves agreed, "and you need to stay where you are." The message—and the caution it contained—was unmistakable.

"Not a problem," said Dan, working to make his voice amiable. "But Walker and Claire are out there alone, keeping an eye on that black ship. If they need me, I'm going—and I won't be asking permission."

There was silence, and then Hargreaves grunted. Dan took that as acceptance even if it wasn't exactly agreement.

The police boat Hargreaves commanded, the *Lindsay*, was a sixty-three-foot catamaran with a top speed of almost thirty knots. Hargreaves told Dan they were heading south down Laredo Channel and were due to dock at Shearwater in a couple of hours. Even if she was not held up there, it would take several more hours for her to reach Dan—if she did. More likely Hargreaves would stop at Ivory Island or Bella Bella and launch the big rigid inflatable boat, or RIB. It could hold several men and, at forty-five knots, could travel much faster than the catamaran. It was also much easier to hide.

An hour after their first conversation, Hargreaves called him back. "I've got three guys headed your way in the RIB. I'm putting them onto Dowager Island, just north of Thistle Point. There's a beach they can haul out on there and it looks like they'll be able to walk over to the south shore and get in behind a group of offshore rocks. Should be able to get a good view of Shoal Bay from there."

Dan smiled with relief. Not only was Hargreaves sending the

troops, but they were going to the same spot Walker had chosen to watch from. It was better than he could have hoped for. "Thanks, man. Any idea of the ETA?"

"Well, it depends on how easy the walk is. They should be on the island about half an hour from now. Maybe a half-hour walk?"

"Great. I really appreciate this."

Hargreaves grunted again. Dan was beginning to think that might be his normal form of communication.

▶ It was a little over two hours later when Dan heard from him again.

"That crew boat your people saw just arrived in Shoal Bay. The guys have it tied up at the wharf." Hargreaves was on the phone with Dan and he was relaying the information from his team on the ground.

"They see that guy with the short white hair?" Dan asked.

"Hang on. I'll check."

This three-way relay thing was not the most direct method of communication, but it was the only one that ensured privacy.

"Nope. They've got seven guys who look like loggers. They're all standing out on the wharf," said Hargreaves.

"Watch for the guy with white hair," Dan said. "If he's there, there's a good chance those guys aren't loggers."

"Okay. I'll tell them." There was a pause, then Hargreaves cut the connection.

▶ Dan called Walker back. "The crew boat's in Shoal Bay. They've got seven guys that look like loggers out on the wharf."

"They got the white-haired guy there?"

"Nope. Just the loggers. Think they could be the real thing?"

Walker looked at Claire. He knew she had heard. He had seen the quick clench of fear when he mentioned White Hair. He raised his eyebrows in query. She shook her head.

"Don't think they're loggers," he replied.

"Yeah. That's my guess too," Dan said. "Those two dinghies still with the black ship?"

"Yeah."

"Okay. Call me if anything changes. If we can put White Hair in Shoal Bay, it might be a good time for me to come and get you, but if he's still there, I think you're better off staying put."

▶ Walker and Claire stared at the black ship. Walker had collected some berries and he still had some dried salmon left, but the planned meal of oysters and mussels had not happened. They had both lost their appetite with Dan's call.

"None of this makes sense," Claire said, looking at Walker. "They can't be loggers. What would loggers be doing at Shoal Bay? Why would they come and visit the black ship?"

Walker shook his head. He had asked himself the same questions and he hadn't been able to come up with answers.

▶ Dan was frustrated, and being frustrated made him restless and impatient. He didn't like being a bystander. He didn't like knowing the action was just a few miles away and having no role in it. He didn't like having a growing list of questions he couldn't find the answers to. And he hated the thought of the girl being out there on her own—or almost on her own. He didn't know her, had never met her, but the knot in his gut was growing bigger every second, and memories of Susan were impossible to still. He hadn't been there when she needed him. He couldn't let it happen again.

Even knowing Walker was with her didn't help, because he didn't feel right about Walker being there either. The man might be superb at looking after himself in this environment, but that didn't mean he was equipped to take on a group of armed thugs. Apart or together, neither Walker nor the girl had any way of protecting themselves if things went wrong. That was his job—or at least it had been—and here he was, sitting on his ass doing nothing. Waiting for Hargreaves to tell him what was happening in Shoal Bay. Waiting for news on White Hair. Waiting for Walker to report on the black ship. Waiting, waiting, waiting. The need to act vibrated through his brain and ricocheted down his nerve endings. It swam through his blood, heating it to fever pitch as it throbbed below his skin and snaked along his muscles. It was going to drive him crazy.

Half an hour later, he had the answers he needed. White Hair was in Shoal Bay. Hargreaves had called him back with that information after the guys had seen a man matching the description coming down the wharf from the old lodge. And the black ship was still anchored. He had checked that with Walker. Now he was in the Zodiac, throttle open as wide as it would go, heading for the island that matched the description and location Walker had given him. It was the best chance he had of getting Walker and the girl off that island and into relative safety on *Dreamspeaker*, and he was going to use it.

Running flat out, Dan figured he could reach them in maybe thirty minutes. There was some risk involved, because he had no way of staying in contact with either Walker or Hargreaves while he was on the water—he only had one hand-held radio, and he had given that to Walker—but he figured he was okay. White Hair was accounted for and from what Hargreaves had told him, it seemed likely that both he and his "loggers" were going to be at Shoal Bay for a while. Besides, until he reached the island Walker and Claire were on, he was just a guy out fishing. Once he was there he would see for himself how things were, and he would have the radio. Unless, of course, things had changed. Unless Walker and the girl were not there when he arrived.

It took him nearly an hour. A heavy chop in the channel slowed him down and he had to cut the engine when the island came into view. He needed to see if there were any signs of trouble, and he didn't want to create a wash that could alert someone on the black ship. Staying close to the shore as he approached would have given him some protection and allowed him to check for signs of activity, but there was maybe a mile of open water he had to cross. No choice but to crank up the motor again.

He made it with no problem. The island was like all the other islands off this part of the coast: lichen-covered rocks with patches of moss, tufts of grass, the odd clump of dark shrubs, and a few wind-twisted trees. There was a slight breeze, but it was barely enough to stir the leaves. Dan coasted in and let the inflatable bump gently up to the rocky shore. He couldn't see any sign of either Walker or the girl, but there was no point in getting out. If they were still here, they would come to him. If they weren't, or if someone else had got to them first, there was nothing he could do here that would help them. Either way, it wouldn't take long for him to find out.

His ears were just getting used to the quiet after shutting off the motor when Walker spoke.

"Nice boat."

The disembodied voice came from above and to the right, and even though Dan had been hoping to hear something, it jolted him.

"Jesus! You scared the hell out of me," he said as he scanned the rocky slope above him. "Where are you?"

"Up here."

"You okay?"

"Yeah."

"Black ship still there?"

"Yeah."

"Any activity on it?"

"Nope."

Dan shook his head. Getting information out of Walker was like shucking wild oysters for pearls: a lot of work with little chance of reward. He wasn't even sure he needed more information. What he did need was to get Walker and the girl back to *Dreamspeaker*.

But what he wanted was to see the black ship for himself.

"Is there an easy way up?" he asked.

▶ Walker pointed out the trail he had taken and Dan headed up. He slowed as he reached the summit. He didn't know how close the black ship was or how exposed he might be. Plus, the girl might not be expecting him.

She was sitting in the shadows, watching his approach.

"Hi," he said. "I'm Dan." He stopped and waited for her to respond. Considering all she had been through, she was undoubtedly exhausted and scared and maybe near breaking point. There was no need to add to her stress.

There was a faint rustle as she stood up and stepped out into the light.

"Thanks so much for coming." She walked toward him. "I'm Claire."

The greeting seemed formal and was at odds with her tousled hair and rumpled clothes. Shadows rimmed her eyes and there were lines of tension drawn around her mouth, but in spite of that, she looked surprisingly healthy. She also looked . . . what? Open? Warm? Maybe both, although neither was exactly right. It was something more than that. Perhaps "real" was the closest he could get, but whatever it was, he found himself drawn to her in a way that he would have had difficulty explaining—or even admitting—to himself. And that smile. It was amazing, especially considering the circumstances. He felt himself respond to it instantly. It was like Susan's . . . He shut off the thought before it had time to complete.

"The black ship . . . ?" he asked.

Her smile dimmed, and she turned to point back at the trees.

▶ Walker was right, of course. The black ship was still anchored and there was no sign of activity. At least, not that Dan could see. He checked the angle of the sun for possible reflection, then raised the binoculars he had brought with him. They were surveillance binoculars, 20x50 power. He didn't have a tripod, but there were plenty of rocks scattered along the ridge that he could use to keep them steady. At this distance they wouldn't let him see much detail, but they would help some.

He let his eyes drift slowly from bow to stern, then top deck to waterline. There was a forest of antennae. He counted two radar, a couple of satellite phones, a satellite dish, GPS, SSB, VHF. The works. Nothing unusual and nothing useful. A rigid-hull inflatable maybe twenty-five-feet long swung on davits above the upper deck, and two dinghies floated off the stern, just as Walker had described. Nothing special about them either. He couldn't make out the name or port of registration. Just a faint tracery of lines on the stern. Same thing for the registration number. No flag either. Nothing.

He was about to turn away when movement caught his eye, and he quickly swung the glasses forward. Someone was coming out of the wheelhouse. Dan was too far away to make out his features, but as he watched the man walk aft along the deck he felt a faint shiver of recognition. There was something familiar there. Nothing specific. Not at that distance. More a combination of shape and movement: top-heavy with an odd mincing twist to his walk. That and a heavy thatch of thick, dark hair. Probably curly from the way it caught the light. He had seen him before. But where?

The man disappeared into the cabin a few seconds later, and when he failed to reappear Dan slid back down to join Walker and Claire. They had both caught his reaction when he noted the movement and now they were staring at him, waiting to hear if he had seen anything. He shook his head. "Nothing happening. Time to get out of here." He turned to Walker. "Got the radio handy?"

Walker passed it over to him. Dan had left the SSB radio open back on *Dreamspeaker*, as well as the VHF, in the hope that he could hear and speak directly to Hargreaves from the hand-held. He didn't want to think about what it would cost him when the bill came in, but whatever it was, it would be worth it if it worked. It did—sort of. Hargreaves's voice faded in and out and sounded weird, but there was enough to make out the gist of what he was saying.

Hargreaves still had White Hair at Shoal Bay. The guys could see him clearly. He was standing on the wharf, supervising the retrieval operation. The "loggers" had been sorted into teams: three men in each of the two aluminum dinghies that belonged to the crew boat, and one standing up on the wharf. There was another man there too. A heavy-set, swarthy-looking guy with his hair pulled back into a ponytail. The men in one of the boats had pulled up a black metal canister. It was obviously heavy and they had had trouble getting it into their boat, but they had manhandled it in and were in the process of bringing it back to the wharf. The other boat was still pulling chain. They were taking it slow and being very careful.

"The dark guy has to be White Hair's pal," Dan told Hargreaves. "The description's right on." He looked over at Walker and Claire.

"We'll be leaving here in about five minutes. Should be back on board in about an hour. I'll keep in touch." He slid the radio into his pocket and started down to the shore. "Okay, guys. Follow me."

He was about to step into the Zodiac when he realized that Walker hadn't moved.

ELEVEN

▶ "You'll be a sitting duck out there!" Dan shook his head in frustration as he took in Walker's imperturbable expression. The man was still perched up on the knoll where he had been when Dan first arrived.

Walker shrugged. "Who's going to care about a crippled Indian in a beat-up canoe?"

A smile masked the cynicism, but Dan heard it. He wasn't buying.

"Oh, bullshit! Don't give me that crap. These guys are serious. We might not know what they're up to, but we do know they don't want any witnesses. If they see you out there, they're going to try to get rid of you."

Another shrug. "I'll wait till dark. Stay in close."

"Close to what? There's a mile of open water out there!" Dan turned to the girl. "Can you talk some sense into him?"

Claire blinked at him in surprise. "Me?"

Dan nodded at her, taking in her reaction. Other than a brief acknowledgment when he first saw her, Dan had barely addressed a word to her—the situation they were in didn't exactly encourage the niceties—so it was hardly fair to expect her to jump in now. But Walker liked her, and he might listen to her reasoning. He watched as she looked back and forth between them, silently urging her to add her encouragements to his. Meanwhile, Walker continued to sit on the rocky outcropping above them, a slight smile playing across his face. He was relaxed, at ease, even comfortable. Dan, on the other hand, was so tense his back felt rigid, his arms and legs frozen, hands clenched at his side.

"No," she said. "I don't think I can." She met his stare full on. "He knows what he's doing."

Dan snorted. "Yeah, right." He turned away abruptly and let his gaze wander out over the water, trying to reconcile himself to the inevitable. There had been a time when he could simply impose his will on others, Walker included, but it seemed that time had passed. Now he had no choice but to respect the decision this taciturn, solitary man had made. Walker would stay on the island, at least till nightfall, and then leave in his canoe. Dan was not even sure where he would go when he left. Walker hadn't said he was going back to his home— wherever that was—but he hadn't agreed to come to *Dreamspeaker* either.

Dan turned back to find both of them watching him and threw his hands up in a gesture of surrender. "Okay. I give up." He turned and reached down into the Zodiac for the radio he had just taken back.

"Here. You may as well keep this. At least let me know where you are. Call me if you need help." He scrambled up a few feet of rock and held it out so Walker could reach it.

There were a few seconds of hesitation and then it was removed from his hand.

"Thanks."

"Yeah. Make sure you use it. I'll be waiting to hear from you."

Walker smiled but said nothing.

▶ Dan, with Claire sitting quietly beside him, made it back to *Dreamspeaker* in well under an hour. With no radio to keep him informed and no need for a quiet approach, he simply ran full out the whole way. The speed and power helped him deal with his frustration and took his mind off Walker.

He barely glanced at Claire. He knew she was on the edge of exhaustion, her skin wan beneath streaks of dirt, her hair lank, and her eyes ringed with a bruised, bluish tinge. Yet she hadn't complained, either on the island when he had told her they could not take her kayak with them or here in the dinghy, where she was forced to brace herself against the constant pounding. And she had showed spunk when she stood up for Walker. He wondered whether Walker had told her that her boat had been sunk or whether that would become his job. He hoped not. He was not good at giving bad news and he hated having to do it.

Back at *Dreamspeaker*, he helped Claire on board, dug out a towel and a clean T-shirt, and then pointed her to the shower. Once he heard the water running, he returned to the galley, put on a pot of coffee, and made up a couple of sandwiches. He was not sure she would be able to stay awake long enough to eat them, but she needed food. She looked like a starving waif.

While he was waiting for her to finish her shower, he headed forward to the wheelhouse and called the *Lindsay*.

"Any change?" he asked Hargreaves.

"Nope. It's starting to get dark so the guys can't really see well, but it looks like they're either slowing down or close to finished. They've pulled five canisters up so far and they're working on a sixth. They've got them all lined up along the dock."

"Have they opened any of them?"

"Nope. Just put 'em down real careful and left them. Looks like the guy with the ponytail is in charge of that end of things."

"So what's the plan?"

There was a pause and Dan could sense Hargreaves deciding how much he should share.

"Figuring it out as we go. Technically, we've got nothing on them."

Dan got the message. He wasn't going to get much. "Keep me in the loop. I've got the girl on board. I don't want to risk running into trouble."

"Yeah. Okay. You got the Indian too?"

"No. He stayed with his canoe."

Hargreaves was quiet for a minute as he considered that, then asked, "Has he got a radio?"

"Yeah. I gave him my hand-held."

"Huh. You keep me informed too, okay?"

"Yeah."

He headed back toward the galley. The shower had quit and there was no sound coming from the head. He stuck his head around the open stateroom door and saw a pile of clothes on the floor but no sign of the girl. He found her sitting at the table in the galley. She had already finished half of a sandwich and was well on her way to finishing it off. Her hair had been roughly toweled and it stuck up in spikes all over her head. The T-shirt he had given her was at least three sizes too large and the neck hung down over her shoulders, but her eyes had lost some of the bruised look and her color was better.

She held the half-eaten sandwich up in the air. "I hope this was for me?"

Dan eased himself in to the other side of the table. "I figured you might be a little hungry."

She grimaced. "Hungry? I'm starving! I could eat wood chips and grubs."

He smiled and pushed the other sandwich across to her. "Want some coffee?"

The corners of her mouth lifted in the beginning of a smile, and once again he found himself responding to some unidentifiable magnetism. He felt ridiculously pleased that he could put her at ease, but at the same time he felt perilously close to his own demons. He knew he'd have to be careful.

"I'd love some, but I think I might fall asleep before I can drink it."

He shrugged and stood up to reach the coffee pot. When he turned back to the table, her smile had disappeared again and she was staring up at him, her eyes huge and dark.

"Will they find us here?"

He sat down and slid a cup across the table. "No. Not likely. They have no reason to come this way. And even if they do, they won't know you're aboard. I talked to them back there at Annie's boat—you know Annie, right?" He didn't wait for an answer. "They think I'm just a guy passing through on my way down south."

"You talked to them?" Her voice rose in pitch.

"Relax. It's okay. I don't know how much Walker told you, but I'll fill in all the details after you've caught up on some sleep. You're just barely keeping your eyes open sitting there." He reached out a hand and helped her up, then led her down the passageway.

He thought she might have been asleep before he closed the door to the stateroom.

▶ Walker didn't answer until his fourth call, and Dan worked hard to keep the frustration out of his voice. "Where are you?"

"Heading your way."

"You going to make it tonight?"

"Probably not."

Dan shook his head. "Where the hell do you sleep? Under a rock?"

He didn't expect an answer and he got none. "I'll leave the radio on. Be careful. Call me if you need me."

▶ He dug a beer out of the refrigerator and turned on the stereo. He figured Claire would probably sleep through a brass band playing a Sousa march on the deck, but he kept it low anyway. Didn't need volume to let the sweet sounds of Coltrane's saxophone seep into his soul, and it helped him think. He dragged a notebook out of the drawer and started to make some notes.

Coltrane had morphed into the plaintive wail of Charlie "Yardbird" Parker's alto sax and Dan still had nothing. There were too many pieces of the puzzle missing. He needed a place to start. He closed his eyes and let his mind drift with the music. A faint image pulsed and coiled on the inside of his eyelids, gradually coalescing into the shape of the man he had seen on the black ship. A memory feathered through his brain, but it twisted out of reach and he couldn't grasp it. Who was he?

The last note of Parker's "Ornithology" faded into the night and he felt the silence settle over him, quieting his mind and relaxing his body. It was late. Walker obviously wasn't going to call again. Time to turn in. He pulled a sleeping bag out of a storage locker under the settee and took it up to the wheelhouse. Childhood memories of storm-dark nights and long hours in the wheelhouse watching to make sure the anchor hadn't dragged, checking that the wind hadn't shifted, had spurred him into building a bunk behind the chart table. Tonight there was barely a breeze, and the boat was steady as a rock, but the radio would be only a few feet away. He turned the volume up just in case.

Four hours later, it came to life.

"You awake?"

Walker's voice cut through the layers of sleep like a machete and catapulted Dan off the bunk. He struggled to free his feet from the sleeping bag and fumbled for the microphone.

"Yeah."

"Don't sound it."

"Funny guy. What the hell time is it?"

"White man's time?"

"Ah, shit. Never mind." Dan peered out blindly through the windshield into an ink-dark night. "What's happening?"

"I'm in Shoal Bay."

A surge of adrenalin brought every nerve cell revving to instant attention. He wasn't sure he had heard right. "Say again?"

There was no response, just the faint hiss of the air waves coming from the speaker.

"Are you nuts? Why? Is the crew boat still there?" The questions tumbled over each other as Dan fought to make sense of what Walker was saying.

"Nope."

"They left?"

"Yeah."

"So there's no one there?"

"Couple of guys. They're up at the old lodge."

Dan rubbed his face. Maybe he was having a nightmare. None of this made sense. It was so crazy, it was disorienting.

"What if they're armed? Get the hell out of there!"

"They're sleeping. I can hear them from here."

"Where are you?"

"Down by the float."

"Down by the float." It was ridiculous to simply echo Walker's words, but Dan couldn't find any of his own. "Huh. So now what?"

"Got a bunch of canisters and a box here."

Dan sucked in his breath and his eyes fixed on the microphone as if it were a snake that had come alive in his hand. "They left them there?"

"Yeah. Guess the sleeping beauties are supposed to be keeping watch."

"Walker, leave them alone. You can't open them, and one slip will wake those guards. Then what happens?"

He could hear the smile in Walker's voice. "You got a short memory."

"What?"

"Remember how we met?"

Dan grimaced. This was not going well. He had to find a way to get Walker out of there.

"Walker . . ."

"The box is full of spray cans."

"What?"

"Spray cans. You know. Kinda like paint cans, only little. You got to pull a trigger thing."

"Spray cans." He was back to echoing.

"Yeah. But they're plastic."

"Okay." Dan shook his head. This wasn't a nightmare. It was more like science fiction. Or a scene from *Alice in Wonderland*. Maybe he had fallen down a rabbit hole.

"I opened one of the canisters. It's got a bunch of cooking stuff all packed in foam and plastic."

"Cooking stuff." The repeating thing again. Maybe he *was* the rabbit. "Wait a minute. You opened a canister? Shit! They're going to know. Soon as those guys wake up . . ."

"I closed it again."

"Oh. Right. Sure." Considering what else Walker had done, he supposed that made some kind of sense. Maybe. "So what are you doing now? Are you planning . . ."

"Gotta go. I can hear those guys moving."

The radio went dead, but Dan continued to stand there, staring at the unblinking red light that was the only illumination in the wheelhouse. He was a rational man and his life was based on logic and reason. He remembered taking an aptitude test when he had first applied to the police force. It had been twelve pages of odd, disjointed, seemingly unrelated and irrelevant questions. Crazy stuff. He had thought the whole thing a total waste of time: who cared if he jumped in piles of leaves or rolled up the toothpaste tube? But the next day, when he had been summoned to a meeting with the recruitment-office commander and a staff shrink, they told him more about himself than he had ever thought possible. It was so accurate, so detailed, it was eerie. They knew he was good at math. They knew he liked to work with his hands and was good with tools. They knew he loved puzzles. They even told him he was artistic, although his wood carving was something he had never shared with anyone except Susan. They also told him that he had received the highest score they had ever seen on the deductive reasoning scale. Two days later, he was invited to the police academy.

So what the hell could he deduce from all this? Spray cans and cooking oil? Was the girl wrong? Maybe she hadn't seen a rifle that night when she returned to the bay. But then why were White Hair and his buddy searching for her? Walker believed her, that was for sure. And what about Walker? Was he wrong when he said her boat had been deliberately sunk? Didn't seem likely. Walker was a cautious man who would say nothing rather than go out on a limb. And he knew boats. And the weather. And the ocean.

Dan shook his head to try and clear the fog that was swirling around in his brain. It didn't help. He lifted his gaze to the windshield and tried to peer out into the night, but it was so dark he couldn't even make out the trees on the shore just sixty feet away. Hell, Walker could be ten feet away and he wouldn't be able to see him. And where was Walker? Had he left Shoal Bay? Was he going to come here? Did he need help?

"Shit!" Dan pushed himself away from the console, inhaled as deeply as he could, and breathed it out in a long sigh. "I need a coffee."

He felt his way back to the galley, hearing Claire's soft breathing as he passed the stateroom. At least she was getting some sleep. He knew he wouldn't be getting any more this night, and it seemed like Walker hadn't had any.

He pulled the kettle onto the stove and made himself a cup of coffee. Somehow he had to make sense of all this. He leaned back against the settee cushions and stretched his legs out under the table. The ocean was calm, but it was never still, and the faint rocking relaxed him. Allowed him to let his mind roam free. Let all the facts float and settle. Let his subconscious take over.

► TWELVE ◄

► It all revolved around the black ship.

Dan had moved out onto the deck and was leaning on the rail, watching the trees slowly take shape against a lightening sky. He felt renewed by the freshness and promise that early mornings held. Reveled in hearing the dawn chorus fill the air with birdsong. Loved breathing in the morning breeze that wafted the clean scent of fir and bracken across the water. Three hours of contemplation had not added any new facts, but it had given him a clearer perspective.

Claire had not been mistaken. He had seen and spoken with the men who were looking for her. They had lied to him. And that lie meant Walker had not been mistaken either. Claire's boat had been deliberately sunk. So the black ship was the main player. And the crew boat was part of it. But what the hell were the spray bottles all about? And the cooking oil?

He had been thinking this was drugs. Now he wasn't so sure. It was beginning to take on the shape of something much worse. He remembered the slick, slimy feel of some of the cases he had worked on. They had coiled their way into his gut, taken on a foul smell and taste that seeped into his skin and permeated his dreams. This felt the same.

He needed an edge, a corner, a loose flap that he could use to pry something open. Hargreaves wouldn't make a move unless he had something concrete to go on. He had pretty well said as much last night. And speaking of Hargreaves . . .

Dan pulled his gaze from a pair of gulls, pale against the still-dark shore, and headed back to the radio.

"The guys out already?"

"No, why? Something happening?" There was an odd note in Hargreaves's voice that Dan couldn't quite place.

"Not that I know of. Just wanted to let you know Walker's out there somewhere. Maybe have them keep their eyes open for him."

"That's the Indian, right?"

"Yeah."

"He's in Shoal Bay?"

"Probably not now, but he was there a few hours back."

"Doing what? It was so damn dark last night you couldn't see your hand in front of your face. Hell, it's barely light now. He wouldn't have been able to see his paddle, let alone see where he was."

"He seemed pretty sure about it. Said the crew boat was gone and there were some canisters and a box on the float." Dan figured he should keep quiet about Walker opening the canister. Hargreaves didn't seem like the kind of guy who would be understanding about something like that.

"Yeah. Well, no law against that."

"Depending on what's in 'em."

A vision of Hargreaves and his team opening a box of cooking oil drifted past his mind's eye, and he bit back a grimace.

"Yeah. Well, we'll check them out when we get back."

That was it—the note he had heard in Hargreaves's voice. It was the slight tremolo caused by the vibration of big engines thundering just below the deck.

"Get back? You going somewhere?"

"They've got a freighter changed course south of Rupert. Looks like it could be heading to a rendezvous with a trawler over by Porcher Island. We're headed there now. We'll check it out and be back maybe late tonight or tomorrow sometime."

"Might be too late."

Hargreaves's voice was fading as he moved farther away. "We can keep an eye on them on satellite. Pick them up later if we need to."

Dan bit off his reply and turned off the radio. He couldn't blame Hargreaves for not feeling the same sense of urgency he did. On the other hand, he didn't want to say something he might regret later. He had a feeling he would be needing Hargreaves and his crew again.

▶ A salmon leaped high out of the water, silver body lit by the first rays of the sun. Dan thought about throwing out a line—it would make a nice lunch—but quickly dismissed the idea. The fish would probably sense the mood he was in from five hundred feet away and head straight for the bottom.

There were a lot of things he could handle pretty well, but frustration was not one of them. He hated feeling useless, and that's what he was right now. The girl—he had to start calling her Claire—was still sleeping, and waking her up would be a lousy thing to do. Besides, awake or asleep, he couldn't leave her alone on *Dreamspeaker*. And he had no idea where to look for Walker. He had called him five or six times, but the man always had his radio turned off. So what other options did he have?

He couldn't leave. Not only was it impossible for him to walk away from whatever was developing in Shoal Bay, but he could never bring himself to abandon Walker.

He couldn't move closer to the action. He didn't know if White Hair was out prowling or if the crew boat was back in Shoal Bay, and he couldn't expose Claire to more danger.

He couldn't take the dinghy over to see the canisters for himself. That would almost certainly scare them off, and he might get himself shot in the process.

He couldn't do any damn thing except wait . . . and he hated waiting.

His foot brushed against a stanchion and he aimed a vicious kick in its direction. It connected much harder than he had planned and his reward was a stabbing pain in his toe. "Damn, damn, damn, damn . . ." He held on to the railing and hobbled toward the door, his face twisted into a grimace.

"Are you okay?"

Claire was standing in the doorway, watching him, a wary look on her face. She was wearing the T-shirt he had given her last night; her hair was disheveled from sleep, but the color had come back to her face.

He fought to change the grimace to a smile. "Yeah. I'm fine."

"Okay. If you say so." She didn't look convinced.

He followed her inside, bracing himself against the wall to keep the weight off his foot. "My foot slipped. Guess I need to be more careful."

"Either that or get softer stanchions," she said, moving past the table so that he could slide onto the bench. The wariness had been replaced with the hint of a smile. "My turn to make coffee. You'll have to point me to the supplies."

The pain in his foot gradually faded as the coffee brewed and he eased his toe around inside his shoe. Nothing broken. It had been a stupid thing to do. He had been lucky.

Claire slid onto the bench across from him. "Have you heard from Walker?"

He looked at her. "He called last night."

"And?"

"He was in Shoal Bay."

"Shoal Bay?" Her voice echoed the confusion on her face. "But why? He knew I was coming here with you."

Dan looked out the porthole. A gull was skimming the water, its wings spread in an effortless glide. He realized she had naturally assumed that Walker had gone to Shoal Bay to check on her, which meant she didn't know about her boat. If she had known, she would not have mentioned Shoal Bay without some acknowledgment of its being sunk. That meant he would have to tell her. Shit.

"Did Walker tell you about your boat?"

"My boat? Do you mean *Island Girl* or the kayak?"

"Not the kayak. The boat you had in Shoal Bay. *Island Girl.*"

Her chin lifted in acknowledgment, and then, as his words registered, her gaze narrowed. "Had? She's still there. I was going back to her when I saw those men."

It was Dan's turn to nod. "I know. But she's not there anymore." He took the plunge. "We think those same men you saw towed her out and sank her."

"What? Sank her? What are you talking about? Who towed her out? What . . ."

He watched her struggle as she tried to take it in. This had been the part of the job that he had hated: the pain and discomfort of being the bearer of bad news. He had hated seeing the sudden look of vulnerability that turned bright eyes dull and made taut muscles slack. It drove a knife into his gut in a way few other things could. On the job, he had used it to fuel his anger and drive his determination to solve the case. Out here, he could only fight a sudden urge to wrap his arms around the girl across from him and comfort her.

The urge jarred him. He had not thought about touching any other woman since losing Susan. In fact, he had spent most of his days and nights for the past many months thinking about little else but Susan. Now he suddenly realized that he had barely thought about her once since this thing started. The knowledge made him feel oddly guilty and he reached for her memory, teasing it like a sore tooth, running his mind across its rough surface, tasting its texture. It was there, as vivid as ever, but he could sense a subtle change. Not in the memory itself, perhaps, but in him. He felt alive again. Complete. A little older and a little wounded, but the wound was healing, scabbing over. There would always be a scar, but for the first time since he had lost her, he could see past her death to the happier times they had shared.

He brought himself back to the present and to Claire, slumped in shock across from him. While the urge to comfort her was strong, it was not sexual. It was simply a reflex, more paternal than hormonal. Still, he needed to take care that sympathy did not become sex. He knew from his years on the force how easily that could happen when the victim was an attractive woman. He had witnessed it time and time again. He also knew that now was neither the time nor the place to restart his love life. He was grateful for the whistle of the boiling kettle, and he used it to distract himself.

▶ Claire sat silent, her head down and her eyes closed, as Dan pushed a cup of hot coffee into her hands. He knew from experience that there was nothing she could say. Image after image was flashing into her brain only to shatter into a thousand tiny pieces. The idea that her boat had been sunk was incomprehensible to her. The concept was impossible for her to grasp. She could not believe it. She was in shock. Her brain simply would not accept it.

Dan sat quietly across the table from her, coffee in hand, watching her, waiting for her to give him a cue, and after a time she looked up at him, her face once again pale and her eyes once again dark.

"When?"

He knew exactly what she meant. "The day after you saw the men at Shoal Bay. Walker found her in Half Moon Cove."

Talking seemed to help her mind start functioning again, and he could see her searching her memory, trying to recall the details she must have seen so often on her charts.

"Half Moon Cove? That's way east of Shoal Bay, right? Over by Turner Island?"

"Sounds right. I haven't been there, but I talked about it with Walker."

"Is he sure it's her? Maybe . . ."

Dan saw her bite off the rest of the words before the thought could be completed. He was familiar with the pattern, and her actions were so clear, he could almost read her mind. She knew Walker and knew he was familiar with *Island Girl*. Knew he would not make a mistake like that. Tears suddenly flooded her eyes and he watched her shake them away angrily. She was telling herself that crying wouldn't help her make sense of this. Now would come the guilt—maybe it was her fault.

"Maybe I didn't tie her up well enough. Maybe . . ."

Dan reached a big hand across the table and caught one of hers. "Claire. It wasn't you. It wasn't anything you did or didn't do, and it wasn't your fault. Somebody towed your boat out and sunk it deliberately. We don't know why. Not yet. We do know they were looking for you. You saw two of them that night when you were going back to your boat. Walker told me about it. Walker and I saw them again over at Annie's. That means they don't want any witnesses to whatever it is they are up to. You and your boat were a threat to them."

She stared at him. "But why? I didn't see anybody doing anything!"

"I know that. You know that. But they don't, and whatever it is they're up to, they don't want to risk a witness. The black ship unloaded a bunch of canisters and sank them near the shore there in Shoal Bay. There's another boat there now, that crew boat you and Walker saw, hauling them up again. We had the marine police up here yesterday, watching them, but they had to leave before they could figure it all out."

▶ Claire closed her eyes again and Dan could see it was all too much for her. It had to be overwhelming and probably nothing made sense. Shaking her head, she shoved herself up from the table and went out into the salon. The door to the aft deck was open and behind her he could see a lone gull perched on the railing. It watched with bright, black eyes as she approached, then spread its wings and lifted off effortlessly, its protest hurled plaintively into the morning breeze. Dan followed her, not speaking, not crowding her but close enough to let her know she was not alone.

▶ "She was my father's boat."

Her voice was so quiet he had to strain to hear it. She had been leaning on the rail for over twenty minutes, staring blindly out toward the shore, oblivious to the chill of the morning air.

"Your father was a boater?"

"No. He was a fisherman. He spent most of his life on the sea." She looked over at him. "That's where I grew up. We followed the fish. I went to school wherever we were fishing, did correspondence when there wasn't a school to go to, helped where I could." She shook her head. "I loved it."

Dan turned and smiled at her. "So we're both fishermen's brats."

Claire stared at him. "Your dad was a fisherman too?"

"Yep. His boat was the *Betty Jean*. She was a gillnetter. I can still remember every inch of her. My dad sold her just before I finished high school."

She gave him a pale smile. It wasn't much, but at least it was something. It was a start.

▶ THIRTEEN ◀

▶ More than two hundred miles to the south, a float plane banked hard over Lulu Island, and Mike Bryant looked down as the city of Richmond and the great sprawl of Vancouver slid beneath the wings, glass-fronted towers and condos glittering in the sun. He caught a brief glimpse of joggers and bicyclists on the dyke below him and then the pontoons kissed the surface and skimmed across the choppy water of the Fraser River toward the Riverport Seaplane Terminal.

He stepped out into bright sunshine and was greeted by a uniformed RCMP officer, who led the way to a black SUV sitting in the parking lot.

"Thought you might not make it." The uniform had driven him to a previous meeting, but Mike couldn't remember his name.

"Yeah. I was starting to get a little worried myself. It was like pea soup in downtown Victoria. They were just about to cancel when the fog lifted." He peered out the window at the sparkling river. "You've got a nice one going over here."

The drive from the seaplane terminal to Vancouver International Airport took less than ten minutes, and as they drove along the Sea Island dyke, Mike watched the traffic on the river. The intricate ballet of watercraft plying the silty waters never failed to fascinate him. Everything from freighters to ferries to kayaks used the river to access the heart of the city, and, like the city, it never slept. One boat, an old seiner that had seen better days, made him think of Dan, maybe three hundred miles north. They hadn't spoken since Dan called with that wild story about a black ship and an Indian guy and some girl who was being hunted. If it had been anyone but Dan, Mike would have dismissed it all as the crazy ramblings of some dope-smoking hippie, but Dan was one of the sanest and most logical people he knew. If he thought there was something going on, there probably was. Mike had phoned a friend over in the West Coast Marine Division and pulled in every marker he could think of, plus a few he had made up but that sounded good, and as a result had received a promise that Dan would be contacted by one of the big patrol boats. Dan owed him big for that, and Mike was going to enjoy making him pay up. Maybe he could even use it to get him back on the force. He made a mental note to contact him to follow up on the story once he was back at the office.

The car turned onto Russ Baker Way and the river gave way to the warehouses and hangers that skirted the edge of the airport. Mike looked for the increased security he knew was in place. It would be much more obvious in a few days, but even now he could see unmarked police cars in many of the designated police parking spaces, relegating the marked cars to curbside, and there were more security vehicles driving the perimeter. There were even a couple of RCMP cars parked beside the bridge leading over the river from Richmond, although without their lights on they looked more like traffic detail than security.

They passed the glass-fronted airport terminal, where transit police patrolled the crosswalk and the overhead walkway to the Canada Line station, and drove on to the nondescript RCMP sub-detachment building a few hundred yards farther down the road. The rest of Mike's group was gathered in the lobby. They greeted the late arrival with a round of applause.

"Yeah, yeah, yeah. Very funny." Mike pushed past them. "I may strive for perfection, but even I can't control the weather."

He ignored the good-natured rejoinders and moved into the meeting room, where more than a dozen men and a couple of women were already seated around the table. Mike took his place, nodding a greeting at familiar faces. He knew all of them professionally and was socially acquainted with more than a few, but this was not the time for chit-chat, and they quickly settled down to business. This was the final session of the security planning group, and there was no room for error. The leaders of many of the world's largest organizations, including the United Nations, UNESCO, and the World Bank, would be arriving in Vancouver in less than a week. They would be joined by a former US president, the US Secretary of State, a handful of envoys, and several senior Canadian ministers. Following close on their heels, a handful of celebrities slated to perform at the benefit concert that was the only public event of the international conference would descend on the city. The protesters had already started arriving. Most of the bureaucrats and civil servants were already in place. The security requirements were not quite as complex as those required for the G8 summit that Mike had been involved in a few years back, but they were close. And the risks were greater now. It wasn't only the protestors and the lunatic fringe. Terrorism was a very real threat.

FOURTEEN

▶ "I want to see her."

"What?"

The comment surprised Dan. He and Claire had moved back into the salon, where they had been sharing memories of growing up as fishermen's kids. It had stirred up recollections of days spent on net floats, catching shiners and poking at sea anemones as his father and the other fishermen spun yarns and mended nets while they listened to the company radio for news on the returning schools of salmon. It had also kept Claire from thinking too much about the fate of her boat. At least, he had thought it did.

"I want to see my boat. She can't be completely underwater or Walker wouldn't have found her."

"Claire, that's impossible. You know those guys are still out there. They're the ones who sank your boat. You know they're armed. If they see you there, do you think they will hesitate to shoot you?"

She shrugged, her mouth set in a stubborn line. "They could find us here just as easily."

Dan's eyes narrowed. "That's different. If they see *Dreamspeaker* here, it's just me on my way down south—and there is no 'us' because 'we' are not going. Not until this is all over."

She glared at him. "And when will that be? We don't know what's happening out there. It might already be 'all over.' They might be gone."

He shrugged. "The answer is still no—and before you ask, no, you can't take the dinghy." Damn. He was losing his touch. First Walker and now Claire. Maybe it was something in the air up here on the mid-coast.

She looked at him with exasperation. "I wasn't going to ask for the dinghy. I'm not an idiot. But we have to leave here sometime, and when we do, I would like to go via Half Moon Cove and check her out." Her voice faltered. "It's not just memories they took. All my research is on that boat. Maybe I can save some of it."

Dan's frustration evaporated at her words and was replaced by growing admiration mixed with sympathy. Of course she would want to see her boat. In her position, he would want the same, and although she was still battling the effects of shock and confusion, he realized that this girl was tough. She faced life head-on and didn't let it get her down. A wry thought crossed his mind: a few lessons from her might do him good. He smiled and reached out to shake her hand.

"Deal. Look, I know waiting is hard, but right now that's all we can do. If I can't get hold of Walker in the next couple of hours, I'll call the police boat again. Maybe between the lot of us we can figure something out. Okay?"

An apologetic smile quirked the corners of her mouth. "I'm sorry. I'm being a bitch. You've already done more than I could possibly have expected, and here I am plotting your course and arranging your life."

"Hey! No problem. We'll plot that course as soon as we know what's happening and where everyone is." He stood up and scanned the bay through the portholes. "I'll go and check on Walker. How about I show you the laundry on the way and you can get your clothes fixed up. I can't imagine you want to wear that T-shirt for the rest of the day."

▶ It took almost an hour to get a response from Walker, and Dan had almost given up when the quiet voice floated out of the radio.

"Yeah."

"Where the hell are you? I've been trying to reach you since last night."

"Been busy."

"Doing what? You can't still be in Shoal Bay."

"Nope."

Dan sighed. "Walker, this is getting tiresome. I have Claire with me and I have no idea what's happening or where anybody is. At least let me know you're okay."

There was a pause, and he could almost hear Walker thinking before he said, "I'm fine. I'm on the other side of the island. Where Claire took her kayak."

Dan felt a little of the tension go out of his shoulders, although the thought of Walker still being on the same island as the guys from the crew boat bothered him. "You get any sleep?"

"Yeah, a couple hours. Enough."

"So you coming here?"

The silence grew as he waited for Walker to answer.

"Walker?"

"How about you come here?"

"What?" The tension rushed back, a hundred-fold stronger than it had been. Dan could feel it throbbing in the veins in his neck and surging into his skull. "Why the hell would I come there? Are you in trouble?"

"Bring Claire with you."

"Bring . . ." Dan clicked off the transmitter and stared blindly out through the windshield. The sun had risen above the trees and was reflecting off the leaves and the water, turning the tiny cove into a glittering world of light. It was surreal, and it matched this conversation perfectly.

He took a deep breath and pressed the transmitter switch back on. "And why would I bring Claire with me?" he asked, his voice careful and quiet.

"Someone needs to walk across and see what's happening, and I can't do it. Take too long and make too much noise. And you can't leave her there alone while you do it, so that leaves the two of you together. Besides, without her, you have no idea where to go."

Dan let the idea float around his brain for a while. The crazy thing was that Walker was probably right on all counts. It made sense in many ways—and it would get him out of this holding pattern that was driving him nuts—but the risks were enormous. He might be tempted to do it, but all his training and his instincts told him that he should not put Claire, a civilian, a young woman, at risk.

"Too dangerous. What if the crew boat found us out in the open? Or White Hair? We wouldn't have a prayer."

"Already here."

"Who? The crew boat?"

"All of them. Arrived just after sun-up this morning."

"You saw them? Where the hell were you?"

"Just round the point. Taking a nap. They woke me up."

Dan opened his mouth to point out the obvious dangers but decided it would not be worth it. Walker would do what Walker would do. And so far, Dan had to admit, it seemed to be working.

"Walker, I can't ask Claire to go back there. She's spent the last few days running from some guys who want to kill her and she just found out they sank her boat. That's a lot to handle. You think she'll want to walk back into the lion's den?"

"She's a pretty gutsy lady."

The statement hung in the air as Dan struggled with his options. If he did nothing, he might never know what these guys were up to. Even worse, he might hear about some disaster later and have to live with the fact that he might have been able to do something to stop it. On the other hand, the chances that he could actually do anything, even if he did manage to make it over to Shoal Bay, were pretty slim. Still, knowing that didn't stop him from wanting to go there. But what about Claire?

"I don't know. Doesn't feel right—and she's a civilian anyway."

"So are you."

The blunt statement stung. He still hadn't come to terms with that particular situation, had avoided thinking about it. He had given Walker an edited version of his resignation from the force, a version that omitted Susan altogether. He knew Walker didn't buy all of it, but at least he knew that Dan was no longer an RCMP officer.

"Yeah. But it's different for me. I have some training and I know what to expect."

"Why don't you ask her and see what she says?"

Dan snorted. An ex-con was offering him advice, telling him what to do. And he was probably going to do it. Talk about role reversal.

"I'll get back to you." He put the radio back in its cradle.

It took ten minutes of wrestling with his conscience to be able to convince himself to ask Claire. It took her less than ten seconds to agree.

"Sure. Why not? Better than sitting here doing nothing."

Dan stared at her, amazed by her willingness to return to Shoal Bay. "That's my line. I'm surprised to hear it coming from you."

"Why? It's my boat they sunk, my work they ruined, my bay they took over." She had changed back into her jeans and sweatshirt and worked her hair into some semblance of order. She had also shucked the shock and depression.

"You do realize there is more than a little danger involved?"

Her glance slid away from him, but when she looked back, her face was composed. And serious. "Yes, of course I do. I was terrified that first night, when I saw those men and their guns. Nothing like that has ever happened to me before and I had no idea what to do. I was so scared I felt sick."

Dan could hear the slight tremor in her voice as she relived the events.

"And the next morning, when they came looking for me? That was even worse, because I was trapped up in the rocks. But when they left, I knew I had to do something, and once I started moving, it got better." She shook her head as if she couldn't believe it herself. "I don't know why, but even though I was cold, and hungry, and didn't know where I was going, I didn't feel quite as scared. Does that make any sense?"

He smiled. "Yeah. It does. Kind of."

"Well, I feel the same about this. We can either sit here waiting for something to happen, or we can go there and maybe do something. I like that option better."

She had put into words precisely what Dan had been thinking, but still he hesitated. The risks were enormous. Common sense dictated that he haul anchor and head south as fast as he could. That would get Claire out of harm's way and he could contact Mike again, maybe speak to his old team, get them on board, leave the decisions as to what to do up to them. It was not only the safest option, it might also be the best. But it would take time. He was at least three days away from Victoria, and he didn't think they had that long. And then there was Walker.

He looked at Claire again. She was watching him.

"You'll stay with me the whole time and do exactly what I tell you. Okay?"

She nodded, her face completely serious.

"And you wear a jacket with the hood up while we're in the dinghy. Maybe a ball cap under it. Might give us some extra time if they see us."

He was thinking out loud, trying to cover his discomfort and justify doing something he knew he should not even be considering. "And you stay behind me when we're on the island . . ."

It was her turn to reach out a hand and touch his arm. "It's okay. Really."

Dan snorted as he shook his head. "No, it's not," he said. "It's crazy. And dangerous. I could lose my job—if I still had a job. And if something goes wrong, I am probably going to lose my mind—if I still have one of those when this is over." He stood up and ran his hand through his hair. "Come on. If we're going to do this, we'd better get going. Let's get you a ball cap and a jacket."

► FIFTEEN ◄

► Annie struggled out onto the slick, night-damp deck. She had been pulled out of deep sleep by a noise that threatened to break her eardrums as it reverberated through her boat. Once she was outside, the pounding only intensified. Now the vibration traveled up through the hull to the soles of her feet in time with the assault on her ears. She clutched a tattered robe to her throat with one hand and grabbed her shotgun with the other as her worn slippers slapped along the deck. The moon was behind a thin cloud, and only a silver gleam stippled the water as she peered down into the blackness, trying to make out who, or what, was there. She was more than willing to fire the gun, but she thought there was a chance it might be Walker again, maybe with news of Claire, and she didn't want to shoot him.

"Walker? That you? Goddamn it! You gotta stop sneaking around at night, scaring the shit out of people!"

The pounding continued unabated, but above it she could hear another noise and she strained her ears to identify it. She thought it sounded like an animal in distress, an eerie keening that rose and fell with the waves. It set her teeth on edge.

"Walker?" She made her way back along the deck, trying to see past the curve of the hull. There seemed to be a blacker patch within the deep blackness of the shadow, but she couldn't be sure, and in any case, the pounding was going to drive her insane.

"Shut the fuck up!" she screamed down into the darkness. The noise stopped for perhaps ten seconds, then started up again, more frantic than before, and the weird howl that accompanied it swelled to a crescendo. In the lull, the howling had sounded more like sobbing.

"How the hell can a person get any sleep with this shit going on," Annie muttered to herself as she stomped back to the wheelhouse and pulled the big spotlight from its holder. "It ain't right."

She moved back out onto the deck, flipped the switch on the spotlight, and held it over the railing, watching as the brilliant white beam of light erased the shadows. It revealed a tiny, battered rowboat with a single occupant: a skinny, oddly twisted old man, sitting hunched on the single wooden seat. One gnarled hand clung tightly to the ladder that hung down from her boat almost to the water and the other held an oar. He was smacking the butt end of that oar against the hull, rocking himself back and forth, his eyes closed and a dark trail of what could be blood twisting down his sleeve. His long hair was plastered in wisps across his head, and his open mouth was uttering the weird, hysterical, unnerving cry she had heard.

"Tom? What the fuck are you doing here? Tom! Tom!" Her voice rose in pitch as she tried to get him to look at her.

She could hardly believe her eyes. Old Toothless Tom was a fixture for those few people who, like her, had made their home in these waters. A hermit. A loner who kept completely to himself. She had only seen him on a few occasions, when she had been heading over to the store at Dawson's Landing. Each time, he'd been standing out on the shore in front of his ramshackle cabin, hurling invective at some invisible adversary or pleading with some equally invisible friend. His thin, querulous voice would drift out over the water, rising and falling in time with his waving arms and the writhing undulations of his body as if he were performing a grotesque and macabre dance.

"Tom! Tom! You stupid old bastard. I know you can hear me."

Again there was no response, and he didn't give any signs of stopping his compulsive pounding. Maybe Tom wasn't his name, just what everyone called him. As far as she knew, he had never spoken to anyone else either. She wasn't sure if he had ever left that dilapidated piece of shit he lived in, grubbing for a living in the confines of the tiny dent in the shoreline that surrounded it. The few times she had seen him, standing on the rocks as she motored past, he had never waved. Never called out. What the hell would bring him out in the middle of the night? Was this something those "voices" he talked to were pushing him into? And how the hell could she get him to stop that infernal racket?

"Tom!" No response. "Tom!" Still nothing.

"Fuck!" Annie could feel the tension building behind her eye sockets. She had to get him to stop. She looked frantically around the deck, and her eyes settled on a pile of wood she had dragged up, piece by piece, to burn in the stove. She hated to lose any of it after the work it had taken to get it up onto the deck, but she had to do something. She snatched up the biggest piece she could reach, balanced it on the rail while she lined it up with the dinghy below, and let it fall. If it hit the old bastard on the head, too goddamn bad—at least it would shut him up.

It dropped squarely onto the bow of the tiny boat, setting it rocking and almost tipping it over, then bounced up against the metal hull of her old workboat, where it made a noise louder than Tom's oar before splashing harmlessly into the water.

The old man looked up in shock, toothless mouth open in mid-wail, and rheumy eyes wide with fright.

"What the hell do you want, you silly old fuck?" Annie shouted down to him. "Stop banging on my boat."

"He's dead!" The sound was something between a scream and a wail, and the words were distorted by his lack of teeth.

"Who's dead? What the hell are you talking about?" A cold worm of fear shivered to life as she wondered if he was talking about Walker. Of the few people living here, Walker was the one Tom would be most likely to know and recognize. Walker was always out paddling that canoe of his, visiting every tiny nook and cove.

"Dead! Dead! Dead!" The quavering voice rose and fell, the rocking was starting again, and she thought the oar pounding was next.

"Okay! Okay already. You already said that." Annie cut him off in mid-ululation and leaned over to rattle the ladder. "Tie that piece-of-shit dinghy up to the ladder and get up here. I ain't standing out here all night."

She moved back from the rail, far enough to be out of sight, hoping his need for contact would make him move, hoping he could keep himself together enough to do it. Could he even climb the ladder? He had to be in pretty good shape to have rowed all the way here, but maybe he was exhausted.

For several minutes she heard nothing but an occasional moan, but at least the pounding hadn't started up again. She was about to step forward and see what he was up to, maybe prod him some more, when she heard a creak from the ladder and the sound of feet climbing up the rungs.

She moved back into the cabin, turned on the light, and poked at the firebox on the stove. She certainly needed a cup of tea, and maybe he could use one too. Might even help settle him down some. The kettle was still hot and she pulled a china teapot out of a cupboard, dropped a couple of tea bags into it, and filled it with water. She knew he had reached the deck: she had heard him scramble over the railing. She could feel him peering in though the porthole, watching her, but he didn't come in. It was unnerving, but it matched the man. He was crazy. A real loony. She could not imagine what kind of horrific event, real or imagined, had made him set out in the middle of the night and reach out to another human being.

She took two cups off their hooks and set them on the table, then, as an afterthought, reached up for the sugar bowl and placed it beside them. Maybe that would bring him in. The poor old bastard had to be hungry. There was a can of milk already open in the fridge and she added that to the homey tableau. Lastly, and with a good deal of reluctance, she dug out a box of chocolate-chip cookies and put a few of them on a plate. She really hated to use up the cookies. They were her special treat. She only bought one box a month, over at the floating store, and she only allowed herself one a day, just before she went to bed. Still, if it got the old bastard off the deck and settled down a bit, it would be worth it.

She sat down on the bench, poured herself a cup of tea, and

waited. She had drunk half of it before Tom finally sidled into the doorway, and she was almost finished before he found the courage to move in and join her at the table, sliding awkwardly onto the bench across from her and perching on the edge of it, his thin body tense and coiled, poised to run.

She ignored him. Picking up the pot again, she filled both cups, then pushed one slowly across the table toward him. For several minutes he simply sat motionless, staring at the cup as though he expected it to come to life. Then, with a darting glance at her, he snatched it up with both hands.

Still she stayed silent, quietly pushing first the sugar bowl and then the milk toward him, but avoiding the eye contact she thought might frighten him. He stared at those too before reaching grimy fingers into the sugar bowl to pick out three sugar cubes. He held them for a few seconds, then dropped them one by one into his cup and watched with rapt attention as they dissolved into the pale liquid. She waited till he looked up again, then pushed the plate of cookies over. This time the fingers moved more quickly.

"Who's dead, Tom?" She kept her voice low, hoping not to set him off again, but she heard the first moan start even before she had finished speaking.

"Tom! Who's dead?" This time she smacked her hand down on the table to accompany her yell, cutting off the moan in mid-quaver. "Who?"

He stared at her in shock, his eyes wide. "Don't know," he whispered. "Man."

"A man's dead?" she asked. "A man you don't know?"

He nodded, wrapping his thin arms tightly around himself as he rocked to and fro. The half-eaten cookie sat forgotten on the table. Annie breathed a sigh of relief. Tom knew Walker.

"Man. Floating." The words were disjointed, unfamiliar in his mouth.

She looked across at him. He was a pathetic figure: scarecrow thin, dirty, and obviously terrified, hands rough and scarred, sparse gray hair lank and stringy, thin strands meandering across his mostly bald head. He could have been Dickens's model for *Uriah Heep*, she thought, except he didn't match the unctuous part.

"Where did you find this man?" She had to keep him talking. If he stopped, he was going to start the moaning and rocking again.

He writhed and twitched, his eyes sliding from side to side. "In water. On rocks."

"In your bay?"

He rocked back and forth in what she thought was a nod.

"You've never seen him before?"

He shook his head so violently, his whole body shook with it. "Don't know! Never seen!"

"Huh." She didn't know what else she could ask him. Or what she should do. She wished Walker would come back. He would figure something out. He had that quietness that gave confidence.

Thinking of Walker made her think of the man Walker had called for help—and the reason he had called him. Maybe this dead man was somehow mixed up with what had happened to Claire's boat. And what about Claire? Where was she?

"You sure it was a man?" she asked.

He stared at her for a minute as if confused, then nodded. "Man. Man."

"How do you know? Was he naked?"

"No! Has clothes! Pants. Shirt." He patted himself as he spoke, indicating each item.

"Tom, women wear pants and shirts too," Annie said.

His agitation increased. "Not woman! Man. Has beard!"

"He has a beard?" So not Walker, or Claire, or the guy Walker had called in—what was his name? Dan. That was it.

Tom nodded vigorously. "Beard. Long beard. Red. Red hair."

"He had a red beard?" Tom nodded again, his eyes tightly closed.

This seemed much too vivid, much too detailed, to be some figment of imagination, even in a brain as troubled as Tom's seemed to be. Certainly his agitation was real, and Annie thought the fact that he had come here, and was talking to her instead of to one of his "voices," also pointed to his story being true, even if hard to believe.

The bigger question was what to do about it. She supposed she could always go over and see for herself, but what would that accomplish? She had no desire to see a dead body, and other than reassuring herself that Tom was in fact speaking of reality, it would do nothing to help her figure out the next step.

Maybe she should go over to Dawson's Landing. They had boats stopping at the floating store all the time. They might have heard if someone was missing. Might even know who this dead guy was, and they could contact the RCMP to come deal with it. But that would take time, and what would she do with Tom?

Once again she wished Walker were there, but she had no way to contact him: he didn't have a radio, and she didn't know where he lived. That left his friend, Dan. He had told Walker that he was no longer with the RCMP, but he must know a lot of them and he would certainly know how to handle something like this. She could call him, although she recalled Walker saying it was dangerous to use the radio because those men might hear it. The radio was public, and anyone could listen in on a conversation. She would have to be careful what she said. Maybe she could make up a story that would bring him here—something completely different but important enough to make him agree to come. She looked at Tom, sitting across from her, his eyes tightly closed as he rocked endlessly back and forth. That dark stain on his sleeve was almost certainly blood, but it didn't look fresh and she had no desire to check it out. On the other hand, it did give her an idea. A medical emergency. That might be the perfect excuse to get on the radio and call for help. She wouldn't even have to give out her location because he had already been here. She searched her memory for the name of Dan's boat. She had only glanced at it when he first came in. What the hell was it. *Dream* . . . something?

SIXTEEN

▶ The morning was in full bloom, sun stabbing through the trees with tongues of light, gulls wheeling lazily over the water. As Dan and Claire got under way, Dan kept the revs on the outboard low to keep the noise down and whenever he could, he kept close to shore.

Claire sat huddled in the front of the dinghy, the visor on the ball cap Dan had given her pulled low over her eyes and the hood of a green rain jacket up over her head. She looked both awkward and ridiculous in the oversized clothing, but Dan's initial feelings of sympathy were more than offset by the concern he felt growing with every turn of the motor. She had been so sure that this was something she wanted to do. So certain she could handle it. Now he could see her fear building with every slap of a wave against the bow, and he was aware of the worried glances she was throwing his way.

The entrance to the passage that lay to the south of Claire's Cove, as he called the little bay where Claire had hidden in her kayak, opened up, and Dan cut the revs even further as he let the dinghy idle along its southern shore. He had loaded a fishing rod and tackle box on board before they left, and now he placed the rod in the rod holder and fed out some line. It wasn't much, but at least it provided some kind of cover story. He felt almost as nervous as Claire looked and he asked himself for perhaps the twentieth time if he should simply turn around and go back to *Dreamspeaker*, fire up her engine, and head south.

"You don't have to do this, you know," he said, leaning forward to peer under the visor at her pale face.

She flashed him a strained smile. "Thanks, but I think I do. I need to see them for myself." She looked across the water toward Spider Island. "I'll be okay once we get there. It's just sitting here thinking about it that's getting to me."

He sat back, still not happy with what they were doing, although perhaps a little reassured by the knowledge that this was her decision as much as his. He wasn't normally an indecisive man, but the fact that there were no clear-cut courses of action open to him bothered him almost as much as the feeling that he was endangering the life of a young woman he had just met.

But he had been right in thinking she was tough. No matter how frightened she might be, she had made her decision and she was not going to back out. Now he needed to do the same. His hand reached back for the control stick and he turned the dinghy north. "Okay. Let's see if we can find Walker."

He let Claire guide him in, knowing she was familiar with these reef-infested waters. As he was coming to expect, there was no sign of Walker on the shore, and no sign of his canoe either. Dan assumed— and hoped—that the man was up in the trees somewhere, watching them. On the plus side, there was no sign of anyone else.

They skirted the reefs Claire must have paddled past just days before and idled toward the rocks where she had stashed her kayak. True to form, Walker appeared as they approached, moving quietly out of the trees where he had been hidden by the long shadows cast by the early-morning sun. He turned and pointed east along the shore to where the jumbled rocks became a low cliff overhung with hemlock trees.

"Go past those trees. There's a ledge where you can climb up. Good place to hide the dinghy."

▶ If it weren't for the black ship and those damn canisters, Dan thought as he scrambled up from the ledge after tying the dinghy to a low branch, this would be a great place to spend some time.

The moss-covered ground was soft underfoot, and the sun filtering through the trees was warming the air and filling it with the rich scents of late summer: salmonberries and salal, hemlock and fir, bracken and fern. Claire had been right again. It was less nerve-wracking now that they were here.

He made his way back to Claire and Walker, keeping the water to his left as he threaded his way through the trees. He had let her out below where Walker was standing, and now the two of them were sitting side by side in companionable silence, watching him as he approached.

"You make that much noise when you were sneaking up on bank robbers, you wouldn't have caught many." Walker's lopsided smile took the sting out of his words.

"Don't think I ever had to scramble over a bunch of rocks to catch any," Dan replied with a grin, matching his tone to Walker's. "Those bank robbers tend to be city slickers."

He looked at the two of them sitting there, Walker leaning back, relaxed, and Claire hunched forward, looking out over the water. They made an odd couple, the big, dark Native with his crippled legs and cynical smile and the slim, blond girl with her tousled hair and determined face. Claire's nervousness had all but disappeared and she and Walker looked like they could be out for a picnic instead of risking getting shot. And it wasn't just that she was now here on the island and committed to walking across that had relaxed her, he realized. It was Walker's presence. There was something about the man's calm confidence and quiet demeanor that was contagious. He felt it too.

Dan was still thinking about Walker as he and Claire started down the trail a few minutes later—although he was not sure it really could be called a trail. It was just another small dip in the land, no different from many others except for its course and direction, strewn with fir cones and leaves now that it was dry. He would never have noticed it if they hadn't pointed it out to him, but he was pretty sure Walker would not have missed it. And not just because of his familiarity with this watery maze of islands. The man's powers of observation were incredible. Not much would escape him. It was a skill Dan admired and had worked hard to acquire, but he had never approached Walker's expertise and he knew he never would.

Or Walker's ability to concentrate, for that matter, he thought wryly as he almost ran into Claire, who had stopped ahead of him.

"What's up?" he whispered, keeping his voice low as sudden tension sang along his nerves. He bent to peer through the trees. "Hear something?"

She shook her head. "No. I just wanted to stop and listen. See if I could. Hear something, I mean." She gave him a quick apologetic look. "It's something I do on the boat. Helps me figure out what's happening."

He nodded, chiding himself for letting his mind wander. He was supposed to be the pro, but Claire was handling this better than he was. This casual walk through the woods had lulled him into forgetting why he was here. He was used to rushing in, full of adrenalin, heart pumping, weapon drawn. This whole stealth thing was unfamiliar. It demanded the patience he had so little of, yet he needed to stay nothing less than fully alert. He owed that much to her and to Walker. And to himself. He could not afford to lapse into daydreaming now.

Almost an hour later, they stopped for perhaps the fifth time. The forest remained quiet except for the occasional flit of a bird and the faint sighing of the wind high above their heads.

"How much farther?" Dan whispered as he peered through the trees.

"Maybe half an hour. It opens up a bit as we get closer, so we'll have to slow down."

Another twenty minutes passed before she reached out a hand and stopped him. A new sound rode on the air, low and rhythmic, pulsing gently through the earth. It was the wash of waves on a gravel beach. They were close.

They moved off the path and deeper into the forest, creeping down toward the edge of the meadow, working their way through the trees. They were slightly below the lodge and off to one side, almost directly across from the wharf where the crew boat was tied. It appeared empty, as were the three dinghies tied in a row behind it. Twelve canisters lay scattered across the heavy wooden planking, seven of them open and empty.

Dan pushed Claire gently to the ground and sank down beside her. He had been planning on sending her back as soon as they reached the lodge, but now he realized that until they knew where all the men from the crew boat were, it was safer not to move around. They would have to wait here and hope that Walker was okay on the other side of the island.

They only had to wait a few minutes. It was very quiet in the bay, no sound except for the whisper of waves surging up onto the gravel, but gradually Dan became aware of a low noise coming from the lodge. It was almost a buzz, and he thought at first that it could be bees deep within a hive, although there was an odd, rhythmic, chanting quality to it. More like kids in a kindergarten class, reciting lines, though the sound was pitched too low. He looked at Claire to see if she had heard it. She had, but judging by the look on her face, she too was puzzled.

He checked behind them, then indicated to Claire that she was to stay where she was. If he could work his way back behind the lodge, maybe he would be able to see what was causing the sound. He had only gone a few yards when a sudden screech of wood against wood tore through the silence, and then came the pounding of running feet as a group of seven men burst through the door and raced out onto the deck. Dan froze as they spread out, then watched helplessly as two of them headed straight toward where Claire was crouched in the sparse undergrowth. There was no time to react, no way to give her a warning—and nothing either of them could do. Mentally he willed her lower to the ground, pushed deeper into the tangled salal.

Seconds later, before he could force himself to take a breath, the two men stopped, turned, and dropped into a crouch. Looking around the meadow, Dan could see that the others were doing the same. What the hell was going on? They were all well-dressed, mostly in slacks with shirts and sweaters, although two wore tailored suits. Definitely not a logging crew.

"Again!" The voice was sharp and oddly abrupt.

Dan swung his head back toward the lodge, where White Hair was now standing on the edge of the deck, a stopwatch in his hand. He didn't wait to see if the men had heard him, but turned away and walked back inside. The men followed.

It could have been a rehearsal for a play. It was certainly a rehearsal; that much was clear. But a rehearsal for what? As soon as the last man had disappeared, Dan carefully made his way back to where Claire was crouching and dropped down beside her.

"Is that the man you saw?" he asked.

She nodded. "I think so. I really only saw his hair, but he was tall—and he sounded odd when he spoke. Not an accent, exactly, but sort of clipped."

Dan nodded. "It's the same guy who came to Annie's boat when Walker and I were there. He had a buddy with him, but the buddy wasn't one of those guys who came out of the lodge. Maybe they left him behind today."

He hoped that wasn't true. If the other man wasn't here, he could be out somewhere looking for Claire and that would put Walker at risk.

"There was a second man on the deck of the lodge that night," Claire said. "I heard him talking, but I never saw him."

"Probably the same guy. They seem to stick together."

There were three more of the "rehearsals" over the next half hour or so, then they stopped and were replaced by the odd murmuring Dan and Claire had heard earlier, broken by the occasional scraping of chairs and the sound of footsteps. There were also metallic sounds that Dan thought might be from weapons being assembled, although he didn't mention that to Claire.

It was frustrating to be so close and yet have no way of seeing what was happening, and it was obvious they weren't going to learn much more staying where they were. Not only was it unproductive, but the risk of being discovered was too great. Dan had just reached out a hand to touch Claire's shoulder and urge her to leave when he saw movement, and one of the men emerged from the lodge. He was dressed in gray slacks and a light sweater, and he stood on the deck for a couple of minutes, scanning the bay as he lit a cigarette. Then he stepped down onto the path and started toward the wharf, turning left just before he reached it to head out around the far side of the bay. In minutes they had lost him in the trees.

"Anything out that way?" Dan leaned close to Claire, keeping his voice to a bare whisper.

She shook her head. "There's a bit of a trail—probably a deer trail—that goes out to the point." She was silent for a few minutes as they watched to see if the figure reappeared, and then she turned toward him. "You get a really good view of the channel from out there. I used to walk out there once in a while just to see what was happening. You can see right out to Hecate Strait to the west and, if you look south, way down to Goose Island. Maybe he's checking for someone. They could be expecting a new arrival."

He nodded. It was possible, although he couldn't see it. Whatever this was, it seemed like a pretty well-planned operation. It didn't seem likely they would want to add anyone new to the mix. It was hard enough to organize and control even a small group, and there were already at least nine men here.

Claire's sudden intake of breath alerted him to new activity.

"There's a different guy coming back," she whispered.

Dan nodded in agreement. The newcomer was clearly visible as he emerged from the trees. He was taller and heavier than the first man, and he was wearing chinos and a dark-green polo shirt. As he came closer, Dan saw that the polo shirt had ridden up where it had caught on a belt holster. There was a gleam of dark metal that winked with every swing of the man's arm as he took the steps two at a time, crossed the deck, and disappeared into the lodge.

So they had mounted a lookout, they didn't want visitors, and they were armed. Now Dan surely had more than enough to get the full attention of his former fellow officers. Sergeant Hargreaves would have to make a return trip—and quickly.

SEVENTEEN

As soon as the lookout disappeared, Dan tapped Claire on the shoulder and beckoned her back into the trees. There was nothing more to gain by staying here, and there might be a lot to lose if the meeting broke up and the men started wandering.

Claire and Dan moved quickly, stepping back out from the trees and onto the relatively easy ground of the path as soon as they had lost the sound of the ocean. They recrossed the island in less than half the time they had taken on the outward trip and found Walker sitting where they had first seen him several hours earlier.

"Must be nice, sitting out here in the sun," Dan said. "You fight off any bad guys while we were gone?"

Walker smiled. "Nope. Figure they were all out there following you. Sounded like an elephant coming back along that path."

"Yeah, right." Dan dropped down onto the ground beside him and watched as Claire moved past them to scan the water beyond the trees. "You see or hear anything?"

"Nope. Could be they've called off the search. It's been a few days now. Maybe they figure there's nothing left to search for."

"Yeah. Or maybe they've got a deadline and they need to concentrate on preparing for whatever it is they're planning." Dan hitched his shoulder back toward Shoal Bay. "There's nine or ten of them over there, a couple of lookouts and the rest of that crew boat, plus White Hair. Looks like they're rehearsing for something."

"Huh. You see any weapons?"

"Just with the lookouts. Nothing bigger than a handgun. But there was something happening inside the lodge that sounded like they might have been assembling weapons of some kind."

"So they'll probably be ready pretty soon."

"Yeah. I gotta get Hargreaves back down here."

▶ Dan retrieved the dinghy from its hiding place and pulled it back along the rocks. As soon as Claire was aboard, he turned to Walker, wanting to convince the man to come back with them but not sure if there was any chance he would succeed. Walker did his own thing, and even though he had been the one who had reached out for help when Claire was missing, he kept his own counsel. On the other hand, Dan knew he needed a sounding board, someone to run his ideas by, and Walker would be perfect. It was worth a try.

"You want to come with us? No point in hanging around here."

"No point in hanging around your place either." Walker was still comfortably relaxed on the grass.

"I could really use your help figuring this out."

As he said the words, Dan felt a start of surprise, and he realized they were a first for him. He had never asked for help before, not on the job, not from his friends, not even at home with Susan. Had he changed that much or was there something about Walker that invited trust? And how could that be when the man was an ex-con?

Walker was looking at him, the dark eyes suddenly intent. A long moment later, he twisted to his feet. "Yeah. See you over there."

"Hey, you can come with us. Leave the canoe here. I can bring you back whenever you want. It'll be faster and safer that way."

"That's okay. I'll be fine. I can make it in an hour or so."

He was already making his way down to the shore, and Dan was pretty sure arguing would be useless. Besides, Walker was probably right: he would be fine.

In fact, he arrived at *Dreamspeaker* little more than an hour after Dan and Claire. The three of them gathered in the salon to eat a pizza that Dan had dug out of the freezer and heated in the microwave. It was the first time Walker had been on Dan's boat, and he shook his head as he took in the array of appliances in the galley, the flat-screen TV hanging on the bulkhead, and the combined washer/dryer that sat behind the open door of the laundry locker.

"Tough way to live," he said as he made himself comfortable on a leather swivel chair. "Not sure you should be consorting with the lower class."

Dan smiled. It did look pretty fancy, even to him, but at the time he outfitted the boat, he had simply agreed unquestioningly to every suggestion Mike or the guys had made. It was as if he had been on autopilot. A robot. Maybe it was the funk he had been in. Maybe depression had taken away his ability to make his own decisions. Maybe his unconscious was trying to recreate the domesticity of the life he had lived with Susan. In any case, *Dreamspeaker* was now equipped with every appliance he could possibly think of and a few he hadn't known existed.

"Yeah," he nodded, keeping his face serious. "Got to watch who you associate with." He chewed the last of his pizza and let his eyes wander around the cabin. "Haven't used half of this stuff, but I guess it might come in handy someday." He slid his plate onto the side table and reached for his glass. "So," he said. "Where do we go from here?"

"What do you think they're doing?" Claire asked, her face suddenly tight.

He took his time answering. It was a question he had been asking himself ever since he had responded to Walker's call and met up with him over at Annie's boat, and the answer had been slow in coming. Now, for the first time, he put it into words. "I think they're rehearsing for some kind of attack."

The statement was greeted with utter silence.

For Dan, the idea had been growing over the last few days, coalescing as he wove the pieces together but never becoming totally coherent. Now, as he said it out loud, it finally took form and became real. It made sense of a lot of things. The sunken canisters would have contained equipment or, more likely, components that had to be assembled. The crew boat would have brought the team that was to do the assembly or make the hit or both. The logger disguise might even have been a last-minute idea in case someone came looking for Claire—although it was a good way to move around in these waters anyway. And that odd chanting they had heard? That would have been part of the planning, maybe counting out the sequence of events or the timing of the action. All of that would fit with the men running out of the lodge, and with White Hair and his stopwatch.

But what kind of attack? And where? He had been away from things for too long to know what was happening back in the city—or in the world, for that matter. And he still wasn't sure how the cooking oil and the spray bottles fit in—although he had an idea about that too. One he really didn't like.

On the other hand, he suddenly realized, the event didn't matter. He had to keep reminding himself that he was no longer on the force. The where and when were someone else's problem. All he could do was let them know what was happening. The rest would be up to them.

"We have to get the marine guys back," he said. "We've got to stop this." He pushed himself up from the chair and headed forward to the wheelhouse.

▶ The *Lindsay* didn't respond to Dan's call, which didn't really surprise him. Even though he had a good antenna mounted on a mast that reached high above the cabin roof, the SSB had a pretty limited range. And it was maybe a good thing in some ways, he told himself as he returned the microphone to its cradle, because now that he thought about it, he was pretty sure Hargreaves would kiss him off. He still had nothing but a hunch to go on, and he didn't think Hargreaves was the kind of guy who gave much credence to hunches—especially from a civilian.

That left Mike, and he hoped he had made it back to his office. It meant using a phone, which was not as secure as he would like, but he could work around that. He and Mike were close enough that they could read between the lines, and they had developed their own shorthand over the years.

Dan picked up the handset and punched in the number. It was answered on the first ring, and he heard Rosemary's cultured voice float out of the speaker. It had the odd metallic quality that always seemed to go with recorded messages. *You have reached the voice mail of Detective Mike Bryant. Please leave your name, number, and a brief message and your call will be returned as soon as possible. If you wish your call to be redirected, please press zero now.* Shit!

Dan slammed the handset back onto its holder. Now what? Where the hell was Mike? Or Rosemary, for that matter? And what fucking good was all this fancy radio equipment if he couldn't reach anyone? He looked at the electronics shelf of the navigation station: SSB, satellite radio, radio telephone, VHF, GPS, radar, depth sounder, computer, electronic chart display—the list went on. The place looked like a techie's wet dream. And none of it was of the slightest use in this situation. Maybe he should stop being so picky and just try to reach one of the guys in the squad instead.

His phone book was in with the rest of his papers, packed into a metal box that he kept in a storage bin under the floor boards. He ran back, pulled up the hatch, dragged it out, and lifted it onto the counter. This could take a while. The stuff wasn't sorted into files; he had just thrown it all in before he left.

"*Dreamspeaker. Dreamspeaker.* You there?"

The unexpected sound of the radio caught him by surprise, and he turned so fast his elbow caught a corner of the box. It tumbled off the counter and dumped its contents on the floor behind him as he raced back to the wheelhouse.

"This is *Dreamspeaker.* Over."

Who the hell was this? The voice sounded husky, and although it was distorted by static, he thought it sounded female. It certainly wasn't Rosemary and he knew there were no females in the crew of the *Lindsay.* In any case, the call was coming over the VHF, so it had to be someone fairly close. The only woman he had met around here was Annie, but why would she call him?

"About time you answered. I've been trying to reach you all morning. You under way or anchored?"

That was a strange question, and he wondered what difference it could possibly make.

"Anchored," he replied, his voice cautious. "Why?"

"I got a problem here. Old Tom's hurt bad."

"Old Tom?" Who the hell was Old Tom? Could there be another boat called *Dreamspeaker*?

Walker suddenly appeared beside him and grabbed the microphone from his hand.

"Annie?"

"Hey, Walker. That you?"

"Yeah. What's up?"

"Need some help here. I ain't no doctor."

"Jesus! What happened?"

"Don't know. You know how Tom is. He won't say."

"How'd you find him?"

"He found me. Rowed himself over, but he looked damn near dead by the time he got here."

"Shit! Look, I'll call you back. I gotta talk to Dan. Stay by the radio, okay?"

"Okay, but don't take too long. He ain't lookin' too good."

Walker handed the microphone back to Dan. "We gotta go, man."

"Yeah. But we've got this other problem and it isn't going to wait. I've got to get hold of Mike, get some help in here." He looked at Walker. "Why don't you take the dinghy? I can give you a first-aid kit—"

Walker cut him off. "Won't work. If we have to take him over to Dawson Inlet, I can't run the boat and look after him too. Shit, I can't even move him by myself."

"I can help." Claire had overheard some of the conversation and had come to see what was happening. "I've got my first-aid ticket. I needed it to get the contract with Fisheries."

"That's great," Dan said, relief shading his voice. And it was. Claire knew Annie and she probably knew Old Tom too, whoever he was. She could look after him—or at least provide assistance if it was something serious.

"Grab a jacket and some supplies. You'll have to take the long way round so you aren't seen by the Shoal Bay crowd or the black ship, so you could be gone for a while."

Walker was already shaking his head. "Still need you. We might have to lower him down by rope. Can't carry him down those planks."

Dan hadn't thought of that. But if he left *Dreamspeaker*, he would be out of reach of the radios until they got back. No way to get hold of Mike. No way to talk to the *Lindsay*. Would he still have time to contact them and get something going after they had taken care of Old Tom? He had his doubts. The planning he had seen was too good. These guys were getting ready to act.

And if the black ship was monitoring the radios—and he was pretty sure they would be—they would have heard Annie's call. He knew White Hair would have noted the name on *Dreamspeaker*'s stern when he had stopped at Annie's, looking for Claire. But White Hair was busy running the operation in Shoal Bay, and he might not have told the crew on the black ship. That might give them a little time before someone put two and two together and realized that he wasn't just out here to fish, but it made everything more urgent.

Dan could feel the tension building in his chest. He couldn't just let these guys take off and do whatever it was they were planning to do, but he really didn't have any choice. An injured man had to come first. He reached for the handset again and passed it to Walker. "Call her back. Tell her we'll be there as quick as we can."

► EIGHTEEN ◄

► At the last minute, Dan remembered his chart book, although he knew that with Walker aboard, they probably wouldn't need it. Still, he would rather be safe than sorry. He added it to the already bulging bag of first-aid equipment and dragged it out to the dinghy.

"You okay with leaving *Dreamspeaker*? We could be gone a while," Walker said as he watched Dan and Claire load the gear.

"Can't be helped. We need the speed, and she's fine here. The anchor has a really good hold and that line to shore stops her swinging. Could probably leave her here for winter if I had to."

Walker nodded and started his slow descent down the ladder.

By two o'clock they were winding their way through a series of narrow passages that were so small they didn't even appear on the chart. They were shallow too, and several times Dan had to lift the leg out of the water so the propeller didn't scrape on a rock. More than once he thought they would have to go back, but he trusted Walker's knowledge and if Walker said this was the safest route to get them where they needed to go, he was not about to question him. He knew they had to keep well away from both Shoal Bay and the black ship, and it was making the trip much longer and slower than he liked, but the fact was they really had no other choice.

And if it hadn't been for that damn black ship and the men in Shoal Bay, the entire trip would have been pure pleasure—a voyage of discovery that Dan was sure he would never forget. As it was, it seemed almost schizophrenic, a part of him filled with apprehension, another part entranced by the sights and smells of the trip itself.

It was obvious Walker knew the whole area as well as Dan had known his backyard, and in his terse, laconic way he provided a commentary that, while it probably didn't stop her worrying, at least appeared to take Claire's mind off what was happening in Shoal Bay. "Big mama bear there," he said, pointing ahead to what looked like a dark rock on the beach. It was only when they came right up to it that the rock came to life, and they watched a black snout lift into the air, sniffing the wind.

"How'd you know it's a mama?" Dan asked, watching the bear carefully as they passed by her no more than thirty feet away.

Wordlessly, Walker turned and pointed to two smaller rock-like forms behind and to one side of the big bear. Two miniature black heads had lifted to look at them, and as they watched, one of the two young ones stood up and started to amble along the beach.

"Swallowtail."

Walker's quiet announcement a few minutes later drew their attention to the tumbling flight of a brilliant yellow butterfly.

Later, Dan would not be able to figure out when he stopped worrying and let the peace of the afternoon steal into his soul. Maybe it was their proximity to the shore, which put them in almost intimate contact with the wildlife as they wove through the narrow passages. Maybe it was the serenity, which they could discern even above the steady hum of the motor as they idled over rocks and reefs. Maybe it was Walker's quiet voice, pointing out a weasel or a mink scouring the beach, or the plummet of a tern as it dove for a fish, or the magnificent sweep of an eagle flying low overhead.

Whatever it was, he suddenly found himself in a time warp, transported back to a land where humans held no sway. The sky and sea were full of birds: terns, oystercatchers, mergansers, and cormorants. Weasels and mink scoured the beach. Bears foraged on the shore, and the wind carried the slightly astringent scent of hemlock and cedar. It was magical and oddly euphoric.

▶ As they exited the narrow passage just a couple of miles from the place where Annie's boat was anchored, they picked up speed and Dan was snapped back to the present. He remembered entering this channel just a few days earlier, although it seemed much longer ago than that. Within minutes they had turned a bend and the big old workboat appeared, looming up against the far shore.

A decrepit wooden rowboat was tied to the bottom of the ladder, blocking their access. Dan figured they would have to move it before they could climb aboard, but Walker directed him around to the shore side of the hull and up onto a patch of shingle where two wide wooden planks formed a steep walkway up to the deck, providing relatively easy access to the rocky beach. Annie was standing at the top of it.

"Took your time," she said.

"Still quicker than my canoe," Walker answered.

"Huh." She turned and disappeared into the cabin. A few seconds later they heard an odd moan. It wavered in pitch and then was cut off by another voice, this one obviously Annie's.

"Shut the fuck up!"

Dan grinned as he looked over at Claire, who was just stepping off the planks and onto the deck. "Don't think I would want Annie as my nurse," he said sotto voce. "She doesn't seem to have terrific patient skills."

She smiled. "I doubt Tom is a terrific patient."

"You know him?" Dan was surprised, although he didn't know why he should be. She had spent a good few months in the area, and now that he thought about it, it seemed obvious that she would have come across him. But she hadn't said anything till now, and he had simply assumed she had never met the man.

"Of course. We all know him—or at least we know who he is. He's a hermit. Lives in an old shack made of driftwood on Starfish Island. I've never talked to him . . . don't think anyone has. And I've never seen him out on the water before, either."

"Huh. Must be something pretty serious to drag him all the way here."

She nodded in agreement just as Annie re-emerged from the cabin.

"You wait out here. If you all come in, you'll set him off again and he'll start that moaning shit. Drives me nuts." She pointed a grimy finger at a porthole as she turned to go back inside. "I'll open that so you can hear. May take a while to get him talking."

"Talking? I thought he needed medical help," Dan said to her back as she disappeared through the door.

She stopped and backed up. "Not the kind you can give him!" She gave a harsh laugh and shook her head. "I lied when I told you he was hurt. Made that up—although he scratched up his arm a bit getting over here. But he ain't sick—at least, no more than the crazy old bastard always has been. I just needed to get you over here, and I remembered Walker saying it might not be good to talk on the radio. I figured saying he needed help might do it." She spread her hands in what Dan figured was the closest to an apology he was going to get. Her eyes slid across to Claire. "I figured this dead guy might be tied to what happened to your boat."

"Dead guy?" Dan, Walker, and Claire spoke in unison. "What dead guy?"

"I'll get him to tell you," Annie said as she disappeared inside.

A second or so later the porthole opened, and Dan could faintly make out someone hunched over the table. His back was to them, but Dan could see enough to tell that the man was both skinny and filthy, and the shirt he was wearing was so threadbare, it looked as if it might fall off at any moment. He also stank: his sour body odor drifted out the opening with Annie's voice.

"Tom."

There was no answer.

"Tom." Annie's voice grew louder and sharper. "What'd the dead guy look like?"

The ululation caught them all off guard.

"Jesus!" Walker breathed. "Sounds like an animal caught in a trap."

"Probably how he feels," murmured Claire. "Stuck inside a little cabin with someone he doesn't know—and having to talk and tell her his story. Must be tough for someone like Tom."

"Yeah. Poor bastard."

Dan thought Walker might have been joking, but his face was full of compassion.

"Tom!" Annie's voice was now a yell. "Cut it out. What'd he look like?"

The shriek subsided to a moan and gradually faded to the occasional wheezing gasp.

"Dead!" the reedy voice quavered.

"Yeah, I know he's dead, but who is he?" Annie asked. "What's he look like?"

"Man! Dead!"

"Yeah. Okay. Anything else?"

There was a pause, a snuffle, and then the answer came. "Red hair. Beard."

Another pause, then, "Wood shirt."

"Wood shirt? What the hell is a wood shirt?"

Annie's patience was obviously wearing thin and her voice was rising. Tom's moan started up again.

"Okay. Okay. Wood shirt. What color was this wood shirt?"

There was a silence lasting several seconds and then Annie's voice could be heard again. "So where is this guy with the red hair and the wood shirt?"

Another pause, another moan, then two words that turned into a shriek that set their teeth on edge and drove them all back from the porthole. They also sent Annie back out of the cabin with Tom's words twisting on the air behind her.

"In water!"

"He's off again," Annie said as she joined them on the aft deck, as far away from the shrieking as they could get. "But at least it's the same story. I thought at first it might be one of his invisible friends he was talking about." She saw Dan's puzzled look and gestured at Walker. "Ask him. We've all heard him talking to them."

Walker nodded. "Yeah. But this seems pretty solid. I mean, red hair and a beard? But what the hell is a wood shirt?"

"He's talking about the same thing I'm wearing," Annie answered, pointing at herself. "You couldn't see him from out here, but he kept pointing at me when he was saying it. Finally figured out he was pointing at my shirt." She shook one of her lapels. It was made from a heavy flannel cloth in a green-and-blue plaid design. "Loggers wear them."

Dan looked at her shirt. "Yeah. It's called a lumberjack shirt." He smiled. "Lumberjacks are loggers and loggers cut wood. A lumberjack shirt—a wood shirt. Guess that makes some kind of sense."

"So where's this dead guy supposed to be?" asked Walker.

"Said he found him floating in the water by his shack."

"Where's that?" Dan asked.

"About five miles up that way." Walker pointed northeast.

"Huh. Maybe it's someone from that crew boat," Dan said.

"Could be, I guess." Walker didn't sound convinced.

"He's not from the crew boat."

They had completely forgotten about Claire. Now they all turned to stare at her. She was clinging to the stern rail, looking as if she had seen a ghost.

"Claire?"

She continued to stare off into the distance, her face ashen.

"Claire? Are you okay?"

"His name is Robbie. He's my boss."

NINETEEN

"Jesus! Yeah, you told me your boss was coming up," Walker said. "You think this could be him?"

Claire swayed and Dan stepped toward her, gripping her arms to steady her. She stared up at him, a pleading look on her face. "I completely forgot about him! How could I do that?" Her eyes were begging him for forgiveness, for help, for relief from a sin she seemed to think was so huge, it was unforgivable. "I didn't even think about him once."

"Why would you, with everything else that's been going on?"

Claire pulled away from him, then buried her face in her hands. "Oh, God! This is insane."

She started to crumple to the deck and Dan reached for her again, pulling her to him. He felt a brief moment of resistance, but then she leaned into him and pushed her face into his shoulder, her body racked with sobs. Instinctively, Dan's arms wrapped around her, cradling her against him, and he lowered his chin to rest gently on her head. He inhaled the scent of her hair: fresh, clean, a mix of sunshine and the ocean that seemed to run along his nerve paths like a mild electric current. Over the top of her head, his eyes met Walker's and he saw not only concern but also approval. That was . . . interesting. He was not sure if he approved himself. If he had still been on the job, he sure as hell wouldn't be doing this. She was both a witness and a victim. But to hell with the job. He was out of that now. Those rules no longer applied and this felt right. And good.

He held her and let her cry, listening as Walker and Annie discussed what they should do.

"Sounds like him, huh?" Annie's attempt at a whisper sounded more like a croak. "I guess you'll have to go over to Tom's shack and check it out. Better make it soon too. The tide'll be turning in half an hour, and if there's a body floating there, it'll be carried out on the current and you ain't never gonna find it."

Dan met Walker's gaze and a silent communication passed between the two men. There was no doubt that Walker thought Tom's description of the body made it pretty well a certainty that it was Claire's boss, but it needed to be checked out, and they needed to do that as quickly as possible.

There was no way Tom was going to go back to his shack until he was convinced the body was gone, and Annie couldn't—and wouldn't—leave him. That meant Walker had to go, as he was the only other person who knew where Tom lived. And he needed Dan to help him move the body if they found it.

But they needed Claire to go with them. Robbie was her boss, and she was the only one who could identify him. A troubled silence fell as the two men looked helplessly at her shaking form. It was something that neither of them could find the courage to ask her to do.

"You have a camera?" Dan asked Annie quietly. If they could take photos, they could get the ID later—assuming the body was still in decent shape: immersion in salt water meant rapid decomposition, and scavengers would not be slow to use the opportunity presented.

She shook her head. "Nope."

"It's okay." Claire's voice was muffled against his chest, but she had obviously picked up on their concern. He felt her take a gulp of air, and then she lifted her head and looked up at him. "I can do it."

He started to shake his head, but her hands pressed against him and stopped him.

"Really. I'll be okay." She moved away from him, and he felt a chill on his chest. He touched his shirt, feeling the dampness from her tears.

"I'm sorry," she said as she saw his gesture, and he felt a surge of . . . what? Concern? Compassion? It couldn't be anything more than that. He barely knew her.

He wanted to hug her to him again but knew she wouldn't allow it. All he could do was watch helplessly as she straightened her shoulders in an effort to prepare herself for what lay ahead.

▶ The three of them crowded into the dinghy and stowed the tarp and rope that Annie had provided under the seat. Annie stood at the top of the plank walkway, watching them go. Tom, of course, didn't make an appearance, although his moans followed them as they moved away.

Dan would have liked to keep Claire close to him, but the requirements of the dinghy made that impossible. Instead, she sat by herself on the thwart in the center of the boat, her shoulders hunched, a forlorn and lonely figure that wrenched his heart. He half hoped that Walker would provide some distraction with more of his commentary, but he too remained silent, his eyes focused on the water ahead.

▶ The body was easy to spot, floating face down among the rocks close to shore. It was almost directly in front of Tom's shack, so it couldn't have moved much since Tom had seen it, and Dan wondered if the shirt was caught on something that was holding it in place. They would have to drag it to shore if they were going to be able to wrap it up, although what they would do with it then, he had yet to figure out. They could maybe drag it over closer to Annie's boat and leave it on the shore till they could get hold of someone from the coast guard or the police to come and get it, but a tarp wasn't going to keep animals away.

Over the top of Claire's head, Dan saw Walker nod toward a shingle beach where a huge driftwood log lay half buried. It was well past the body, and if they could get Claire to wait there, they could spare her the worst of it.

The dinghy bumped gently as Dan brought it up to the beach. He stepped out and reached down to Claire. "Give me your hand." He spoke to her gently, as he would to a child. "You can sit here. Walker and I will take care of everything. We'll come and get you when we're ready for you."

She looked at him mutely, then stepped slowly out of the dinghy and let him lead her, unresisting, to the log. Her quietness was so out of character that it worried him and he exchanged a glance with Walker. They couldn't leave her alone for long. They would have to work quickly.

The two men returned to the dinghy and headed back to where the body floated face down in the water. Close up, the red hair was obvious, although checking the beard would have to wait until they could get the body to shore. The limp form was hung up on some kind of underwater obstacle, and even though Dan jockeyed the dinghy back and forth, a patch of jagged rock that lay just below the surface repelled his efforts to get in close enough to get a hold. He was starting to get frustrated when Walker solved the problem in the simple, direct fashion Dan was beginning to expect.

"Hang on a minute," he said as he removed his shirt, pulled off shoes and jeans, and slipped overboard into the water.

Dan shook his head. It was typical Walker: no discussion, no argument, he just did what needed to be done.

"You want to find a place to beach the dinghy, I'll try and work this guy free." Walker already had a solid grasp on the "wood shirt" that still clothed the body, and as Dan watched he ducked underwater, presumably to see what was holding it. Dan quickly turned the dinghy and took it back to the first landing place he could find, hauled the tarp and rope out, and dragged them back along the beach toward the gruesome scene.

By the time he got there, Walker had worked the body free of the rocks that were holding it and was guiding it in. Dan shucked his own jeans, put his shoes back on, and waded in to help, gasping as the cold knotted his muscles and puckered his skin.

"Jesus! How can you stand this? It's freezing!"

Walker smiled. "Hey, we Indians are tough. Not like you wimpy white guys."

Dan snorted. "Yeah, right." He knew banter helped to keep his mind off what they were doing, and he guessed it was the same for Walker. "We need to get him somewhere we can slide him out onto the tarp."

They clambered carefully over the slippery rocks, gently easing their burden toward an area of sloping sandstone.

"Can you hold him for a couple of minutes?" Dan asked as they neared the edge. "I'll get the tarp and spread it out."

The body was heavy. Robbie—if it was Robbie—was a big man and he was still fully clothed. The sodden flannel shirt, heavy jeans, and boots added to the weight, and the frigid water was rapidly draining Dan's energy, to the point where it took all his strength and determination to keep going. Several times he came close to quitting, but both the thought of Claire sitting by herself on that lonely beach and the sight of Walker's blue lips and clamped jaw made him keep going.

In the end, they had to pull the tarp into the water and slide it underneath the corpse. The muscles in Dan's legs were starting to cramp, and pain knifed down his calf. He lost his footing more than once and his ankle stung where he had grazed it against the rough edge of a rock. Across from him, Walker stumbled several times and Dan realized that he too was nearing the end of his endurance. As soon as the top edge of the plastic had been secured by tying it to a rock, he staggered out of the water and flung himself down on the ground, panting and shivering.

"You okay?" he asked when he had caught his breath enough to speak.

"Yeah," Walker answered. "Better than that guy, anyway."

They both lay there shivering for a few more minutes, and then the cold drove Dan into action. He tugged his jeans back on and went to collect the clothes Walker had left in the dinghy.

"Better get these on. You're starting to look whiter than me." He handed the bundle to Walker, then went to finish securing the tarp and its macabre burden. Those thoughts of Claire, waiting just a few hundred yards away, were urging him to finish things up.

▶ "I'll go get Claire."

Walker nodded his agreement and Dan started back along the shore.

They had managed to drag the body completely out of the water and Dan had wrapped the tarp tightly around it. Now it lay trussed with only the head exposed. He had little doubt it was Claire's boss, Robbie: once they had rolled him over and seen the wild red beard, it seemed impossible for it to be anyone else. After all, how many men with red hair and a beard could there be in this remote area? What had been less obvious—and much more troubling—was the deep indentation in the back of his skull. It was hidden beneath the mass of thick, curly hair, but Dan had felt it when he positioned the head in order to make it easily visible for Claire to look at when she came over. He had no forensic training, and he supposed there was a chance the injury could have happened post-mortem, but the weather was good and the sea was calm. It was hard to see how anything could have hit hard enough to cause that kind of damage.

Claire was still sitting where they had left her, staring out over the water.

"Claire? You okay?" It was a stupid question, but he couldn't think of anything better.

She turned toward him, her face still damp with tears, and nodded without speaking.

"Do you think you can do this?"

He wondered how many more times he was going to have to ask this girl that same damned question. He had asked it when she was stuck on that bloody island, watching the black ship. He had asked it when he took her back to Spider Island and got her to walk to Shoal Bay, to the very place some guy had been waiting for her with a gun. And now here he was, asking it yet again in order to get her to look at the dead body of someone she had probably known and been friendly with. He felt like an asshole, but he knew it was something that had to be done, and she was the only one who could do it.

She still didn't speak, but he saw the slight rise of her shoulders and the pale, resigned smile as she stood up. He reached out his hand to steady her as she staggered slightly on the rocks and then moved it to her waist to support her. He could feel the tension in her body, her muscles stiff with the effort of holding her emotions in check.

Walker stood up as they approached, blocking her view of the corpse. As she got nearer, he stepped back to let her pass but stayed close. Dan moved up on her other side and reached forward to turn down the flap of tarp he had folded over the dead man's face. He heard the sudden intake of breath and turned to look at her face.

"Is it Robbie?" Dan asked quietly.

She nodded.

"You're sure?"

She nodded again and turned away.

Dan watched her stumble back across the rocks. Her shoulders were hunched, and her hands were clenched into fists. He looked at Walker. "We need to get her back to Annie. She can't stay here. Want me to wait here while you run her back in the dinghy?"

"No. You go. I'll wait."

Dan was about to argue but thought better of it. He was getting by far the best of this deal. He nodded, caught up to Claire, gently took her arm, and led her over to the dinghy. As he pushed off, he heard Walker call out to him, "Hey, white guy. Don't get lost." Even in these circumstances, Walker could make him smile.

▶ Annie was sitting out on the aft deck. She stood and walked out to the top of the walkway as they approached, her eyes holding a question as they stared down at Dan. He gave her a brief nod and watched as she reached out to pull Claire toward her, enfolding the younger woman in a rough bear hug as she stepped onto the deck.

"You staying?" she asked Dan, her chin resting on Claire's head and her voice muffled.

"Can't. I have to go help Walker."

"Go. I'll look after things here."

"Thanks, Annie. We shouldn't be too long." Dan had come up with an idea for how to secure the body. He would tow it to a piece of shoreline nearer to Annie's boat and bury it under rocks. That should protect it from animals, although he couldn't slow decomposition. It would also allow Tom to return to his cabin. "How's Tom doing?"

"Still moaning, but he's okay. I'll try and get some food into him in a while. Stupid old bastard."

Dan smiled. Annie might pretend to be tough, but there was a softness there that was unmistakable and heartwarming. He turned to Claire and took her hands in his. "I'll be back as soon as I can," he told her. He was rewarded with a wan smile.

▶ It took longer than he had planned to find a place to bury Robbie. Either the shore was too steep or the rocks were too big. Finally he found a site that might work. It was above the high-tide line, on a sloping ledge of dark rock, and Dan climbed up onto it. He had to reach above his head to pry some rocks loose and then pass them one by one down to Walker, who arranged them carefully around and over the body. It was far from perfect, but it would have to do.

As he slid back down, Dan heard Walker begin to chant. The sound was eerie, almost hypnotic, and it grew until it seemed to fill the air and the water and even reach down into the rock itself. The rhythm was so ancient, so primal, so fundamental, that Dan felt his body start to rock and weave in unison.

As the last sound faded, the two men stood together on the edge of the land and looked out over the water. Words were inadequate. And unnecessary. A man had died. A spirit had been freed and sent forward on its journey. There was nothing else to say or do.

Silently, they made their way back down to the dinghy. Dan held it steady as Walker climbed in, then cast off the rope that tethered it before stepping in himself and pushing off. He put his hand on the controls, but instead of starting the motor, he let the boat drift out on the waves. Walker sat quietly, watching him.

"You still chewing on a problem?"

It was a statement more than a question and Dan nodded in acquiescence. "Yeah."

"Think you can fix it?"

Dan shrugged. "Not really. These guys are pretty well organized. I can't get hold of anyone, and even if I could, they probably wouldn't listen to me. And I don't think they could get here quickly enough to do anything anyway, so I guess it doesn't really matter. And they look ready to move. They're not going to hang around once they've got those canisters organized. I figure by tomorrow, next day at the latest, the black ship and the crew boat will be gone."

Walker nodded and inclined his head toward the shore. "What're you going to do about him?"

"Nothing I can do there either, except tell Mike or the coast guard about it—whoever I can reach first. They can take it from there."

"You figure it was the same guys?"

"Yeah."

They sat quietly for a few minutes, and Dan watched the water move around them as he struggled with the concept of being a bystander rather than a player.

"Be a bitch to just let them go."

Dan's head snapped around as he heard the softly spoken words. They certainly weren't what he had expected to hear from Walker, although they echoed his own feelings perfectly.

"Yeah," he said, his voice betraying his wariness.

Walker smiled. "Wanna stop them?"

"Stop them? Are you fucking crazy? We can't stop them—that's what's driving me nuts!"

"Yeah. I know. I've been watching it eating at your gut."

"Yeah. Well. Guess I've got to learn how to deal with it."

"Uh-huh."

"Fuck off!" Dan took a deep breath. He was letting both the situation and Walker get to him. "We've got to get back to Claire."

"Yeah. Nice girl, that." Walker's face was expressionless, but Dan heard the smile behind the words.

"Yes, Walker. She is. Now let's drop it, okay?" This was getting way too personal. He reached for the starter. "In fact, let's drop everything and get back to Annie's."

"We can stop them, you know."

Dan's hand froze in mid-air. Walker was serious.

"Yeah? And how are we going to do that?"

Walker outlined his idea as they sped back.

► TWENTY ◄

► The lineup for customs and immigration at the main terminal at the Vancouver International Airport was slowly thinning. The passengers from the big Cathay Pacific arrival had mostly been processed and were now milling around the luggage carousels while the next group, off an Air Canada flight from Mexico City, moved steadily forward, passports in hand. Jason Colwood glanced up at the clock on the wall of his booth. He had been on duty for almost three hours and was due for a coffee break. He beckoned to the next person standing in the line. The man was dressed in a slightly rumpled business suit and was obviously traveling alone. He had his passport ready in his hand, open to the photo page, and as he approached, Jason could clearly see the cover: Mexico. Well, that made sense seeing as the flight had originated there. Jason reached out a hand for the passport as he took in the face of the man who now stood in front of him: dark eyes, sharp nose and high cheekbones, black hair and light-brown skin. He glanced down at the photo and then back up again. Definitely the same man, and he appeared to be totally at ease, perhaps even a little bored, certainly a bit impatient. Who wouldn't be after a long flight and then standing in line for half an hour or so? He slid the passport into the reader and watched the screen as the data appeared: Juan Luis Rodriguez Vargas. Age 42. Married. Born in Tapalpa in the state of Jalisco, Mexico. Businessman. There were no cautions. Juan Luis had visited Vancouver twice before.

Jason looked back up from his screen at the man standing across from him and made his decision. "Good evening, Señor Vargas. *Bienvenido a Vancouver.*"

The man smiled. "*Gracias, señor.*"

Jason handed the passport back, nodded, and turned to look at the next people in line: a family with two fractious young children. Juan Luis Vargas, more properly known as Mohammed ibn Saleh ibn Tariq al-Nasiri, took the passport and slid it into the inside pocket of his jacket. He would not be needing it again.

A car, its windows darkened, was waiting for Nasiri outside the terminal. The driver lowered his sign, bowed his head in deference, took the suitcase and stowed it in the trunk, then waited while Nasiri slid through the open door onto the back seat. He wouldn't be needing the suitcase again either. The Mexican clothing he had filled it with would be worn by whoever was returning there with the passport he had used. A fresh set of clothes lay on the seat beside him and he used the drive into downtown Vancouver to change. He was booked into the same hotel he had used on his last two visits, Days Inn Vancouver. It was perfect for his needs: not high-end enough to attract clients requiring their own security details, not low-end enough to attract trouble, and only two blocks to the massive Vancouver Convention Centre, with its glass walls and picturesque views across the harbor. With the main event starting in just three days, the hotel would be full of bureaucrats, civil servants, and journalists. He would blend in perfectly. The message light on his phone was already blinking when he entered his room.

▶ Mike Bryant moved out onto the walkway in front of the Vancouver Convention Centre and gazed out over Burrard Inlet. Across the water the lights of West and North Vancouver glittered brightly. Even after an exhausting seven hours spent organizing the inspection of every square inch of the more than two hundred thousand square feet of meeting space, plus an almost equal amount of service rooms and kitchens, he was still refreshed by the salt air and the luminous glow of the snow-covered mountain peaks that formed a backdrop to the cities that stretched along the North Shore. A warm square of light creeping up one of the steep slopes marked the path of the Grouse Mountain gondola, and the lights on the ski runs on both Mount Seymour and Cypress Mountain were clearly visible. He made himself a promise to visit one of them as soon as this damn meeting was over.

"Hey, Mike. We need you in here."

He dragged himself away from the view and turned to see the broad bulk of Sergeant Grant Fraser standing in the doorway. "Yeah. Coming."

The team had assembled in the wide concourse that ran the length of the main building. Sets of blueprints were spread out over almost every available surface. Mike glanced around, performing a quick head count as he did so. Everyone accounted for.

"So where are we at?" he asked.

Grant answered. "We've checked everything. It's clean."

"Do we have uniforms on duty tonight?"

"Yeah. Three in and four out. Door checks every hour."

"Anyone checked the alarms?"

"Yep. Richards and Ferguson sat in while the manager ran through the system. Everything checks out."

"So we good to go?"

Grant turned to the group. "Guys?"

There was the rustle of paper as notebooks were opened and pages checked, then one by one the men reported.

"Yeah."

"I'm clear."

"All good."

"Same here."

By midnight, the convention center lay quiet and dark. Mike made his way back to his hotel, stripped down to his underwear, and fell into bed. Even if he was able to sleep—something he doubted—he would be back up at five the next morning to monitor the check-in procedures for participants in the preliminary meetings. So far it had all been routine. Everything had checked out fine and he thought they had all the bases covered. But he still couldn't shake the feeling that something was wrong.

▶ Javier Fernandez sat quietly in the salon of *Snow Queen*, legs stretched out in front of him and a glass of single-malt scotch by his side. He had acquired a taste for the stuff on one of his trips abroad and knew he would never go back to the aguardiente of his native land. It was two hours since he had placed his call to the hotel in Vancouver. Nasiri should be calling him back very soon.

Things had gone well in Shoal Bay. Despite the problem with the girl, whom they still hadn't found, he had been pleased with the day's rehearsals. The men had shown they were ready and they had no problems assembling or handling the various weapons. Fernandez's mouth narrowed in a thin smile as he thought about it. Except for the gas canisters, which Alex and Carlos would fill at the last minute, everything was ready to go. Tomorrow they would load the crew boat and head south.

He stood up and moved to the window. The weather forecast had predicted a front moving in overnight with strong northwest winds and rain, easing by late morning. The men would have to take the crew boat back over early to beat the seas, but once they left Shoal Bay and turned south, they would have the wind and waves behind them. And as soon as they had crossed the open waters of Queen Charlotte Sound, they would gain some protection in the narrow stretch of water that ran down the east side of Vancouver Island. It would all work as he had planned. He could picture the route on the chart he had memorized. The boat would refuel at Port Hardy, then run at full speed down the Inside Passage. It would then turn into Johnstone Strait and pass through the throat of Seymour Narrows, out into the Strait of Georgia, and across to the southern mouth of the Fraser.

The rest was easy. Once in the river they would become invisible. The Fraser was lined with wharves and docks, and constant traffic moved in and out of them. A crew boat's arrival at the public wharf at Steveston was a common event in the working life of the river.

They would not even be noticed, and the vans he had arranged to meet them would also be lost in the normal chaos of loading and unloading.

His thoughts were interrupted as Alex entered the salon. He had been monitoring the radio on the bridge. "Nasiri called. He is in place and he has the rifle."

Fernandez nodded. All the pieces were coming together, exactly as he had planned it. The big man would be pleased.

TWENTY-ONE

▶ Walker's idea was crazy, but maybe it was worth a try. It had to be better than doing nothing, and even if they didn't succeed in stopping the men on the black ship, they might delay them long enough to allow Dan time to contact Mike and get Hargreaves back.

Walker had explained his idea—Dan wouldn't grace it by calling it a plan—as they motored back to Annie's boat, and now the two of them were heading out yet again. They were on their way to some island that didn't have a name, that sat in a river that wasn't shown on any chart, and that was on the other side of two sets of narrows, one at each end of a tidal lake that was reached by a narrow inlet. It would be dark by the time they got there. If he ever tried to explain this to anyone back in the city, Dan thought as he watched the inlet narrow ahead of him, they would have him certified and locked up. They had nothing with them: no charts, no compass, and no supplies, although Annie had lent him a flashlight and an old jacket that he could barely fit his arms into but which she said might come in handy if it got cold. She had also given him a box of chocolate-chip cookies.

According to Walker, the island they were heading for was temporarily home to some twenty or thirty young men—the number changed all the time, so he couldn't be more specific—all members of local Native bands and all of them with troubled histories. Like Walker, they had left their communities to try life in the big city, and, again like Walker, they had gotten themselves caught up in crime or drugs or both. Most had done time in jail, although some had simply found their way home when they ran out of money or alternatives.

"So let me get this straight." Dan was still seriously questioning his sanity for agreeing to this trip. "There's a bunch of kids living on this island?"

"Yeah. Some. Some older guys too. Might even be a few as old as you." Walker looked at him and chuckled. "But probably not."

Dan ignored the jibe. "So what do they do there?"

Walker didn't answer, and Dan thought he might not have heard him over the sound of the motor, so he asked him again.

"Hard to say," Walker finally replied, an intense look gripping his face. "Learn to be Indian, I guess."

There wasn't much Dan could say after that, and the dinghy carrying them moved slowly eastward under the fading sky. Walker spent most of his time peering at the shoreline or looking up at the outline of the Coast Mountains where they were drawn sharply against the encroaching night sky. At times he took one of the oars and pushed it into the water to check the depth or keep them clear of some obstacle. At other times he simply pointed to one side or the other, showing Dan where to steer.

They passed the first of the narrows. It was barely wide enough to allow the dinghy through, and the fast-running water rose up in steep, short waves that hurled themselves against the bow as the boat pushed against them. The water quieted as soon as they were through, and they entered a wide, smooth expanse of ink-dark water that Dan assumed was the lake.

Walker moved back from the bow and sat on the center thwart. He was facing forward, but he turned his head back toward Dan when he spoke, and the dim light caught the flat planes of his cheekbones and the sharp ridges of his brow and nose, giving him the look of an ancient warrior who had stepped out of a legend. He lifted his arm and pointed to a bright star clearly visible above the soaring peak of a mountain.

"You see that star? The one right there over that peak?"

"Yeah. It's called Pollux. It's one of the Gemini twins."

"Maybe where you live. Out here it's *tutu*."

Dan nodded. He was in Walker's territory now.

"Okay. What about it?"

"Keep it dead ahead and you can crank up the speed. Pick up some time."

Dan pushed the throttle all the way to its limit, and the dinghy surged forward and ran through the night. He had learned to use the stars to steer many years ago on his father's boat and it felt good—and natural and right—to be using them again. And for some reason he could not fathom, it somehow relaxed him and eased the worry that nibbled at the edges of his brain.

He felt the movement when Walker shifted again, but it was so dark that the only thing he could see was a disembodied hand as it approached his face. Night had closed in completely and the moon was new; it would not be of any help to them tonight. He slowed, felt the wash catch up, and tried to see what lay ahead.

"You got that flashlight?" Walker's voice reached him over the throb of the engine.

"Here." Dan dug it out of the side pocket, held it up, and felt it removed from his hand. "Where are we?"

"That's the narrows, up ahead." The thin beam of the flashlight illuminated a narrow channel of black water. "Take it slow. There's a big rock a few hundred feet past it. We'll stop there."

The rock wasn't just big: it was massive, a single bulwark of smooth black granite that rose out of the water and soared skyward for maybe twenty feet, almost blocking passage into the waterway completely. Dan shut the engine down, letting the dinghy drift slowly toward it, and Walker reached out his hand to steady them as they bumped up to its menacing face.

"So what do we do now?" Dan asked.

Walker's teeth gleamed at him. "We wait."

The darkness wrapped around them like a blanket as they sat quietly, listening to the water chuckling past. It lapped gently against the hull, setting it rocking so slightly they could barely feel it. On the nearby shore, a breeze stirred the branches and whispered through the leaves. Somewhere, an owl hooted, then another.

And another.

A shrill whistle shredded the silence, and Walker answered it with one of his own. Minutes later came the muted splash of paddles.

The two canoes that slid out of the night were almost alongside before Dan saw them. Each contained a lone paddler, both of whom greeted Walker like an old friend, with warmth and, Dan thought, a large degree of respect. Dan they ignored completely.

They positioned themselves one on each side and reached out to the dinghy, holding it steady as Walker carefully lifted his legs over the adjoining gunwales and into the starboard canoe, then slid his body across and settled himself on its forward thwart. Once he was in place, he used his hands to pull the canoe backward till he was even with Dan, then looked at him.

"Wait here. I'll go talk with them."

"Jesus! How long you going to be?"

He shrugged. "Not long. I'll come and get you if everything's okay."

"What?" Dan found it hard to believe that Walker was simply going to paddle off into the night and leave him sitting out there alone.

Walker grinned. "Don't forget, white man. Out here, they think you're the bad guy!" He pushed off, and the darkness swallowed him. The sound of the paddles faded, and a few seconds later his voice drifted across the water.

"Don't worry. I'll be back."

Right. Sure. He was going to be back, but he didn't say how long he was going to be. What now? Did he really expect Dan to just sit and wait?

Once his initial shock at being left alone had worn off, Dan realized that that was exactly what Walker expected him to do. And there was nothing else he *could* do. He didn't know where he was, and while he could probably find his way back once it was light, he sure as hell couldn't do it in this blanket of darkness. Shock turned to anger, and he was tempted to hurl an oar against the rock and scream curses into the night, but common sense prevailed and the anger quickly evaporated into frustration as he sat helpless in the dark.

And although it seemed impossible, he thought it was getting darker. At first he put it down to his imagination, but then he realized that the stars had disappeared. Great. That was all he needed. He'd just sit out here in the middle of nowhere and wait for the wind to pick up and the rain to start. Hell, maybe there would even be a thunderstorm! He couldn't even try for the shore. This was near the end of a fjord, and the sides were steep, the land dropping almost vertically into the water.

He raged and seethed for a while, but gradually his emotions calmed and the sounds of the night infiltrated: fish rising, water chuckling, roosting birds softly chattering. His mind finally quieted and he settled himself into the bottom of the boat, leaned back against the thwart, and let his thoughts drift with the night air, to his father, Mike, Susan, Annie, Old Tom, Claire, Walker . . . so many lives being lived in so many different ways. He had never really thought about it before—too busy doing to simply be. Did people really choose their lives, he wondered, or did their lives choose them, sort of evolving over time? Make a spur-of-the-moment choice about something—go to the city, apply for a job, submit an application—and the rest would just follow? Surely Annie must have made a deliberate choice. And Walker had certainly made one when he decided to return home after his years in jail. Even Old Tom would have had to choose to make his way up here.

He wondered if he'd ever made a deliberate, thoughtful, careful choice that had required him to shut one door of opportunity in order to open another. To give up something of value, something familiar, for the chance to achieve something else. He had joined the police force as much on a whim as anything else: it had seemed like fun at the time. True, he had also left the police force, but that had been a reaction, an escape rather than a choice. So too was buying *Dreamspeaker* and moving aboard—and that was mostly Mike's doing anyway. So what did all that say about him, if anything? And what choices could he make to get his life back on track? Something to think about.

He settled himself a little more comfortably and made Annie's jacket into a pillow for his head. Too bad he couldn't see the stars anymore. It would have been nice to just watch them overhead. Hadn't steered by the stars in a long time. Had to do that more often. Switch off all those fancy electronics and trust himself. Maybe he and Claire . . .

He woke to a violent rocking and found Walker trying to clamber back into the dinghy, his progress hampered by Dan's body, which was sprawled across the bottom of the boat.

"Remind me not to use you for guard duty," Walker said as he worked his way to the bow. "You think you can stay awake long enough to run this thing?"

"Yeah." Dan blinked and pushed himself up into a sitting position, then moved up onto the thwart. "What's happening?"

"They're in."

"They'll do it? Hey, that's great. How're they going to get there?"

"They've already gone. Went right past you while you were snoozing."

"They're paddling?" Dan couldn't believe it. "Shit! It's gonna take them till daylight to get there!"

Walker laughed. "They'll be back here before dawn."

Dan had no answer for that. It didn't seem possible, but he knew the distances Walker could cover, and the speed at which he could paddle. He had seen it for himself. He reached for the starter.

"You want to untie us?" Dan said as he moved his hand to the throttle.

Walker's peal of laughter echoed off the steep cliffs.

"You lasso that big rock or something?" Walker asked when he had caught his breath. "You're not tied up, white man. You've been sitting in a back eddy. It'll hold you against that rock for as long as you want to stay there."

Dan stared at him for a minute in confusion, looked up at the blackness that loomed ahead, more solid than the blackness of the night, then shook his head and pushed the starter button. He was a complete neophyte out here. All that time spent on his father's boat, all the navigation equipment and electronic gizmos, all the charts and tide tables—and still he felt out of his element. He didn't have even a small portion of the knowledge and ability that Walker and his friends had and he never would.

And as for his powers of observation . . .

"So what're they going to do when they get there?" he asked, changing the subject. "They can't just climb aboard."

"Don't know," answered Walker. "They'll think of something."

"Jesus. I don't like it, Walker. Maybe we should stop them. If they get caught . . ."

Walker interrupted. "You don't have to like it. And you can't stop them. This is their decision, not yours. They know the score. They made the choice. They'll handle it."

And there it was. All the stuff he had been struggling with ever since this had all started, laid out in front of him in a few simple, uncompromising words. He was not in charge. He had no authority. He was not a cop anymore. He couldn't just rush in and take control of the situation. Like it or not, he was just an ordinary guy, a private citizen no different than Walker—or Annie or Claire, for that matter. He could only do what he could do. The realization should have depressed him, but instead he felt strangely relieved.

"Can you see where you're going?" Walker's voice brought him out of his reverie, and he was suddenly aware that he had the boat moving without any idea of where he was or where he was going.

He jerked his hand off the throttle and peered ahead, trying to see some kind of landmark but coming up with nothing. "No. Too dark."

"Look again. Over there, a bit to your right. See that shine? That's the narrows."

Dan looked again and finally saw the faint glimmer of light that danced along the ridges of moving water. How the hell did Walker do it?

They stayed silent as the boat moved steadily down the lake, Walker occasionally giving corrections to the course, and just before they arrived at the last set of narrows, the clouds cleared away and the stars shone out to limn the water with silver.

A single canoe was waiting for them once they had made it through the narrows. It too had a lone occupant, and he made no move to approach them as they slowed to a stop, seeming content to stay some distance off. Walker looked over and lifted his hand in greeting, then turned back to Dan. "Think you can find your way back to Annie's from here?"

"What? Where the hell are you going now? You want me to go back to Annie's by myself?"

Even as he said the words, Dan knew how inane they were. He sounded like the kind of man he despised. He should have figured this out by now. The fact that he hadn't was a testament to how lost he felt in this environment. Of course Walker would want to go with his people, guide them, lead them, help out where he could. And Dan couldn't go with him. Not only would he not be welcome—as Walker had pointed out, he was one of the bad guys as far as they were concerned—but the motor on the dinghy made far too much noise. And he had to go back to Annie's anyway. Claire was still there, waiting to hear what they had done with Robbie.

Walker was looking at him, watching him struggle past the layers of doubt, waiting patiently for his answer, no doubt well aware of exactly what he was going through.

"Yeah," Dan said as he breathed in a lungful of air and gathered his scattered thoughts. "Sure. Of course I can find my way. That's as long as the sky stays clear until I get in the channel."

Walker looked up. "It'll stay clear, long as you don't fall asleep again. Just take it easy till you get out of the inlet, then go a bit to starboard. You'll see the channel open up easier if you keep to this side."

He turned toward the waiting canoe, gave a short whistle, then sat quietly and watched as it moved toward them and slid alongside. As it came close, Dan could make out the features of the man who paddled it. He was considerably older than he had expected, long hair heavily streaked with gray and deep wrinkles seaming his face, although they could have been due as much to exposure to the elements as to age. Still, Dan figured he had to be well into his second half-century.

Walker introduced him. "This is Percy. He runs the camp back there. He looked after me when I came back. Taught me what I needed to know."

Dan reached out a hand in greeting. "Good to meet you." He nodded at Walker. "You did a hell of a good job."

Percy grinned. "He tells me you did a pretty good job too—for a white guy."

Dan snorted. "That's not what he said at the time."

Walker laughed. "That's not what I thought at the time." He took an oar and placed it so it rested sideways across the two boats. "Hang on to this. I'm gonna get in with Percy." He eased himself up till he was sitting on the oar, then slid across into the other boat.

Within seconds the canoe had disappeared into the night, but Walker's voice came drifting back over the fading splash of the paddles: "See you in the morning, white man."

Dan had lost all track of time, but it seemed like many hours had passed since they had set out from Annie's. It had to be almost morning now. He squinted down at his watch. It was not yet eleven o'clock.

► TWENTY-TWO ◄

► Dan found the trip back to Annie's surprisingly easy. He had been caught off guard by Walker's suggestion that he make his own way back in the dark, with no charts, no compass, no lights. Nothing. But when he had forced his mind past its initial resistance and taken stock of exactly where he was, he realized with both surprise and pleasure that it was something he could do. Risky, certainly, but far from impossible. Hell, Walker and his friends were doing it without a second thought.

At first he was nervous. He kept his speed down and stayed close to the shore, but as the inlet widened and he moved out into more familiar territory, he found the stars provided just enough light to give form to the land. The odd sense of relief he had been feeling ever since Walker's pronouncement that he was neither in control nor responsible persisted, and the steady hum of the motor slowed his brain in much the same way as listening to the soaring jazz notes of Charlie Parker.

He thought there was a chance that it was already too late, that Walker and his bevy of canoes might find Shoal Bay abandoned and the black ship long gone. But probably not. The men at the lodge had given off a sense of purpose, but not of real urgency. And they had only opened five of the canisters. More than half had remained sealed when he and Claire had left . . . was that only this morning? Seemed impossible.

So what would happen if the men were still there? Walker figured he and his friends could stop them, but how? They had no weapons, and Dan doubted they even had any tools—not that tools would help them. Maybe they figured that just by being there, they would disrupt things enough to throw the schedule off. Might work, too, as long as White Hair and his pals held off from using their weapons. Come to think of it, they hadn't actually used them at all so far, and while Dan was pretty sure one or more of them was responsible for Robbie's death, they hadn't used a gun to kill him—unless it was the butt. But that was hardly a guarantee they wouldn't use weapons tonight on the slow-moving canoes.

Still, Walker might have numbers on his side—he had said "they" when he talked about his friends, like there were quite a few involved, and Dan thought there were probably at least enough to make it unlikely they could all be taken out, even with guns. And if White Hair and his boys couldn't take all of them out, it would leave witnesses, and one thing for sure was that these guys didn't seem to want any of those. They certainly had no qualms about removing them, either. They had gone hunting for Claire and had made sure Robbie was removed from the picture. Not that that would have been difficult. They would have approached him the same way they had approached Annie's boat, gone aboard, hit Robbie over the head, and then shoved him overboard. God knows what they had done with his boat—sunk it, maybe, or set it adrift on an ebb tide. He would have to tell Mike to get the coast guard and the marine guys to look for it.

So the bad guys might not shoot at Walker and his group. Hard to hit a moving target, even if they could see it clearly, and almost impossible in the dark unless you had a night-vision scope, and that seemed unlikely. So Walker and his friends might be okay. Hell, if the guards were asleep, as they had been the night Walker had snuck into the bay, maybe they wouldn't even be noticed. But then what? What could they do that would stop them? Steal the canisters? Possible, but surely that would make enough noise to alert even sleeping guards. Set the crew boat adrift? That might slow them down, but they had dinghies and radios and it wouldn't take long to track the boat and bring it back. And the crew boat might not even be there. It could have gone back to the black ship. In fact, Dan figured it probably had. And that was a problem of a completely different kind.

Dan's mind shifted to the black ship. It had looked harmless enough, sitting quietly at anchor. Not much activity except for the one guy he had seen come out of the wheelhouse. The guy who had looked familiar, with black curly hair and an odd rolling walk and the . . . wait a minute. Harry! That was his name. Harry Coombs. Dan had seen the name in any number of files. Had seen the man himself two or three times, although always at a distance, never face-to-face. Harry Coombs was a wheeler and dealer with a long history of questionable associations and activities. He was suspected of trading illegal weapons to terrorist organizations and smuggling drugs for the Mexican cartels, but although the police had come close, they had never managed to nail him with anything. Harry "Houdini" Coombs. The escape artist. The slick con man with the jovial manner, who laughed as he slipped through every net they had set up. What the hell was he doing here, floating around in this isolated archipelago? Must be drugs or weapons. Maybe both. But why would he hang around? That didn't make sense. The trade would have been made when the canisters were dropped. It would be more logical for Harry and his black ship to get as far from Shoal Bay as they possibly could. Logic said they should have left as soon as they had sunk the canisters. And who the hell was White Hair? If Dan remembered the file correctly, Harry preferred to work alone.

The channel leading to Annie's boat opened up, steel gray against the solid black of the land, and Dan turned the dinghy into it. It was rougher here with the wind coming in off the open ocean and kicking up a chop, and within minutes he was drenched with cold spray. He thought about slowing down but knew he couldn't afford the extra time. His sense of urgency had returned with his recollection of Harry Coombs and it increased as he came nearer to his destination. He might not be able to control things, but there were still things he could—and should—do. Like Walker and his friends, he had a role to play. He had both the contacts and the means to reach them, but only if he made it back to *Dreamspeaker*. He now had more than enough to convince Mike and get him on side, and Mike in turn could use the information on Coombs to get the marine guys in place, and then Dan's responsibility really would end. But until then he had to keep going. It was no longer just about stopping whatever Harry and White Hair and their buddies were up to. It had become much more personal than that. It was about Walker and the men who had willingly gone with him in order to right a wrong. And it was about Claire and all that had been done to her.

The wind was steadily picking up, and he thought there was a thin veil of cloud forming, too thin to block the stars but enough to dull their brilliance. His wet clothes clung to his body, leeching whatever warmth he still had left after sixteen or seventeen hours mostly spent on the water, and the resulting chill drained the last of his energy. He was shivering as much from fatigue as from the cold, and he knew he couldn't continue much longer. Yet he also knew that somehow he had to find a way. There had already been at least one death. With Walker and his friends out there, he didn't want there to be any more.

Despite the hour, light glimmered through the portholes on Annie's boat, and both Annie and Claire were out on deck to greet him. He wondered if that might be less about welcoming his arrival and more about keeping as far away from Tom as possible, but whatever the reason, he was happy to see them. He turned the dinghy in behind the boat, let it idle up to the planks, and turned off the motor. The sudden silence rang in his ears as he sat there, clinging to the rough wood, his muscles aching and his body stiff.

A beam of light tracked over him. Annie was making her way down the planks, a flashlight in her hand.

"You okay?" She leaned down to peer more closely at him. "Give me the line. I'll tie you up."

He reached down, his numb fingers scrabbling in the pool of frigid water that filled the scuppers to find the end of the rope. When he finally managed to grab it and fish it out, cold arrows of pain shot through his hand as he passed it up to her.

"Got the stove going in the galley," Annie said as she tied the dinghy to one of the planks. "Kettle's hot."

"Thanks, Annie." Damn, that sounded wonderful. "Just give me a minute to get my legs working and I'll be up."

"Huh." She stared at him for a moment longer, then turned and made her way back up to the deck.

It took him longer than a minute and he had to use the planks to pull himself upright, but he finally managed first to stand and then to move. He hadn't realized how long he had been sitting in the same position—and the cold wind hadn't helped. He would have to get back to his judo. He had let it slide since he'd moved aboard and he was paying the price physically and mentally. He flexed his shoulders a couple of times, rotated his spine, and cautiously stepped onto the planks. Thank God Annie had tied a rope from the railing down to a conveniently located log. Without it to hold on to, he was not sure he could have made it.

When he finally reached the deck, Claire was waiting for him, her arms wrapped around her body to keep herself warm.

"You must be frozen," she said, looking at his wet clothing. "Annie says she can probably dig you up something to change into."

"Sounds good—although I'm not sure I'd fit into anything of Annie's—unless it's a dress."

She snorted. "Does Annie look like someone who would own a dress?"

He chuckled and reached out to put his arm around her shoulders, turning her toward the cabin. "Doesn't seem too likely, does it? Let's see what she has in mind." The casual embrace felt awfully good.

The warmth of the cabin wrapped around Dan like a soft blanket as he stepped inside. It felt wonderful, although it made his clothes feel even wetter and colder, if that was possible. He briefly considered joining Old Tom, who was still sitting in the same place at the table, hunched as far into a corner as he could get, but he didn't want to soak the cushions with his wet clothes and there was still that eye-watering smell to deal with. Instead, he stood awkwardly in the doorway, dripping on the wood floor, until finally Annie came to his rescue.

"I've got a shirt and pants might fit you," she said. "Come on up front." She started forward, then turned to look past him at Claire. "You want to make the tea? It's up there in that cupboard."

Annie dug out the clothes and pointed him to the shower. Heated by the wood stove, the water was blissfully hot, and Dan reveled in the warmth that cascaded over his shoulders. He would have liked to let it run for hours, but he forced himself to limit it to a brief rinse. There would be time for indulgence once he got back to *Dreamspeaker* and got hold of Mike.

The pants were a pair of gray, elastic-waisted sweatpants. They were old, loose at the waist, and several inches too short in the leg, leaving his ankles bare, but they were clean and dry and comfortable. The shirt was a "wood shirt," one of her ubiquitous lumberjack shirts in faded green-and-black plaid, and it was tight across his shoulders, but it too was clean and dry and felt wonderfully warm. He toweled off his hair, stuffed his wet clothes into a plastic bag, and made his way back to the galley.

Annie's trademark cup of tea was waiting for him, along with a plate of cookies. Belatedly, he remembered the bag of cookies she had given them earlier. It must be floating around in that pool of water in the bottom of the dinghy. He had forgotten all about it.

Mercifully, Tom was quiet, his eyes tightly closed, but he was still rocking compulsively, his arms wrapped tightly around his thin body. Dan noticed that Annie had opened all the ports in what was probably an effort to clear the pungent smell of sour body odor, but it had been only partially successful, and both she and Claire were standing near the open door, about to move back outside to where the air was fresher.

"You and Walker take care of things?" Annie obviously didn't want to mention the body, perhaps afraid that it might either upset Claire or set Tom off again.

"Yeah," Dan said. "It's safe for Tom to go home. His cove is clear again." He glanced at the hermit, who appeared not to have heard, then at Claire, who had turned to stare out into the night. He knew he needed to explain to her what he and Walker had done with—and for—Robbie, but now was not the time. He took a sip of the hot, sweet tea. "I need to get home too. I've got to talk to a friend of mine."

"You'd have to be crazy to go tonight." Annie gestured into the darkness. "Darker than a coal mine at midnight—and that wind's not gonna let up till morning."

They had moved out of the cabin and were standing on the lee side of the boat, where it was relatively quiet and calm, but they could feel the slap of the waves coming up through the hull and the deck rocked under their feet.

"Can't be helped," Dan said. "I don't have much choice." He felt better about his chances now that he had dry clothes and a warm drink.

Annie didn't agree. "Won't help if you get lost or flipped or sink. And you'd have to fight that wind all the way. Take you till morning to get there." She looked out into the night. "Might as well stay here and sleep for a couple of hours. You can still leave before dawn. Wind might be down by then too. You'll probably get back quicker that way than if you leave now."

Her argument made sense and Dan realized he didn't need much convincing. In spite of his need to get back to *Dreamspeaker*, he knew what she was suggesting was the wisest course and he found himself surrendering willingly to her urgings. Minutes later, Annie led him back through the galley to the salon, where two long cushioned settees beckoned. By the time Annie came back from her stateroom with a pillow and a blanket, he was already asleep.

TWENTY-THREE

▶ Walker sank quickly under the waves. He was *sat'sam*, the spring salmon, his body sleek with silver scales. The black water wrapped him in its embrace, enfolded him, caressed him. He moved through it, powerful muscles surging through its currents. This was his home.

His hand touched the smooth black hull and he rose to the surface. He was at the stern, hidden from anyone on the deck by the curve of the transom. Just below him, twin propellers sat idle on the end of their shafts. On either side, through-hulls provided passage for the exhaust.

Walker had told Percy and the others to give him half an hour. More than that and hypothermia would claim him. As it was, his skin had lost feeling and he could feel the cold cramping his muscles. Soon it would penetrate deep into his bones, burn along his sinews, sear his nerves. Then it would send shards of ice into every cell. The myth of *sat'sam* could only sustain him for so long.

He had long since stripped off his clothes, wanting the speed and freedom that bare skin would give him. His only burdens now were the long strands of bull kelp he had tied to a rope he had wrapped around his waist and the knife he had strapped to his wrist.

There was no sign of movement on the black ship, although he thought there would almost certainly be someone on watch. Most likely they were sitting in the comfort of the bridge, watching the radar for intruders. On a night like this, it made sense: it was too dark outside to see anything without the help of technology. Fortunately for Walker and the rest of his small group, technology was much too sophisticated to notice something as primitive and small as a wooden canoe. Or a swimmer. And for that he was very grateful.

He slid under the surface again, feeling his way along the hull to the propellers. There were two of them, attached to pod-like structures that hung beneath the hull. It was impossible to see through the night dark water, so he worked by feel, praying that the numbness creeping into his fingers would hold off long enough for him to finish. Strand by strand, he pulled the kelp from his waist and wove it around the blades, wrapping it tightly around the curved metal and up and down the shafts. He lost count of the number of times he came up for air, but finally he was finished. He had built up a smooth, intricate covering and tied it off by weaving the ends back in. Satisfied, he moved on to the exhausts. They were larger than he had expected, and there was a heavy mesh screen just inside each one. It was an odd configuration and one he had never seen before. He figured it might explain why the engines were so quiet, but it meant there was nothing he could do there. Again he moved forward, his hand sliding along the hull till it found another opening. He wasn't sure what it was for, but it was big enough to reach his hand into, and his fingertips touched heavy rubber. It was some kind of valve or through-hull, a flap that allowed waste or water out but blocked it from coming back in. He took the knife and pushed it in as far as it would go. Cutting the rubber would be impossible, but if he could jam the flap open, it could cripple the ship, even sink it.

He had done all he could do. The dangerous tendrils of fatigue were already creeping into his brain, weaving dream into reality and reality into dream. *Sisiutl*, the sea serpent, beckoned him down to the depths, and the pale face of *Bukwas*, king of ghosts and lurer of drowned spirits, laughed at him through the waves. For a moment he thought he could feel the brush of soft hands caressing his hair, and then all of them were willing him to sleep.

He shook his head and fought to clear his mind as he pushed off for the shore. He had left Percy with the canoe, hidden among the rocks. Percy would be watching for him and would come if he signaled him, but any signal that would alert Percy could also alert the men on the black ship, and he could not, would not, do that.

Walker sucked in a lungful of air and slid under the water. Silently he prayed to the Creator, willed himself to transform once again into the magnificent *sat's@m*, giver of life, strong and sleek, girded with muscle, armed with scales. He was too cold to feel his muscles respond.

▶ The return of warmth to his legs came with stabbing pains that shot along his nerves and set them on fire. His back arched with agony, and his hands reached out like claws in an effort to stop Percy from rubbing life back into them. A rivulet of blood crept down his chin and started to meander down his neck from the split his teeth had opened in his lip as he fought to stop from screaming.

He was more dead than alive when Percy fished him out of the water, dragged him up on the shore, and covered him with a blanket, but he knew he needed to get the circulation in his legs going enough to let him get back into the canoe. They needed to get out of the bay.

Three more canoes were waiting for them around the point. They slid out of the darkness as soon as Percy and Walker threaded their way through the rocks and turned into the channel. Percy steered alongside the first and Walker forced his aching body to lean close to it.

"It's quiet. The crew boat is tied alongside. Two lines. Keep it between you and the black ship." He spoke in a whisper, even though they were out of sight of the two boats. Sound carried well over water, and the night was quiet. No point in taking a chance.

Percy released the canoe he had been holding on to and let himself drift as he watched it move into the night, followed by its two companions. Further talk was unnecessary: they had discussed their options earlier and knew what they were going to do. But that didn't mean there was nothing more to be done, and both men lifted their heads and spread their arms wide, offering up a silent prayer to the Creator, calling on the ancestors to lend their blessing to this enterprise.

As soon as the three men had disappeared, Percy turned his canoe east and slid his paddle deep into the water. He had done all he could. It was time to get back to camp. Walker sat huddled in the bow, his head bowed and the blanket wrapped tightly around his trembling body.

The three canoes crept around the point and slid in among the same rocks that had hidden Percy. They rested there for a minute or two, then one at a time moved out, each paddler watching the canoe before to see if it caused any sign of activity on the black-hulled ship that lay at anchor in the middle of the bay. Nothing stirred. No light showed in any of the windows. No sound drifted across the water. No shadow moved along the decks.

They joined up again on the far side of the crew boat. They had made the first move without a problem, but this was when they were most vulnerable and they could not afford even the slightest misstep. If they were discovered now, it would not only mean they had failed, it would also put them and the four brothers who were still over in Shoal Bay in jeopardy. And if Walker's guess was correct, maybe many others too—men they didn't know, people they had never cared about. White people. City people. People who had never cared about them and even some they may have robbed down there in the city they had left behind.

They were nervous, but it didn't show. This was exactly the kind of adrenalin rush they had lived by in the city and they knew how to control and direct it. They moved with speed and caution and, although few of them were ready to admit it, a kind of eager anticipation that they thought had been left far behind. These were, after all, the very same skills and actions that had gotten them into trouble just a few months ago, and it was bizarre and a little unsettling to be offered the opportunity to use them again, this time on the side of justice, to help others rather than themselves. The first man to silently scale the smooth metal surface of the hull reached the deck. He was grinning as he turned to help the next.

It took only moments for the two men to climb the rail and flatten themselves on the narrow side deck, where they blended into the darkness and the shadows. They lay there, motionless, until they were sure they had not been noticed and then one of them reached an arm back down to grasp a water-filled plastic bottle that was being passed up from the canoe below. He passed that to his partner and reached for another. More followed, until each man had three bottles. The smaller of the two men then eased his body over the cockpit coaming and dropped silently into the well. Again he waited, listening for the slightest sound, straining to detect any movement, but nothing stirred. Satisfied, he lifted his head till it was barely above the lip, then slid his hand forward along the deck until his fingers touched the raised metal of a filling cap. Perfect. He rubbed his fingertips lightly over the surface and felt the groove that ran across the center. The blade of the knife he carried in his jeans pocket was polished and honed, and in anything other than this pitch-dark night he would have worried about it throwing off a reflection, but that would not be a problem here. Sound, however, might be unless he took care to avoid it. He dug the knife out, opened it up, and reached his hand out along the deck again.

Twenty minutes after they had entered the bay, the three canoes were back out in the channel, heading home to the camp.

▶ In Shoal Bay, four tiny vessels slipped quietly through the night. They approached from the west, hugging the shore, careful to maintain silence and stay out of the sight of any guard who might be sitting out on the point above them. One by one they slid past the rocks, then turned and sped across the open strip of water that stretched between them and the wharf, where they slid between the creosoted timbers to gather again in the heavy black shadow beneath. Silent and motionless, they peered out at the dark lodge at the top of the bay, searching for any sign of life. Above their heads they could see four canisters gleaming dully through gaps in the wood. One appeared to be open.

Two of the men left the group and guided their canoes up onto the shingles at the head of the wharf, using the deep shadow of the timbers overhead to stay hidden. One at a time they climbed out, lifted their small boats up to rest on the rocks, then crept into the open.

Keeping their bodies low, they ran up the path and out along the top of the wharf until they reached the canisters. It took only seconds to realize that they were too heavy to pass down to the tiny canoes below, but locked containers were a challenge both men had dealt with many times before. Working silently, they opened each one and passed the contents down, one item at a time. Waiting hands received them, and there was a soft splash that blended with the restless slap of the waves as the men waiting below dropped each one into the water. A few items from each canister were carefully wrapped in a blanket and laid in the bottom of one of the canoes, just as Walker had asked.

TWENTY-FOUR

▶ It was late when Dan woke up, much later than he had planned. The wind had not quit. In fact, he thought it might have strengthened and he could hear the rain drumming on the cabin roof. That and the rocking of the boat were probably what had kept him asleep long past the time he had wanted to be up and gone. It had kept everyone else asleep too. There were no sounds of life that he could hear and he knew he was not the only one who had had an exhausting day yesterday.

He pushed aside the quilt Annie had put over him and rolled off the settee. He had slept in the clothes he had been given, but there was no way he could wear them outside in the dinghy. In this weather, he would be hypothermic within half an hour. He needed to find where she had put his stuff and see if, by any miracle, it was dry. He glanced at his watch as he moved toward the galley. It was after seven o'clock, although the rain and clouds were holding back the daylight.

The galley was empty and the only sound was the occasional tick from the cooling wood stove. He guessed that Old Tom had left sometime in the night, but he wasn't about to go outside to see if his rowboat was gone. He would find out soon enough. He sat for a minute and looked around. No sign of his clothes, and he wasn't about to go exploring the boat. If he stumbled into Annie's stateroom and woke her, she would probably shoot him! So now what?

His eyes lit on the kettle. Coffee would be good—actually, more than good. Even tea would be okay. He stood up and moved across to the stove. There was a box of wood by the door and a cast-iron poker lying on the grate. Dan grinned. There was nothing like killing two birds with one stone, and he could certainly plead innocence if he just happened to make a lot of noise opening the stove door. After all, he had never used this stove before.

It didn't take long to get the firebox roaring and he really did have to struggle to get the wood in. In fact, it required much use of the long cast-iron poker, which clanged loudly every time it hit the heavy metal of the stove. Annie appeared just as he was closing the damper. Unlike him, she had changed before she went to bed, and it was hard to believe this was the same woman who had greeted him the night before. Gone were the boots and the heavy work pants. Now she wore a long pink flannel nightdress that she had covered with a faded robe, and her feet were pushed into a pair of ancient fleece slippers. With her face softened by sleep and her hair free to fall across her shoulders, she reminded him of a favorite aunt he and his mother used to visit: he could see the woman's face but couldn't remember her name, although he was pretty sure it started with an *H*—Holly, Hilary, Harriet . . .

Annie interrupted his reminiscence by grabbing the poker from his hand and replacing it none too gently on the grate.

"Lot of work to get that stove going." Her eyes were fixed firmly on his face and he worked hard at looking innocent.

"Yeah. Guess I haven't done it for quite a while. I've got a Dickinson. Runs on diesel." He looked away from her to glare at the offending wood stove. "Sorry for the noise. I didn't mean to wake you."

"Huh." She lifted the kettle and took it to the sink to fill.

Dan thought she was going to call his bluff, but instead she changed the subject.

"Guess Old Tom took off."

Dan glanced at the now-vacant place at the table. "Guess so. He wasn't here when I came out. Think he'll be okay?"

Annie shrugged. "Should be. He's weird, but he seems to make out all right." She set the kettle on the stove and leaned over to peer out the porthole. "Maybe the rain'll clean him up a bit. Sure did stink."

Dan smiled. The sour odor Tom had brought with him still lingered in the cabin and he guessed Annie would be doing some cleaning of her own later on.

"At least he's going the right way. The wind will be pushing him. Like I said last night, I'm going to have to fight it pretty well all the way."

Annie's head snapped around and she stared at him. "You still figuring to go out in this?"

"Don't have a choice. I've got to get back to my boat."

"Yeah." She snorted. "Don't think that's going to happen till this blows over. Look outside."

Dan shrugged and tried to make light of it. He really didn't have a choice. "It's not that bad."

Annie wasn't buying it. "Right. Why don't you step out onto the deck and say that?" She gave a harsh laugh. "And while you're out there, make sure you look right out into the channel. I'm protected by the point here. It'll be blowing twice as hard out there. You'd be lucky to get twenty feet."

Dan leaned over to peer out past the whipping branches of the trees to the waters of the channel, where the tops of the waves were churning with white foam.

"Shit. How long you think it's going to last? You said last night it would quit by this morning."

Annie shrugged. "So I was wrong. Up here you can never be certain of anything. Probably blow over by the end of the day. Maybe earlier. It ain't nothing serious."

Well, maybe it wasn't to Annie, but it was to him.

"Think I could use your radio?"

"You're welcome to try. Not going to get much reception in this. Probably can't even reach Dawson's Landing."

"Jesus. You're just full of good news this morning."

She grinned at him. "Can't control the weather."

There it was again—the control thing. First Walker, now Annie. Seemed like a theme was developing.

"Who's trying to control the weather?"

Claire appeared in the doorway of the salon. She was dressed in yesterday's clothes, her face flushed with sleep and her hair tousled.

"Ask him." Annie flipped her thumb toward Dan. "Says he's going to head back to his boat."

Claire frowned and bent to look through the porthole. "In this?" Her voice was incredulous.

Dan sighed. Never mind a theme. This was a litany. "Hey, gimme a break here. You both know how important it is that I get back to my boat. How else are we going to stop these guys?"

Claire's face softened as she took in his concern. "This will slow them down too, you know. The crew boat might be able to make a bit of headway, but it would be slow going and a very rough ride."

Dan inclined his head, acknowledging her logic. "Yeah. I guess it might even be enough to disrupt their plans."

That was if Walker and his friends hadn't already disrupted them. And where was Walker, anyway? When he'd disappeared last night, he had said he would see Dan this morning, but he wouldn't be able to fight this weather either. Dan could only hope that he and his group had made it back to safety.

As if she had read his thoughts, Claire asked, "Where's Walker? He didn't come back with you last night."

Dan shrugged. "Your guess is as good as mine—actually, probably a lot better. He took off last night. Said he'd see me today." He didn't want to tell her about Walker and his friends going to the black ship. It would be too hard to explain and it would probably upset her. Hell, thinking about it upset him. There were so many things that could have gone wrong. "Hope he's okay."

"He probably went back home. He'll be fine." She turned away from him and looked out at the slanting lines of rain. "Did you . . . have you . . ." Her voice faltered.

"Robbie is buried back a bit along the shore. We wrapped him up so he's protected from the weather and we covered him with rocks to protect him from animals. He's fine there, and once I can get hold of someone—police or coast guard—then they'll come and get him." He put his hands on her shoulders. "They'll look after him properly. Take him back down to Victoria. Contact his family."

She nodded but didn't speak.

"Walker sang a chant for him." He wasn't sure why it was important to tell her that, but somehow he thought it was.

Her eyes welled with tears, and she gave him a tremulous smile. "That was kind. Robbie would have liked that."

TWENTY-FIVE

▶ Fernandez woke early. He seldom slept more than five hours, and the rising wind had pulled him from his bed earlier than usual. The ship was restless, bucking hard against its anchor, but inside it was quiet and dark, the rest of the men asleep in their berths and the weather blocking out even the faint glimmer starlight might have provided.

He dressed quickly in his normal attire of black trousers and black polo shirt, slid his feet into a pair of canvas deck shoes, and made his way toward the salon. The aroma of freshly brewed coffee caught his attention as he passed the door to the galley and he stopped. Someone else was awake. He checked the gold Rolex that circled his wrist: 3:50 AM. Alex would have gone on watch at 2:00 AM. The man had been with him for four years now and he had complete trust in him. He would not leave the bridge until his watch was over at 6:00 AM, certainly not for coffee. The other men were thugs hand-picked for the job and had spent most of their time over in Shoal Bay. They were unfamiliar with both the *Snow Queen*'s layout and the onboard equipment and were unlikely to be doing anything in the galley. Gunter did not drink coffee, so that left Harry and his captain, neither of whom Fernandez trusted.

He opened the galley door. Harry was standing at the counter, wrapped in a black silk, monogrammed robe, a carafe of coffee in one hand as he reached for a cup with the other.

"Jesus! You scared the hell out of me. Thought everyone was sound asleep." Harry lifted the carafe. "Want some coffee? I just made it. Took me twenty minutes to figure out how this thing works and another ten to find the bloody coffee."

Fernandez shook his head in refusal and watched as Harry rooted through the cupboards, searching for sugar. Harry's thinly veiled complaints about the absence of his crew were becoming increasingly annoying.

"You are up early."

"Yeah. Couldn't sleep. Must be this damn wind." Harry leaned over and peered blindly out of a porthole. "Need to get back to the city. Should have left days ago. All this time cooped up on the boat is driving me crazy." He turned back to Fernandez. "We're leaving today, right?"

Fernandez watched him, but did not speak. His silence made Harry nervous, and that made him more talkative.

"Been here too long, man. I've got stuff I need to be doing, people I need to see. We should have been back already. People will start wondering where I am." He paused as another thought came to mind. "This weather isn't going to be a problem, is it? The guys are going to be able to get down there all right? There isn't much time to spare with this thing."

That question finally provoked a response, and Fernandez pushed past Harry to peer out the same porthole the little man had just vacated. Even in the darkness, the white foam that surged along the wave crests was visible as it caught the faint glow from the masthead lights. His mouth tightened, and he turned and walked out the door without saying a word, leaving Harry staring after him. Halfway down the hall, Harry's voice caught up to him.

"Arrogant bastard."

The words registered, but Fernandez barely noticed them. Harry meant nothing to him. He had been a means to an end, useful for a while but now no longer needed. Once this was over, he would have to be dealt with.

Moving swiftly back through the boat, Fernandez knocked on the door to the bridge. It opened almost immediately and Alex stood back to let him in, clicking on the safety of the big Zamorana 9mm handgun he always carried as he returned it to the holster that rode under his arm.

"Any trouble?" Fernandez took in the faint glow from the array of instruments stretching right across the navigation station. No blips showed on either of the two radar screens as they painted the contours of the bay with an eerie green brush. No alarms were sounding on the GPS and no hazards or anomalies showed on the depth sounder.

Alex shook his head. "Quiet as a church. Ain't anyone around. Even if there was, they wouldn't be out in this shit."

"How bad is it? Will it be a problem?"

"What, the wind?" Alex knew exactly what he was talking about, and he reached over and pressed some keys on the computer, then waited till a new screen appeared. "Wind's northwest. Might be a bit rough going over to the lodge, but it'll be behind them when they head down south." He shrugged. "Should be okay for loading. That wharf gives a bit of protection and it's in behind the point."

He reached up and switched on the weather station. "The last update was an hour ago. Said it should ease up by late morning, early afternoon." The two men stood quietly and listened as the bored voice of a weather forecaster confirmed Alex's report.

When it was finished, Fernandez clapped him on the shoulder. "*Bueno*," he said and left the bridge as abruptly as he had arrived. He would wake the men early. They were going to need to gain time in any way they could, and from the sound of it, leaving early was going to be about the only way they could do it. He didn't return to the salon. He had no wish to run into Harry again and he preferred the solitude of his own cabin anyway.

At 5:00 Fernandez once again opened his cabin door and moved down the passageway. This time his destination was Gunter's cabin, just two down from his own. The door was opened so quickly in answer to his knock that he knew the German had already been awake.

"*Buenos dias.*" Gunter's accent lent a harsh, guttural quality to the Spanish greeting, making it almost unrecognizable.

Fernandez acknowledged it with a slight inclination of his head. He had no time for pleasantries. "Wake the men early. This weather will slow them down. Wake Carlos now and the rest in half an hour. Tell Carlos to pack up some food. They can eat when they get over there."

Gunter nodded an acknowledgment.

▶ The men gathered in the salon. There was no chatter. One look outside had told them that the hard day ahead had become harder, but their goal was in sight. They would do what they had been trained to do, what they had been preparing for, what they were paid for. Gunter joined them, followed by Carlos and Alex, who had just come off watch. All of them would be on board the crew boat for this trip.

Gunter did a brief head count. All were accounted for. Satisfied, he gave a quick nod and watched as Carlos led them outside, where the wind and rain caught them with a hissing, malevolent fury, shocking them out of their morning comfort and driving them across the heaving deck. The transfer to the crew boat slowed them down as the men staggered to the railing and waited with hands clenched and muscles tensed, poised to leap the gap between the two rolling hulls whenever they came close enough together to make bridging the distance possible. The rain made the metal decking of the crew boat slick, and more than one man slid heavily into the side of the deckhouse as he landed, adding his curses to the howl of the weather.

Back in his cabin, Fernandez listened to the muted sounds of the struggle taking place outside and mentally rehearsed the plan yet again, searching for any weakness and finding none. Nasiri was in place, his credentials ensuring he had the ability to move freely through the city. The target was already in Vancouver, his arrival confirmed by an informer who worked in a hangar at the south terminal of the airport. Another informer had confirmed that both American and Canadian security forces had checked the venue and had given it their approval. The same forces had tested the emergency evacuation plan and a trial run had been conducted. This too had been confirmed by the informant and was exactly as expected. The men who had just left were trained and would be well equipped, and Fernandez had no doubts regarding either their ability to perform their tasks or their dedication; they had been specifically chosen because of those exact traits. It was unfortunate that they would be sacrificed in this operation, but it was for a good cause, and in any case, they were expendable and easy to replace.

The knock on his door came sooner than expected and he checked his watch. He had given explicit instructions that the ship was to leave as soon as he had spoken with Nasiri at seven o'clock. It was only six-thirty. Unless it was another of Harry's pointless interruptions, this could only be bad news. One look at the man standing outside his door and he knew the answer. He gestured Gunter into the cabin.

"The crew boat will not start. Joaquim thinks it is the fuel." The German's voice was expressionless.

"Can he fix it?"

"He is trying, but in this weather . . ."

"Sabotage?"

The German shrugged. "He thinks not. The sea is very rough. It is possible that the motion dislodged something in the fuel tank and the line has been blocked."

Fernandez crossed to the porthole and peered out, but all he could see was the rain and the churning foam of the waves. "Tell him to keep working on it. The men can help him. They must leave here by seven at the latest." He turned back and added, "Send Alex to me."

He waited till Gunter had left, then slammed his fist into his palm. There could not be a delay now. It threatened everything.

Alex's knock came seconds later.

"Last night. You are sure there was nothing?"

Alex gave his usual shrug. "It was dark. Real dark. But those radars can see everything out there. They were set down to close range, and the alarm was on as well. It never went off. And I didn't see or hear nothing either." He waited to see if there would be a response, but there was only silence, so he continued, a plaintive note creeping into his voice. "It was real rough out there last night. Would have had to be something big to be moving around in that. Wasn't nothing."

Fernandez dismissed him with a wave of his hand. "Very well. Go and help Joaquim." He checked his watch again. Almost seven. Time for Nasiri's call.

Fernandez had not bothered to learn the captain's name, but the man was on the bridge, working at the navigation station, no doubt entering their course back down to Vancouver. Fernandez barely glanced at him as he shouldered him aside and moved to the radio.

"I require privacy," he snapped as he picked up the handset. He ignored the man's sharp intake of breath, listening only for the click of the door as he left.

At least Nasiri was ready. His call came in as scheduled, and it was good news. He had checked the location and verified the lines of sight. He had confirmed the broker's appointment that had been arranged more than two weeks ago and that would ensure access to the office that overlooked the east side of the conference center. His weapon had been delivered as arranged and had been checked and sighted. It was all satisfactory. Today he would confirm the distance from the window of the office to the emergency exit and verify the assigned vehicles and drivers. Feeling slightly mollified, Fernandez closed the connection. He had not informed Nasiri of the crew-boat problem. It was something he did not need to know, and it would only distract him from his job.

Harry was still in his stateroom, lounging on the settee in his silk robe and watching television, when Fernandez walked in. "You could knock first, you know," he said.

"There is a problem," Fernandez replied.

Harry turned off the television and sat up. "A problem? What problem? Has the crew boat left?"

"The crew boat will not start."

"What? What the hell are you talking about? Crew boats always start. They're the toughest, most reliable boats around. I'll send Richard over; he knows engines, he'll be able to—"

"We have to make a backup plan." Fernandez was not interested in Harry's ranting. "We will call in another crew boat." He paused as another thought struck him. "No. I think perhaps a helicopter would be better."

"You can't get a helicopter here in this weather, for God's sake." Harry's voice was contemptuous. "And it would have to come out of Rupert anyway. That's the only place that has the big ones that might handle this, and it's about three hundred miles away. Maybe more. Take hours. And where would it refuel? There's nowhere they could go. Even Shearwater's too far. Have to go to a marina—maybe Pruth Bay or Namu, but they're probably shut by now . . ."

Fernandez let Harry ramble on, but he had stopped listening. If a helicopter was not feasible, another crew boat was the only other option. They could not use *Snow Queen*. Not only could he not risk being seen with the men, but he needed to get down to Vancouver. *Snow Queen* should have already left. Taking her to Shoal Bay would take time that he could not afford. There had to be a better way.

"Call a new crew boat. Send it to Shoal Bay. If they get this one started, we will cancel it."

"Shoal Bay? What good will that do?" Harry was spluttering. "How will your guys get to Shoal Bay if the boat isn't working . . ." He was talking to an empty space. Fernandez had already left.

"Bloody hell." Harry shrugged off his robe. "It's starting to come apart."

▶ Silence fell in the salon as Fernandez appeared. The men who had returned to *Snow Queen* had no idea who he was and no desire to talk with a stranger. They noted his presence with wary eyes, watching him pass with taciturn hostility. Fernandez ignored them and walked straight out to the stern deck. Where the hell was Gunter? He was supposed to be directing things. He continued on along the side deck, his eyes squinting against the driving rain. Alex almost knocked him over as he ran back from the crew boat in an effort to escape the weather.

"Shit! Sorry boss. Didn't expect to find you here." Alex's gaze slid around him to the open door to the salon. "Did the men see you?"

"It is not important now. Where is Gunter?"

Alex frowned and tilted his head toward the crew boat. "He's keeping an eye on things over there."

"Any success?"

"Nothing yet. Joaquim thinks water has got into the fuel tanks."

"*Mierda!* Okay, get Gunter. Send him to my cabin." Fernandez pushed his way back through the heavy silence in the salon. He had reached the companionway when he felt a vibration ripple through the soles of his shoes: *Snow Queen* had started up her engines. Imbeciles! Would nothing go right this day? Yesterday he had told Harry they would leave at seven, right after the call from Nasiri, but surely the little prick should be smart enough to figure out that they could not go until the men had left. Had he even called for another crew boat yet? Fernandez flung open his cabin door and headed for the intercom, wheeling as Gunter entered behind him, water dripping from his chin and fingertips.

"Is it fixed?"

"No. I do not think it can be started. The tanks would have to be drained."

"*Joderse!*" Fernandez snarled. He strode over to the window and stared out at the foam-streaked water. There had to be something he could do.

"Could the inflatables make it?"

Gunter paused for a minute, then shrugged. "Not the little ones, but the big one up on top, I think perhaps. If it went a little slowly. But it would be very rough and it would be dangerous. The men would probably be very seasick."

"Get it launched. And get rid of that damn crew boat. Sink it. Let it go. I do not care—just get rid of it. I will have another one sent over to Shoal Bay to collect you from there."

The German nodded and left. It was more than twenty minutes later when Fernandez finally heard the metallic clang of the locking mechanism on the big davits on the upper deck being released, followed by the thump of heavy boots as the men struggled to lower the big rigid-hull inflatable over the side. And it was another twenty before the throaty roar of a big inboard/outboard motor signaled their departure. They had lost almost two hours, but they could still make it.

TWENTY-SIX

▶ Nasiri left his room as soon as the phone call with Fernandez was done. He headed down to the waterfront. There was a café in the lobby of the hotel that he had checked out yesterday and it would be perfect for his needs. It provided a clear view of the elevators leading to the office tower above, and he could see out through the wide glass windows to the east side of the convention center. Wearing a black gabardine raincoat over a pin-striped gray suit, black wingtips, and white button-down shirt, he was indistinguishable from the hundreds of other businessmen heading out for a day at the office. The fact that the place would be swarming with security people was almost a plus.

Sitting in the café sipping his coffee, Nasiri let his gaze wander along the outer perimeter of the conference center, where early-morning joggers and eager tourists braved the fine mist of rain that silvered the city and the waters beyond. It was an impressive building, big and solid yet somehow delicate. Angled windows on the prow front were cantilevered out over Burrard Inlet, and the curving planes of the living roof blended with the treed expanse of Stanley Park immediately to the west. Glass walls reflected the harbor and the decorative sails of the cruise-ship terminal that lay to the east. On the wide walkway surrounding it, police and security patrols were easy to pick out. He knew there would be many more the next day, as well as helicopter and marine surveillance, but that didn't bother him. They would be watching the crowds out front and checking rooftops and balconies, not office windows in one of the most prestigious addresses in the city. Besides, if all went according to plan, when the time came their energy would be focused on the chaos that was happening on the other side of the convention center, near the main entrance, where Fernandez's team would be playing out its part.

He slid his wallet out of his pocket and discreetly checked the appointment card he had been given the day before. The name of the financial firm was embossed in black and gold on heavily textured ivory card stock. Below that, a secretary had hand-printed his name and the time of his appointment in beautifully formed, rounded letters. *Roberto Mancera. 10:00 AM*. It was the same name that appeared on the driver's licence and the various credit cards that shared his Italian leather wallet as well as on the registration card at the hotel, where he had willingly provided the desk clerk with his Spanish passport. It appeared again on the sheaf of stocks and bonds that had filled his briefcase yesterday and that he had left in the care of Mr. Jason C. Bainbridge, investment counselor and owner of the elegant card that now rested in his hand. Nasiri smiled as he drained the last of his coffee and signaled the waitress for his check. Everything was in order.

▶   By nine o'clock in Annie's cove, the rain had eased and the wind had decreased and veered toward the east, flattening the seas it had built up the night before. The branches on the trees had gradually stilled and the birds had returned, their calls loud in the newly quiet air.

"You got a radio?" Annie was peering down at Dan as he struggled to untie the dinghy line.

"Yeah."

"VHF?"

"Yeah."

"I'll leave mine on."

Dan looked up at her. "Thanks, Annie. We'll call you when we get back."

"Hmm."

Dan watched her as she stomped away across the deck and disappeared from sight. "She's not half as tough as she pretends to be," he said, turning to check that Claire was settled.

"No, she's not—but don't ever tell her that," Claire replied with a smile. "She'd never forgive you."

They were both wearing dry clothes, bulked up by the addition of the fleece shirts that Annie had insisted on giving them. The weather might have improved, but it was still cold, and they knew they would be drenched by the time they reached their destination even though they planned on taking the circuitous route through the narrow, protected channels Walker had led them on. Was that only a day ago? It seemed more like a week.

Dan finally succeeded in untying the line that held the dinghy to the plank walkway. He passed it to Claire and made his way back to the stern. "Ready?" he asked.

She nodded and released the little boat, and the whine of the outboard shattered the peace of the morning.

They wound through the familiar channels, watching for the rocks and shallows Walker had pointed out. Claire sat in the bow, her gaze on the water ahead as she scanned for dangers. Dan watched Claire, content to follow her directions as she indicated a change of course or speed with quick movements of her hands. Even wearing thick layers of clothing, the slim lines of her body were visible as she leaned and twisted in her efforts to discern the shadowy rocks below the surface, and he found himself enjoying watching her. She had an energy, a vibrancy, and openness that he found irresistible, and a surge of attraction woke from dormancy to warm his interest and heat his blood. He smiled. Maybe there really were second chances in life. A couple of hours and they would be back at *Dreamspeaker*. One phone call to Mike and then his job would be finished. Nothing else he could do. He had learned Walker's lesson well, and although he would have to wait around for the man himself if he wasn't already there, once he had seen him and said goodbye, he would feel free to head back south without his conscience nagging at him. Two, maybe three days, just Claire and him. Could get interesting.

He was so busy enjoying the possibilities that when Claire suddenly jerked back, arms spread wide and fingers white where she gripped the edges of her seat, he pulled the control lever back too far and stalled the motor. The tiny boat lost way and settled down into the water just as the curve of a black hull appeared beyond the point of land ahead of them. The current caught the bow as they slowed and pushed it into the bank, hiding them from the black ship before it came completely into view.

"What the hell are they doing here?" Dan had been flung forward as the bow hit the gravel bottom, and he was pressed against Claire's back, his mouth beside her ear as he whispered the question he knew they were both thinking.

They slid out of the dinghy, leaving it perched on the shore as they crept up to the point and peered through stalks of weedy grass. The black ship was very close, perhaps only a couple hundred yards off the shore, bow out as she hung off a short anchor chain. Light reflecting off the water lit the pale tracery of script etched on her stern:

Snow Queen
Vancouver

Three men were clustered at the stern, peering down at two others who were in a small inflatable, moving slowly along the waterline under the curve of the hull. Dan immediately recognized one of the three up on deck. This close, Harry Coombs's round frame and curly hair were unmistakable, but Dan had never seen either of the other two. He thought one of them might be the captain. The man was wearing white slacks and a white polo shirt with some kind of insignia on the pocket and he appeared to be giving directions to the two below. The third man was standing a little apart, his body tilted slightly away from Harry as if to distance himself. In perfect contrast to the captain, he was dressed head to toe in black, and his dark hair was pulled into a neat ponytail at the back of his neck. His eyes were covered with wraparound sunglasses and the rigid lines of his body suggested a barely controlled rage.

Voices drifted across the water, distorted by the distance but carrying the unmistakable cadence of worry. The beam of a work light, diminished by the light of day, flashed across the hull and then shone down on the surface of the water below the stern. They had to be checking the propeller. There was more talk, perhaps questions or directions and short answers given in low tones. Dan thought he heard the word "seaweed," although he could have imagined it, and then the man he took to be the captain left briefly and returned with a long pole with a hook on the end, which he passed down to the men below. Dan guessed that something—probably the seaweed they had been talking about—had fouled the prop and they were going to use the boat hook to try to free it.

It was not going to be an easy job. The inflatable kept moving out as the men pushed against the hull and they had to use the motor to try to hold it in place. Even allowing for the difficult conditions, they looked awkward, as if they were not used to being on the water and were uncomfortable with it. As Dan watched them struggle, he thought of Walker and how at ease he would have looked in the same situation. Hell, the man had to be part fish. If he had a prop fouled with seaweed, he would probably just dive in and . . . wait a minute. Could this be his handiwork? It was the kind of thing that he might come up with, although Dan had no idea how it could be accomplished. How the hell could you get seaweed onto a prop so it stayed on? And the water had to be cold enough to freeze his balls off! He discarded the notion. Walker might have been here and tried something, but this couldn't be it.

The first piece of seaweed came up on the hook and was passed to the men waiting above. It was shiny and brown, and from his distance Dan thought it looked smooth. He glanced at Claire. "Kelp?"

She shrugged. "Maybe."

She looked as mystified as he was. Kelp didn't wrap around props. It was too smooth and tough.

▶ "Maybe we should move."

Claire's low voice broke into Dan's thoughts. They had been watching the scene on the black ship—*Snow Queen*, Dan corrected himself, which was an odd name for a ship with a black hull—for over half an hour, and it looked like it was going to take a good deal longer for them to finish up. The tall dark man had gone inside and had not reappeared, but Harry and the captain were still out there, peering down at the men in the inflatable, and their body language suggested they were not happy.

"Nowhere we can go," Dan said in a low voice. "If we go back and head round the other way, we have to go right past Shoal Bay."

"What if they come over here?"

Dan shook his head. "No reason to—and we'd see them coming, anyway. We could be out of sight before they got here." He looked back down to the dinghy, sitting on the shore. "We should move the dinghy, though. Take it back around the bend where we can get to it easily. I'll just pull it. Can't start the motor. They'd hear that for sure."

She looked down at the little boat and nodded. "I'll do it. You stay here."

He really didn't think it likely that anyone would come over, but it was a good precaution and he knew Claire would feel more comfortable with the dinghy out of sight. He watched as she wriggled backward down the slope, gently lifted the bow from its resting place on the shore, and nudged it out into the water till it floated free. Wading into the water after it, she turned and started walking away from the point, pulling the tiny boat along behind her like a dog on a leash. She was halfway there when the shriek of a siren cut through the air, and Dan snapped his attention back to *Snow Queen*. A moment later he felt Claire throw herself down beside him again.

"What on earth is happening?"

TWENTY-SEVEN

▶ Fernandez reached the wheelhouse within seconds, the shrill blast of the alarm vibrating through his skull. He pushed his way past Harry, who was standing uselessly near the door with his hands over his ears, and over to where the captain was leaning over the controls, his fingers frantically working the keyboard as he peered intently at one of the screens.

"What is happening?"

His voice, always cold, dripped menace. He saw Harry look at him, worry obvious in the nervous flicker of his eyes.

"It's probably nothing much." Harry gave a strained laugh. "Might be a sensor on the shaft or something. The boys might have set it off when they were pulling off the weeds."

Fernandez ignored him and leaned closer to the captain.

"I asked you, not him."

The man looked up from the controls, his face carefully neutral but dislike and resentment written plainly in the tone of his voice.

"Something in the engine room. I can't be sure from here."

He turned and gestured for Fernandez to accompany him with a careful sweep of his arm that managed to convey contempt within the arc of its polite invitation. Fernandez's flat gaze hardened even further, but he said nothing. The tenuous strands of his patience had thinned to their breaking point. He no longer had any doubt that this was sabotage. The question was by whom.

If the noise on the bridge had been loud, it was deafening in the engine room. Alarms screamed from two speakers, and both engines were running, but they wouldn't be running for long. Water covered the floor. It had already covered the engine mounts and was creeping up the sides of the engine blocks. The captain stared at it for a moment, then reached up to a control panel mounted high on the wall and pressed a series of buttons. The alarms fell silent and the engines died with a series of rough coughs and shudders. The sudden quiet that followed was quickly shattered as another motor started up, this one presumably attached to a pump, because a vortex suddenly appeared on the surface of the water.

"Holy shit!" Harry had followed them and now stood at the top of the stairs, looking down at the flooded engine room. "What the hell is going on?"

"I think perhaps that is *my* question." Fernandez's voice was dangerously quiet as his unblinking stare fixed on the captain. "The crew boat will not start. The propeller will not turn. The engine room is flooded. A little too much for coincidence, no?"

The captain's attention was focused on the water level, his eyes assessing the likelihood of damage to the engines, but he nodded his agreement. "It certainly would seem that way."

"Indeed." Fernandez's gaze had not wavered, but the captain was too concerned with his ship to acknowledge him.

"I'll radio the coast guard. We can't control this when we don't know what's causing it, and we have no hope of reaching a repair facility."

Fernandez moved to block his way. "I think not."

The captain stared at him in disbelief. "We have no other choice. Look at that water. This ship is in danger of sinking, and thanks to you and your bloody scheming, we don't even have a decent dinghy to get us to shore, let alone to civilization." He started to push past on his way to the bridge but froze in horror as Fernandez calmly pulled a small black Beretta pistol from under his shirt and pointed it at him.

"Jesus, man, take it easy!" Harry was still hovering at the top of the stairs. "He's the captain, for God's sake. He knows what's best for the ship."

"But not for me." The gun did not waver, although the muzzle rose and fell briefly as Fernandez nudged the man forward. "You first, my friend."

The captain stumbled up the stairs with Fernandez's gun pressed firmly to his back. As they reached the top, Fernandez stretched out his other hand to grasp the man's shoulder and bring him to a stop.

"Turn off the pumps."

"What?" Harry had taken a step or two back to let them pass, but now he pushed forward again, his voice incredulous. "Are you fucking crazy? You heard the man. We're sinking!"

The sharp click of a safety being released was the only answer he received, and without comment the captain raised his hand and pressed a button on the panel. The silence that followed was broken only by the ragged sounds of their breathing and the gurgle of the water as it started its relentless climb up the engine blocks again.

"Very good." Fernandez once again urged the man forward. "And now we will go to the bridge. You also, Harry." The muzzle moved briefly.

"You bastard." Harry clutched his blue blazer more tightly around his chest. "I'll see you in hell for this."

The three men walked back through the teak-soled passageways and elegantly appointed rooms until they reached the stairs leading to the upper deck and, ultimately, to the bridge. The captain led the way, with Harry so close behind he kept bumping into him and knocking them both off-balance. Fernandez stayed back, keeping himself a steady distance behind them.

"Call a helicopter."

Fernandez stopped at the entrance to the bridge and propped his shoulder casually against the door frame as he watched his words register with the two men standing rigidly in front of the console, staring blindly out through the windshield.

"A helicopter?" Harry whirled around to face him. He was almost apoplectic, his face red and covered with a sheen of sweat. "I already told you that won't work. Sure, the wind's dropped a bit, but a helicopter still won't get here for maybe two hours. Maybe more. We'll have sunk by then. And where the hell could it put down anyway? There's not a flat piece of land within—"

"Tell them to go to Shoal Bay." The Rolex on Fernandez's wrist glinted in the pale light. "We will be there by one o'clock."

"Shoal Bay?" Harry spat the words out. "How the fuck are we going to get to Shoal Bay? We sure as hell can't get there on *Snow Queen*, and that piece-of-shit dinghy hanging off the stern is too small to carry all of us."

"A problem." Fernandez allowed himself a thin smile. "But one I think we can solve." His eyes moved to the captain again. "The helicopter, please."

The captain shot a quick glance at Harry before picking up the radiophone and putting in a call to West Coast Helicopters. The company responded almost immediately, and the conversation could be heard clearly over the speakers. There were no problems arranging for a pickup in Shoal Bay. The wind had dropped enough to allow an MD500D that was stationed at a West Coast Helicopters base in Port McNeill, a hundred and twenty miles south, to take off. It could carry four, and while it would have to stop at McNeill again on the return trip in order to refuel, it could have them in Vancouver before dinner. The company had worked with Harry several times before and did not question the request.

"Well done, Captain. Now just one more thing and we can go." The gun was aimed steadily on the captain's chest. "The anchor, please. Pull it up."

A look of incomprehension crossed the captain's face, and for the first time since he had seen the gun, he spoke out in protest. "Haul the anchor? You can't be serious! The engines won't start. There's too much water. She'll drift out into the channel. It's deep water out there and strong currents. Once she sinks we'll never be able to get her up." He turned toward Harry. "Talk to him, for God's sake. This is madness."

"He's right, Fernandez." Harry's struggle to control his anger played out across his face, but he managed to control himself enough to work a placatory note into his voice. "It won't work. *Snow Queen* is crippled. She can't go anywhere." The anger was creeping back and he checked it again. "Anyway, Shoal Bay's not that far. We can use the dinghy. It's calming down out there. We'll get there in plenty of time."

Fernandez regarded him for a few seconds, his expression inscrutable. After all that had gone wrong, it seemed he was being offered an easy solution to at least one of his problems. "Perhaps you are right, Harry. Go and pull the dinghy up. We will join you in a minute."

Harry appeared to sag with relief. The tension drained out of his body and the anger left his face to be replaced by an eager, almost child-like smile as he straightened and strode out of the wheelhouse, his step full of bounce. The outside deck was narrow here, just wide enough to allow the helmsman to step outside, and it was well over twenty feet above the waterline. For a moment he was framed by the open doorway, the black railing glinting in front of him, his body silhouetted against the restless water. The next he was gone, his body falling forward, its momentum carrying him out over the railing, his legs and feet briefly slowing his progress as they dragged lifelessly over the shining dark metal.

Fernandez turned the gun back on the captain, who stood frozen in shock at the console. It had been an easy shot and perfectly timed, so casual that anyone watching might have believed it had never happened, that Harry had simply slipped and fallen or had descended the stairs to the lower deck. Except for that hard, sharp sound that still reverberated through the still air of the wheelhouse and the acrid smell of gunpowder drifting through the air.

"You are a madman!" The captain was staring at him, disbelief warring with horror on his face.

Fernandez's smile did not reach his eyes. "Merely practical. You heard him say the dinghy can't carry us all." The muzzle of the gun moved slightly. "The anchor, please."

The captain's eyes followed the movement with a kind of fearful fascination before he raised them to meet Fernandez's unflinching stare and then the man turned away and pulled down a knife switch on the console. The distant hum of an electric motor was accompanied by the groan of the chain as it passed over the windlass. That was followed a few minutes later by the solid thud of the anchor as it seated itself in its cleats and then silence as the motor shut off again.

"And now we will go to the dinghy, Captain."

"Are you going to shoot me in the back too?" The man seemed to have recovered from his shock.

"Of course not. There is no need. You are proving to be most helpful. We will travel together to Shoal Bay; then I will leave you."

"Alive or dead?"

"That will depend on you. But we talk too much. The dinghy please. Now."

The unequivocal tone of the demand was impossible to mistake, and with a quick glance down at the gun, the captain moved warily across the bridge and onto the deck. Fernandez followed.

TWENTY-EIGHT

▶ Even before Harry's body had disappeared beneath the surface of the ocean, Dan figured the man was dead. He had seen the telltale arch of his back and the sudden flowering of his jacket as the bullet hit, and he had heard and recognized the sound of the shot even though it was muted by distance. He watched helplessly as Harry tumbled over the railing, gravity lifting and twisting his arms in an eerie ballet before his limp body plunged into the water and sank below the waves.

Beside him, Claire gasped in shock. "Oh my God. We have to help him!"

He reached out and grabbed her arm before she could get up. "We can't help him. It's too late. He's already dead."

He regretted the harshness of his words even before he had finished speaking, but it was too late to take them back. He could see the reproach in Claire's face as she tried to pull her arm away. "You don't know that! It might have been a heart attack. He didn't fall that far. He might have survived it."

"He didn't have a heart attack." Dan tried to think of what he might say to convince her but couldn't find anything except the truth. "He was shot. Didn't you hear it?" He heard her sudden, sharp intake of breath.

"Shot?" She stopped struggling and looked back to *Snow Queen*. "I heard something, but . . ." The sound of the anchor being winched up interrupted whatever she had been going to say. "Are they leaving?"

He carefully pushed the grasses aside to get a better view. "It sounds like it, but that little inflatable is still in the water, and there's something odd about the hull. She's sitting too low in the water."

"Someone's coming out of the wheelhouse," Claire said.

"Yeah. That's probably the captain."

"There's another man too. I think it's the guy with the ponytail."

Dan caught a glint of metal as the second man followed the captain through the door. "Yeah. And he's got a gun, so I guess we know who shot Harry."

"Harry?" Claire was looking at him in astonishment. "You know these people?"

He shook his head, chiding himself for not keeping his mouth shut. Now he would have to explain. "No, but remember when I came to pick you and Walker up off that island and I took a look at the black ship?" She nodded. "I saw the guy who just got shot. He was walking along the deck, and I knew I'd seen him somewhere before. I just couldn't remember where. Then yesterday I figured it out. It was when I was on the job. His name is—was—Harry Coombs. He's a crook. A bad guy. We figured we knew what he was up to, but we could never get anything on him that would hold up in court."

Claire was silent, and he glanced at her. She was looking back at the water, maybe watching the ship, maybe searching for some sign of the man they were talking about, but mostly she seemed to be lost in thought. He watched her for a moment, wanting to find a way to reassure her and also turn that look of reproach into something closer to warmth and . . . was it her approval he wanted? He pulled his attention back to the black ship.

There was still no sign of Harry in the water, and the two men from the wheelhouse disappeared from view as they moved aft along the side deck. With the anchor up, *Snow Queen* was swinging her bow slowly out into the wind. As her stern swung around toward them, Dan saw two more men standing on the aft deck and recognized them as the ones he had seen earlier in the inflatable. Now they looked relaxed and unconcerned, like they were simply waiting for someone; they had made no move to go to see what was happening in the wheelhouse, even though it was impossible to believe they hadn't heard the shots. Which made them part of the gunman's team, Dan thought to himself. How many more were there or had everybody else left with the crew boat? A moment later the captain, still followed by the gunman, appeared from the side deck, and after a brief conversation that he couldn't make out, Dan watched the two men move to the stern and pull both the dinghy and the inflatable up to the grid.

"Are they all leaving?" Claire whispered the same question he had been asking himself.

"Looks like it," he replied.

"But that doesn't make sense. Wouldn't they leave someone behind on the ship? They've hauled the anchor. She'll just drift away."

Dan nodded. He was as confused as she was, but even as they watched, the captain was urged into the dinghy, the gunman followed, and the other two men clambered into the inflatable. Both boats roared to life and motored out into the channel together before turning west and disappearing around a point. Moments later, silence returned.

Dan turned his attention back to the black ship. He couldn't see any sign of life aboard her and couldn't hear the sound of any engine or equipment running. Suddenly his mind slipped back to the night he'd been anchored up north and he had seen the furrowed wake of a passing boat but had heard nothing. He hadn't linked that with the black ship up to now—hadn't had a reason to. He had never seen it under way, but now that he thought about it, he figured this was almost certainly the same ship. It must have some new engine and prop design, one he had never heard of that made no sound. But that boat had been under way and traveling at speed, judging by the wake it had left. *Snow Queen* looked like she was just drifting.

He and Claire lay side by side for a few minutes, staring out at the drifting ship, thinking their own thoughts, feeling the sun warm their backs when it dodged out of the clouds. The wind had veered and was still dropping and *Snow Queen* swung aimlessly as each gust caught her, but she was inexorably drifting out into the deep water of the channel and the current was starting to catch her, pushing her west.

"She looks like she might be sinking and they've abandoned her." Once again, Claire had put his thoughts into words.

He looked at her. "It certainly looks that way, but I guess there's only one way to find out for sure." He pushed himself back from the ridge, stood up, and turned to head down to where the dinghy still sat on the shore below them.

"You planning on just leaving me here?"

He turned to find her still sitting on the grass, her face so indignant that even though her question had caught him off guard, he had to struggle not to laugh.

"Claire, we don't know for sure there's nobody there. You saw what happened to Harry. These guys are dangerous."

"And? What are you going to do if there is someone there? Hit him on the head with your paddle?"

"Claire . . ."

"And what about me? What am I supposed to do here without the dinghy if you get into trouble? I assume you were going to take the dinghy, or were you planning on swimming?"

The indignation had disappeared, and he could see her anger building with every word.

"Claire . . ."

"Men! You're all so damn stubborn." She twisted to her feet, ignoring the hand he extended to help her up. "I'm coming with you."

She brushed past him and he watched as she stalked down the bank to the water and pushed the dinghy out. What the hell? Where had that come from? It was a side of her he hadn't seen before, and oddly enough, he thought he liked it, although now was neither the time nor the place to try to figure out why. He gave himself a mental shake and went down to join her. She was sitting in the bow, facing forward with her back rigid, her shoulders straight, and her gaze firmly fixed ahead, as he pushed out into deeper water and started the motor.

▶ *Snow Queen* was deserted. She was also sinking. Claire had been right on both counts. Her stern was getting low in the water, and she wallowed with each wave that washed past her. Dan made sure Claire stayed with him as he checked the cabins and the living quarters, and once he was sure there was no one left aboard, he left her in the wheelhouse while he made his way down to the engine room.

Even without a light, he could make out the dull glint of water. He reached his hand around the side of the door, feeling for a switch or a panel in case there was still power, and his fingers brushed across a round tube. A flashlight. Even better. He pulled it free from its mount and switched it on. The water was more than halfway up the two engines—if that's what they were. They looked more like big generators, but it didn't matter what they were because they weren't going to be starting again. Neither was a third, smaller engine that sat in the center of the floor and was almost completely underwater, only the top of the engine block still showing. He shone the beam around the walls. Electrical cables and pipes snaked along both sides, and above them heavy shelves with high lips held spare parts and tools. At the front, on a wide ledge and strapped in with heavy steel bands, sat two smaller generators and a bank of batteries.

He turned the beam of the flashlight back to the side of the door-way and located the electrical panel. The switches were all off. He checked the labels till he found a switch labeled Auxiliary Generators and switched it on. Ahead in the gloom he saw twin green lights appear, but nothing else happened. He figured the starter switch was probably up forward, beside the generators, but he had no desire to climb down into that darkness and wade through murky water that was probably knee high in order to find out.

He shone the flashlight down again. The water was higher, but not a lot. Wherever the leak was, it wasn't huge. Why hadn't they tried to fix it? Surely there were pumps. This ship was some rich guy's toy. It would have every possible piece of equipment, all of it top of the line. Suddenly, his brain conjured an image of Harry, tumbling forward, dropping down past the wide side deck, past the shining black hull. This would have been Harry's ship, he realized.

It was exactly the kind of toy Harry Coombs liked to have, and it was registered in Vancouver, where Harry had his sprawling mansion overlooking Horseshoe Bay. Dan had been there once as part of a raid that had yet again come to nothing. And the captain was almost certainly Harry's captain, which meant he would have wanted to save the ship. Probably wanted to call the coast guard, and that would not have suited the fellow with the ponytail. Not if he was the guy behind the Shoal Bay stuff.

"Shit!" Dan flung himself backward and raced to the wheelhouse, ignoring the alarmed look Claire gave him as he blew past her.

"What's happening? Is something else wrong?" Her voice followed him as he scanned the console for the switch he was looking for.

"Only with my brain." He moved to the starboard controls. "If we can get the radio working, we can call the coast guard."

▶ TWENTY-NINE ◀

▶ "But why not just shoot him too? Why force him into the dinghy?"

Claire was straddling the center thwart and scanning the water and shoreline that lay ahead and to starboard of them as she spoke. They were running at less than half speed, partly because they were near the shore themselves and needed to see any rocks or reefs that lay in their path and partly because they wanted to hear any other motor before whoever was using it had a chance to hear them.

"Yeah, I've been thinking about that," Dan replied, his focus on what was happening on the port side. "I think he was the only one who knew how to get to where they were going. Probably Shoal Bay." He hoped he was right. He had pointed the coast guard in that direction.

"Makes sense, I guess," Claire said. She was quiet for a few moments, then asked, "Do you think they'll shoot him too? Once they get there?"

He looked at her. The worry in her eyes made him want to reach out and reassure her, but he didn't know how.

"I don't know. It probably depends on what they plan to do. They may need him to help them."

She nodded, but he knew she wasn't convinced. Neither was he.

"How long do you think it will take the coast guard to come?"

He shrugged. "Depends on where they were. I called it in as a Mayday, made it clear we were abandoning ship. That will make it a top priority. That hovercraft they've got makes pretty good speed, but if they can't get here in good time, they might send out a helicopter." He thought for a minute. "That might even work better for us. They would locate the ship faster, see it was abandoned and sinking, and then head over to Shoal Bay to pick us up."

"Except we won't be there."

"That's true. But the arrival of a coast guard helicopter will certainly screw up whatever they're doing over there, and the fact that they'll be asking for someone called Harry Coombs should really create a problem. Might give the captain an opportunity to get away from the bad guys while they're trying to explain things."

They sat quiet for a while as the water chuckled along the hull and the shoreline slid past. Then she turned to look at him again.

"What if they shoot at the helicopter? Or at the coast guard guys when they get off it?"

He shook his head. "I don't think they'll do that. They don't want witnesses, remember? And the helicopter is going to be in constant radio communication with the coast guard boat, and that won't be far behind." He twisted the tiller to port to avoid a large log floating upright in the water. "Besides, those things carry a pretty big crew, and they're very well armed."

The shore curved south and he turned the dinghy to follow it. It was a little rougher now that they were out of the channel, but the change in wind direction had flattened the waves and the dinghy rode easily. Gulls soared overhead in the clear air, their calls easily heard above the sound of the motor, and occasionally the sun came out to sparkle off the water and warm them. Dan wished he could pretend this was just another lazy day out on the water, but the knowledge of what had happened on the black ship kept intruding.

It was Claire who heard the helicopter first. She searched the air ahead and located it, a tiny speck in the distance, barely bigger than a bird, angling across the wide sky, heading a little east of north.

"There," she said, pointing. "Looks like it's heading in the right direction."

He nodded. "Yeah. Came pretty quick, too. We need to get out of sight. Don't want them thinking we're the ones they're looking for." He angled the dinghy in toward the shore and nosed it in under some overhanging cedar branches.

They turned the motor off and sat and watched as the dot grew larger and slowly turned from the generic black created by distance to a fuselage that was deep blue on the top half and silver on the bottom, with turquoise striping in between. As the helicopter turned, they could make out some kind of lettering above its call sign.

"That doesn't look like a coast guard chopper." Claire was staring at it in confusion.

"No. But it sure looks like it's heading for Shoal Bay. They must have called in their own transportation before they left the ship."

"So he'll get away with killing that man. And I bet he killed Robbie too." Her voice was quiet and filled with regret.

"Not necessarily. We can find out where that chopper came from pretty easily. Those have to be company markings, and there can't be too many operating up here. When we track down the company, we can find out where they took them. Maybe get a name. That gives us—well, gives the police—a good lead."

She nodded but didn't look like she really believed his words.

"Look," he continued, "we have to wait here until they leave, but then we'll get to *Dreamspeaker* and call the police. They may even be able to find out where these guys are going and get there before they land."

She nodded again and they both sat quietly, waiting to hear the chopper leave. They didn't have to wait long. The whine of the rotors and the chop of the blades biting into the air as it lifted off reverberated along the rocky shores and echoed off the cliffs. Minutes later, it appeared above the treeline of the island to the north, hovered for a moment, then turned south. Dan waited until it was completely out of sight, then reached for an oar to push the dinghy into open water.

"Wait." Claire reached a hand back to stop him. "I can hear something."

"Just the chopper. All these channels and islands make it sound like it's coming from another direction. It can trick you."

"No, it's different. Listen."

He put the oar down and turned his head, listening for whatever she had heard, trying to pinpoint its direction.

"Hear that?" There was a sudden surge of sound. "It's not the chopper. I think it's a boat."

Dan swung round and stared at the channel behind them, from where the sound seemed to be coming. It did sound like a boat, and a fairly big one at that.

"That's gotta be the coast guard. Too bad they'll be too late to catch that helicopter, but maybe the captain got left behind." He grabbed one of the overhanging branches and pulled the dinghy farther into the shadows. The coast guard was good at surveillance and would be on the lookout for a dinghy.

The sound swelled to a crescendo, and a bright-silver aluminum boat surged out of the channel and curved north, water foaming on its bow. Inexplicably, it was a crew boat—but was it the same one they had seen in Shoal Bay? Were the "loggers" aboard? It was heading in the right direction, but it was too far away to see how many people were in it. He glanced at Claire. She looked as puzzled as he felt.

"Think it's the same one?" he asked.

She shrugged. "Could be. I really can't tell. They all look pretty much the same."

"Can't be that many crew boats out at this time of year. Not up here. Everything's shut down."

"Maybe they were going to meet up with the people on the black ship and found it deserted and sinking. They would probably figure those guys would head to Shoal Bay and go check it out."

"Yeah, but where the hell have they been? There's nothing else around here. No towns, and the marinas are all closed down. Same with the fishing resorts, and all the logging operations are shut down for the season . . ."

He let his words trail off with the fading of the crew boat's engine. He had thought he had it pretty well figured out, but now he felt hopelessly confused. There was simply too much going on, and most of it seemed focused on Shoal Bay.

The clatter of rotors cut him off as yet another helicopter, this one bright red and with the distinctive white stripe of the coast guard, soared over the crest of the island and swept over the trees above them. The wash from the rotors sent the trees into frenzied motion and rocked the dinghy so violently that he had to grab hold of a branch as it whipped above his head.

"Are you okay?" he asked. Claire had been thrown against the side of the dinghy and had slipped down into the bilge. He reached down and helped her back up onto the thwart.

"I'm fine. Maybe a bruise or two, but nothing major." She nodded toward the disappearing chopper. "It must be getting pretty crowded over there if they're all heading to the same place."

Dan snorted. "Yeah, but my guess is the bad guy has already left the scene."

▶ THIRTY ◀

▶ Gunter Rachmann trained his gun on the man walking ahead of him as they followed the path up to the lodge. He seldom allowed himself to lose control, no matter what the provocation, but today was proving to be a true test of his will. It had started out badly, and it was rapidly getting worse. The trip over had been a nightmare, with most of the men becoming so seasick they were useless, the four containers they had left on the wharf had disappeared without a trace and without the guards seeing or hearing anything, and now Fernandez expected him to get rid of this asshole. He slammed his fist against the door and ordered the startled man who opened it to send Alex out to him.

Alex was quick to answer the summons.

"What the hell is *he* doing here?" he asked as he took in the scene in front of him.

"He came with Fernandez."

"So what are we supposed to do with him?" Alex's voice held a note of contempt. "We don't have time to babysit."

"You will do exactly what I tell you to do!" Gunter snapped, his patience already worn dangerously thin. "And only that. Is everything ready to go?"

Alex shrugged the warning aside. "Maybe two more boxes. They have to dismantle everything before they can get it to fit."

"They must hurry. A crew boat is coming. They must be finished and ready to load when it arrives. Where is Marty?"

"In there. He's helping them." Alex indicated the open door behind him.

"Go back and finish," Gunter said. "And send Marty out here."

"Ah, so that's it." Alex glanced at the captain and grinned. "I will say goodbye to you, then, Captain. I do not think we will be meeting again."

He disappeared back inside and seconds later a small, hatchet-faced man stepped out onto the deck.

"You wanted me?"

"I have a job for you." Gunter nodded toward the man who stood rigid with fear in front of him. "Please take the captain and show him how beautiful the forest is here." The coldness of his voice belied the pleasantness of his words.

Marty nodded in acquiescence and removed a gun that had been hidden in the waistband of his jeans. "As you wish. After you, Captain." He stepped forward and pressed the muzzle into the man's ribcage, pushing him away from the door and along the deck.

"And do not take too long," Gunter snapped. "We do not have much time."

▶ The harsh clatter of rotors slammed into the quiet bay for a second time, beating the air and the rocks and the ground into a frenzy of sound that soared and faded as the chopper negotiated the twisting approach channels. Gunter whirled toward the water, holding his hand out to stop Marty. If this was Fernandez returning, it could mean he had changed his plans yet again and Gunter preferred to be in a position to accommodate him rather than be on the receiving end of his displeasure. Seconds later a helicopter swept around the point, flying close to the water. It lifted as it approached the head of the bay, then hovered over the grassy slope in front of the lodge before gently setting down, red paint and white lettering clearly visible against the dark water. Even before the rotors had come to rest, the doors slid open and four men wearing the insignia of the coast guard emerged.

"Get him inside." Gunter's voice was low and strained. "Get him out of sight—and let the men know. They will need to come out to see what is happening, otherwise it will look suspicious, but make sure there is no loose equipment left in there for these assholes to see."

Marty grabbed the captain's arm and pulled him close, ramming the gun up against his chest. "Come, my friend," he said. "Perhaps your luck has changed, but please don't think of doing anything stupid. I could shoot you before you took a single step." He pushed the dazed man ahead of him into the lodge.

Behind them, Gunter's footsteps crunched along the gravel path as he went down to greet the unwelcome visitors.

"Good afternoon, gentlemen. This is a surprise. How can I help you?"

Two of the coast guard crew were already heading down to the beach, where the small dinghy and the inflatable that had brought Fernandez and the captain rested side by side on the shingles. Neither boat carried the name of the ship they belonged to, but Gunter knew that was only a temporary reprieve: the big yacht tender he had used to bring the men over was still tied to the wharf, and while it also had no name, it did have a registration number.

"We're responding to a Mayday call." The man who replied was obviously the leader. His eyes met Gunter's briefly and then continued to scan the area. "We're looking for a man called Harry Coombs. He said he was abandoning his boat and planned to head this way." His voice held a question, and his gaze returned to Gunter as he waited for an answer. Behind him, two more men climbed out of the helicopter and headed toward the wharf.

"No one has come here." Gunter schooled his face to give no indication of surprise and fought to keep any trace of name recognition out of his voice. Fernandez had been very clear when he'd told him that Harry had been "taken care of permanently," so what the hell was going on here?

Thinking fast, Gunter improvised a story as he spoke. "We are just packing up our equipment. We have a crew boat coming to pick up some of the men." Gunter turned and gestured toward the lodge just as three of his men stepped out onto the deck and stood watching them. Marty had followed his orders, and the timing couldn't have been better. "It should be here very soon."

"Is that your boat at the wharf?"

It was a question Gunter had been hoping he wouldn't have to answer, but now he had no choice. "Yes."

"But you still need a crew boat?"

"We are sending some of the men to check out a possible site."

"So you're part of a logging outfit?"

Gunter shook his head. "Mining."

The man grunted an acknowledgment, then nodded down at the dinghies. "And those? Are they yours too?"

"Yes. We have them to get to shore, and the men use them for fishing also."

"Huh. And what exactly are you looking for again?"

Gunter was saved from having to answer by the swelling roar of an approaching motor, and the two men turned to look out at the channel just as the aluminum hull of a crew boat appeared around the point and made its way toward the wharf. The distraction provided him with a perfect opportunity to terminate the interrogation.

"I will leave you to your search, officer. I must get the men and equipment loaded. We are on a tight schedule and we do not have much time."

The man looked at him for a moment, then nodded. "Please keep a lookout. If you see any small boat out there, radio it in. Use channel twenty-six. We'll be monitoring it at all times."

Gunter nodded. "I wish you luck." He started back up the path, but not before he saw the officer turn toward the wharf and lift his radio to his mouth. He knew the man would check with the crew boat, but that was not a concern. The crew-boat captain knew nothing other than the fact that he was picking up a group of men. His arrival had helped to confirm Gunter's story, but they needed to move fast, before the coast guard decided to check out that registration number.

The canisters were lined up against the wall, closed and locked. The metal surfaces had a dull gleam, probably from their immersion in salt water, and a network of scratches showed as lighter glints.

It made them appear old and well-used, and as he looked at them, Gunter realized they were going to provide reinforcement for his story and be a benefit rather than a risk as the men loaded them onto the crew boat. They were exactly what would be expected from a group of research personnel who would have to have some highly technical and very sensitive equipment with them.

The men had followed him inside, and he beckoned to Alex and Marty. "Is all the equipment in there?"

Alex answered. "Yeah, but it ain't pretty. We just shoved it in wherever it would fit."

"That is not important. We can correct it later. Now we have to leave." He explained the story he had given to the coast guard. "Have the men carry the containers down to the crew boat and load them on. Tell them what I have told you. They are exploring for metal deposits. You go with them. Marty stays with me, but we will be only a few minutes."

Alex gave him a thin smile that didn't reach his eyes. "Gotcha." He moved over to the group of men standing near the door. "Okay, boys, let's lock and load."

Gunter turned to Marty. "Where is he?"

Marty nodded at a door that led off the main room. "He's in there. I tied him up so he couldn't make a noise."

"Do you have a silencer?"

Marty shook his head. "Not on me. It's packed with the other stuff."

Another thing gone wrong. Gunter thought for a moment. "We can not risk a gunshot, but we must stop him from getting their attention. Knock him out. Hit him hard. Make sure he stays out long enough for us to get away from here. After that, it will not matter. And be quick!"

Marty nodded and opened the door. There came the brief sound of his voice, followed by a sharp crack and the heavy thud of a body hitting the floor, and then he came back out, closing the door behind him. He looked at Gunter and shrugged. "He should be out for a long time. Maybe forever, if we're lucky."

Gunter nodded. "Good. Now we leave."

▶ The coast guard lieutenant watched them go as he waited for his team to finish its search of the bay. "Those guys look okay to you?" He was using his radio to talk to the pilot waiting in the chopper.

"Pretty standard bunch of loggers."

"Yeah, but they're not loggers. That white-haired guy said they were miners, some kind of researchers, looking for mineral deposits."

"Huh. Pretty late in the season to be out looking in this area. That stuff takes months."

"Yeah, that's what I'm thinking. And that white-haired guy was a bit odd. Cold. Sort of automatic. He was sure in a hurry to leave. Maybe too much of a hurry. Had an accent of some kind, maybe German or Austrian or something."

"Want me to call the ship and have them check them out?"

The lieutenant thought about it. What was it about the men that bothered him? He looked around the bay again and his eyes settled on the big tender that was still sitting at the wharf.

"Whitey told me they were sending some of the guys out, not all of them. It's odd they would leave the tender there and all take off in that crew boat. Can you read the registration on that tender? Might help to know who it belongs to."

"You got it."

The lieutenant caught the glint of sunlight on binocular lenses as the pilot leaned out to scan the lettering on the bow of the tender.

"Let me know when you have it. I'm going to go check out the building. Maybe there's something up there that can tell us a bit more."

▶ THIRTY-ONE ◀

▶ "Let's get out of here."

Dan pushed the dinghy out from the rocks and started the motor. He and Claire had watched the coast guard helicopter disappear over the top of Spider Island and the crew boat vanish around the bend of the channel that led to Shoal Bay, and now everything had fallen silent again.

"I figure even if Ponytail and White Hair both took off in that first chopper, the rest of them should be tied up there for quite a while. They couldn't take all those canisters with them. I wouldn't mind being over there myself to see what's happening with that crew boat." Dan was shouting over the sound of the motor, and Claire leaned toward him in an effort to hear what he was saying.

"Can you monitor the coast guard radio from your boat?" she yelled.

Dan shook his head. "No. They're on a different frequency."

His words were drowned in the rush of water and the howl of the motor, but the meaning was clear. She shook her head and touched her ear to show she couldn't hear him, then turned away to look out over the bow, watching the shore slip past and the channels open up as they ran south toward *Dreamspeaker*.

The cove he had anchored her in opened up, and they saw Walker even before they saw his canoe. He was sitting on the swim grid, his feet dangling above the water, watching their approach.

"Thought you must have got lost." He took the line Dan passed him and tied it off to the cleat.

"Nice to see you too, Walker." Dan pulled himself up onto the grid, then reached for Claire's hand and helped her out. "Did the boys all make it back home safe and sound?"

"Yep. They were all eating breakfast when I left. Percy sent some along for you." He lifted up what looked like a piece of cedar bark and passed it to Dan.

"What, you want me to eat trees now?"

Walker shook his head. "You've got to learn to look a little closer, white man. Look inside."

"Inside?" Dan turned the square of cedar in his hands and found the opening. It was a bag, made of thin strips of cedar bark, folded and woven with exquisite care. He slid his hand into the opening and brought out two strips of dried salmon. He passed a strip to Claire, who promptly chewed a piece off and said around a mouthful, "This is fantastic. Thanks, Walker."

"Yeah, thanks, man." Dan was enjoying his own mouthful. "And thank Percy for me."

"Will do, but it might be a while before I see him again." Walker smiled.

"Who's Percy?" Claire was looking back and forth between them. "And who are these boys you two are talking about?"

Dan stepped up onto the stern deck. "I'll let Walker fill you in. I've got to get on the radio." He walked away before either of them could protest. No way was he going to be the one to explain it all to Claire.

It took both persistence and time to reach Mike. Rosemary said he was in Vancouver overseeing security for some conference they were having there, and she patched him through to the temporary office that had been set up for the purpose. The desk guy at that office said Mike was over at the conference center and couldn't be reached. Dan said it was urgent, lied a little by giving his old rank, made a couple of vague threats, and was finally patched through to Mike's cell. By that time there was so much static on the connection that he could barely hear anything, but it was better than nothing.

"Dan? Where the hell are you? I can hardly hear you."

"Still up north. Look, we've got a major problem up here."

"You have a problem?" Mike was shouting into his phone, and behind him Dan could hear the sound of heavy traffic and people talking.

"Yeah. Two men dead, maybe three."

"What?"

"Murder." Dan spoke as clearly as he could, keeping it simple and hoping Mike could make it out.

"Murder? Did you say murder?"

"Yeah. Listen, can you get back to your office? We need to talk."

"You serious?"

"Yeah. Go. To. The. Office."

"The office? Oh, yeah. Okay. Give me five minutes, okay? Five minutes."

"Okay, I'll call you in five."

Five minutes later, Mike picked up the phone on the first ring.

"What the hell is going on? Did you say you had a murder up there?"

"Yeah. Actually, two of them and maybe a third."

"You gotta be shitting me! Are the marine boys there?"

"No, but they sure as hell should be. The coast guard's on site though."

Dan told Mike what had happened, giving him the sequence of events as he knew them but omitting the part about Walker and his friends maybe playing a role in sinking *Snow Queen*. He wasn't sure that had actually happened, and even if it had, he wanted to keep Walker out of it. His involvement would only confuse the issue.

"So where is this white-haired guy now?"

"I think he probably took off in that helicopter. You might be able to track it. It was blue, real dark blue, on the top, with a silver belly and a couple of turquoise stripes between. Had a bunch of lettering over the registration number, so I think it was a charter. Came in from the southwest and headed out in the same direction, so probably based on the north end of Vancouver Island."

"Okay, I'll have the guys check it out. What time did it take off from Spider Island?"

"Around two o'clock. The other guy might be in it too. The dark guy with the ponytail. He's the one who shot Harry, and he took the captain with him at gunpoint when he left *Snow Queen*."

"Shit! This is something I don't need right now. It's crazy down here."

"What's happening that's got you so worked up?"

"Hell. It's one of those United Nations/G8 things. Got everybody but God himself arriving here today, and all their goddamn lackeys and mumbo-jumbo artists got here last week. Even got a bunch of superstar assholes going to be doing a concert over at Rogers Arena in a couple of days. All we need now is for Oprah to drop in and really turn it into a circus."

"Sounds like you're having a good time."

"Yeah, right. Anyway, back to your stuff. You said the coast guard was there now?"

"They were when I left. They arrived about the same time as the crew boat and about five minutes after the blue chopper left."

"Huh. I'll call them and see what's happening. Stay by your radio. I'll call you back."

Dan stood and stared out over the water, the phone in his hand. Talking to Mike, giving him the basic facts of what had taken place over the last few days, had felt good. It had made him feel important, although that was too strong a word. Needed, maybe. Part of a team. It had taken him back all those months to when he had been a member of the force, one of the guys, contributing to something. It was a good feeling and he enjoyed the buzz it brought, but at the same time he realized it was a life he no longer wanted. And it wasn't because of Susan and the searing memories that anything to do with his old life usually evoked. It was more about Walker and Claire sitting out there on the stern. Even Annie and Tom were in there somewhere. They had taught him something. Changed something. He couldn't put it into words just yet, but it was there all the same. Something quiet and solid.

The radiophone chimed, interrupting his reverie. It was Mike.

"You got your VHF turned on?"

"Yeah."

"Switch to 83A. The coast guard wants to talk to you. Leave this open and we can have a three-way."

Dan turned the VHF to 83A. "*Dreamspeaker*."

"*Dreamspeaker*, this is the coast guard. Is that Dan Connor?"

"Yeah. Got Mike on the radiophone too."

"Okay. You reported a possible kidnapping. I think we've got the guy you said was kidnapped here with us. He says he's the captain of *Snow Queen*."

Dan inhaled a sharp breath, and a smile lit his face. "Is he okay?"

"Got a hell of a big lump on his head and a headache to go with it, but we've got him up and walking around. Took a while to figure out who he was, but now he's madder than hell."

"Can't say I blame him. You got anyone else there?"

"No. There was a bunch of guys here when we arrived. Odd-looking guy in charge. Had real white hair. Said they were doing some mining research. They looked okay, so we let them go. A crew boat came and got them."

"Shit! You know where they went?"

"No, but we're sure as hell going to find out. We've got the guys back at base trying to track the crew boat now, see where it came from."

"They have any canisters with them? Metal things maybe two, three feet long? Kind of bullet shaped?"

"Yeah." The guy's voice sounded wary. "We thought they were instruments of some kind. You telling me they're not?"

"I'm not sure what they have in them, but it's not instruments. More likely weapons."

"Guns?"

"Maybe. They looked like they were rehearsing some kind of raid when I was there, and it sounded like weapons being assembled."

"Don't have any bullets though." Walker had come into the wheelhouse so quietly that Dan hadn't heard him.

"What? How do you know that?"

Walker held out a bundle that was wrapped in a striped blanket.

210

"Took these from the canisters they left on the wharf." He put it down on the floor.

"Who's that you're talking to?" asked Mike.

"Hang on," Dan said to Walker. This was turning into a circus. "His name is Walker," Dan said to Mike. "He's the guy who called me."

"He was there with you? You didn't tell me that."

"No, he wasn't there. He . . . ah, shit! I'll let him explain later, but he's got a bunch of stuff here he says he got from some of the canisters." Dan glared at Walker as he spoke and received a raised eyebrow and a quiet smile in return. He shook his head in disgust. Walker had always had a knack for driving him crazy. He bent down and opened the blanket. A handful of bullets, all different calibers, gleamed brightly in the sunlight streaming in through the windshield, and a grenade lay beside a small metal canister. In the center was a bottle of what looked like cooking oil, a small spray bottle and a short fuse.

"What the fuck is this?" Dan couldn't quite understand what he was seeing.

"I asked the boys to keep one of everything and bring it all to me when they were done. This is it."

"The boys?"

"What have you got there?"

"Who's Walker?"

It was chaos. Everyone was talking at once, and Dan had no hope of figuring out who was who, let alone answering.

"Okay. Okay. Hang on a minute. I'm not quite sure what we've got here, but it doesn't matter. I'll figure it out and let you know, but right now the priority has to be finding these guys and stopping them before they kill anyone else."

"Yes, you're right." It was Mike speaking. "But you've got some explaining to do once we've got this sorted out. And make sure you stay put. We need you to show the marine guys where this Robbie guy is stashed."

"Yeah, yeah. I'm not going anywhere. Just find these assholes before they do anything else." Dan reached over and turned all the switches to standby.

▶ THIRTY-TWO ◀

▶ "They did what?" Dan lifted his gaze from the blanket with its weird array of objects to Walker's face. He had that *Alice in Wonderland* feeling again and he was the rabbit, falling down that fucking hole. Walker just grinned.

"You're telling me a bunch of punk kids sailed into Shoal Bay in the middle of the night, in a storm, and just emptied out all this shit into the water?"

"Paddled."

"What?"

"They paddled, not sailed."

"Jesus! Fine. They paddled. And then what?"

Walker shrugged. "They went home."

Dan let his breath out in a thin stream, fighting to retain both control and sanity.

"Okay. Fine. And what about *Snow Queen*? They sink her too?"

"No, that was me."

"That was you." God, he was back to the repeating thing. "What exactly did you do? Paddle up and pull the plug?"

"Nah. Stuck a knife up into one of the through-hulls. Jammed it open."

Dan shook his head, trying to clear it. "Walker, the through-hulls are underwater."

"Yeah, tell me about it. Damn near froze to death."

Dan stared at him. "You swam out to it? Are you nuts? You could have died. You should have hypothermia."

The three of them were sitting around the chart table in the wheelhouse, the items from the canisters spread out in front of them.

"Percy pulled me out and fixed me up."

Claire's face was painted with a mixture of amazement and disbelief, her eyes dark with concern. "You really swam out to that ship?"

Walker nodded. "Yeah."

"Was it you who wrapped that kelp around the prop?" she asked.

He grinned again. "Yeah. Worked, huh? Wasn't sure it would. Those were some crazy propellers. They were hung off some kind of pods. Looked a bit like those canisters, only bigger."

"Pods?" Another memory of the silent ship that had slipped past when he was anchored up north ran through Dan's mind. "I've read something about that. Some kind of new propulsion system. It's electric. Run by generators instead of a diesel. Bet that's why it was so quiet."

Walker nodded, suddenly serious. "Yeah. Before this all started, I kept getting this feeling there was something out there, but I couldn't see it or hear it. Must have been that ship."

"God, I hope they get them!" Claire shivered and wrapped her arms around herself. "They killed Robbie."

Dan leaned over and put his hand on her arm. "They'll get them," he said, and as if to confirm his words the radiotelephone peeled a demand.

"*Dreamspeaker.*"

"Dan, it's Mike. We've got them. Picked them up in Port Hardy. They were headed for Vancouver and stopped in there to refuel."

"You talking about the chopper or the crew boat?"

"The crew boat. Haven't tracked the chopper yet. We think it's a charter from West Coast Helicopters. They've got four different bases and it could have come from any of them, so it's taking a while to sort it out."

"Huh. Hope you find it. The main guys are probably on it."

"Well, we've got ten of them in Port Hardy and one of them has real short white hair. The guys up there say he might be German. Got a German name, anyway."

From the corner of his eye, Dan saw the flash of Claire's smile.

"Hey, that's great news. He's one of the kingpins. Anyone have a ponytail? Black hair, pulled back tight?"

"Nope. The rest look like poster boys for a mercenary-recruiting campaign. We think one guy might be from the Middle East somewhere, and maybe a couple more are Hispanic. No ponytails."

"Huh. So Ponytail is still on the loose, and he's the one who shot Harry."

"We're looking, believe me." The intensity in Mike's voice reinforced what he was saying.

"You get the canisters?" Dan asked.

"Yeah. You were right. They had weapons, but here's the really weird thing. The guys are checking them all out now, but it looks like most of them were fakes."

"Fakes?" Jesus, he was doing the repeating thing with Mike now.

"Yeah. The guns are the real thing—AK47s mostly. But the bullets are blanks. Don't know about the grenades yet. They've got the bomb squad coming in to check those."

"Shit! That's crazy. Doesn't make any sense. Why would they go to all this trouble for fakes?"

Behind him he heard Claire say, "It wasn't a fake bullet that killed Harry."

"Yeah. Good point. Did you hear that? Claire says that it wasn't a fake bullet that killed Harry. Wasn't an accident that got her boss Robbie either."

"Claire? Jesus, you having a party up there? First Walker, now Claire. How many people you got with you?"

Dan smiled. "Just the three of us. But back to the bad guys. You've got to find a way to hold them even if the stuff is fake."

"Oh, we'll be holding them. The white-haired guy and two of his pals had the real thing on them, guns and bullets, and none of the weapons are registered. Plus, that guy the coast guard found has an interesting story to tell. We're flying him down now."

"He the captain of the black ship? *Snow Queen*?"

"That's what he says. Guess we'll find out soon enough."

"Yeah. Doesn't sound good, them heading down your way and that UN thing going on. But those fake weapons . . . I dunno about that. Glad I'm not you though."

"Gee, thanks!" Mike signed off with yet another caution about not going anywhere, and Dan turned to find Walker looking at him oddly.

"They were in a crew boat?" he asked.

Dan nodded. "Yeah. Don't know where they'd been because there wasn't any crew boat with the black ship when we saw it, but Claire and I saw it head in to Shoal Bay just after the coast guard got there."

"Couldn't have been the same crew boat."

"Why the hell not? Had to be. How many crew boats are there around here this time of year?"

Walker was shaking his head. "Don't know about that, but the boys took care of the one that was tied up to the black ship."

Dan sat down carefully, working hard to bite off the urge to repeat Walker's words yet again.

"Really. And just how did they do that? Please tell me they didn't just swim out and sink it."

Walker's face crinkled into that same aggravating grin. "Nope. Said they just climbed on board and put a little seawater in the gas tanks. Gonna take a pretty big overhaul before those engines run again."

Dan sighed. "Right. Of course. Why didn't I think of that?"

A peal of laughter raced around the sunlit space and the men both turned to look at Claire.

"What's so damned funny?" Dan asked.

"You!" she answered, fighting for breath. "You should have seen your face when Walker was talking."

"Yeah, well . . ." He struggled between indignation and justification, searching for the words he needed to convey what he was feeling. Finally, he had to settle on simple amusement.

"You've got to admit it *is* a pretty amazing story. Here I am, trying to get the marine guys in here, trying to figure out how to call in markers and arrange satellite surveillance and all kinds of high-tech shit, using some fancy restricted radio to contact some pretty important people, and Walker and his friends paddle over in a bunch of goddamn canoes, jump into the ocean, and solve the problem." He chuckled. "I guess there's some kind of moral to this story—maybe 'the simplest way is the best way' or 'don't use a cannon to swat a fly,' or something."

Walker shrugged. "We just did what we needed to."

Dan nodded. "And it worked."

"But they still have to catch that other guy." Claire's smile had disappeared. "He could still be planning something."

"Pretty hard to do anything without your crew and your weapons," Walker said.

"Yeah," Dan agreed. "But I keep thinking about those damn blanks." He looked back at the stuff spread out on the chart table, rolled a bullet around with his finger, and then picked up a spray bottle and held it up to the light. "What if that whole crew of men and all their weapons were just to create a diversion? Maybe cause a little panic and take attention away from the main event? Don't need real stuff to do that and there's no risk of getting caught before the main event. The men wouldn't even have to know. Probably wouldn't. But it would create panic and pull all the security and cops out to deal with it. Then one guy on his own could deal with the real target."

There was complete silence in the wheelhouse as they all considered the idea, and then Dan voiced what they were all thinking.

"Oh shit!" he said and pushed himself up from the table to run for the radio.

THIRTY-THREE

▶ Nasiri sat at the desk in his hotel room, watching the slow dusk creep over the city, muting the colors of cars and pedestrians and trees and buildings till it all took on the soft gray haze of evening. There was nothing left to be done. He was ready. Yesterday he had broken down his weapon, cleaned and reassembled it, and broken it down again. He had then carefully placed the various parts into the specially designed compartments of his Italian leather briefcase. That same briefcase was now stored in a very secure "safe" room at the offices of Mr. Jason Bainbridge, the financial broker with whom he had an appointment the next morning. The beautifully groomed secretary who had put it there for him had even taken him in to show him just how safe it was. It was not an unusual request, she reassured him. Many of their clients asked that their important documents be placed somewhere for safekeeping until they could meet with their broker. It was a service they were glad to offer and certainly not an imposition.

"Actually," she had said, her voice taking on a note of disapproval, "we probably should have asked all tomorrow's clients to do the same. We've been told there's going to be security screening for everyone coming into the building." She moved from disapproval to indignation. "They're even going to check the staff!"

"For what reason?" Nasiri had injected an appropriate amount of surprise into the question. "Has there been some kind of problem?"

"Oh, no! Nothing that is of concern," she'd reassured him. Lifting a thin, pale hand, she'd pointed a red-tipped finger out toward the wood-and-glass building across the street. "There's a big international conference going on over there and they have some VIPs coming in. Probably politicians." The disapproval had returned. "It's just the inconvenience! I can't imagine how we can possibly keep all our appointments on schedule if they're going to check everyone."

"I see. Well, perhaps I will make sure that I arrive a little early," Nasiri had said. "I would not want to be late for my appointment."

Thinking about the conversation, Nasiri smiled. He would indeed be early. He needed a little extra time to take care of Mr. Bainbridge before Fernandez's men began their little charade out front and the panic started. He needed to be ready when all those security forces rushed to evacuate their important guests.

▶ The Bell 206 helicopter skimmed over the turbulent waters of Seymour Narrows and turned toward the long spit of land that curved out into Discovery Channel just north of the city of Campbell River. It hovered briefly over a strip of marshy grassland, then settled gently onto the tarmac in front of a squat gray building. A sign out front announced it as the home of West Coast Helicopters.

The pilot removed his headset and turned to address his passengers. "We'll be on the ground for about twenty minutes, folks. There's coffee and snacks inside. I'll come and get you as soon as we're finished refueling. Should be about an hour's flying time down to Vancouver."

Fernandez opened his door and nodded for the other two to join him. The sooner they reached the sprawling metropolis that was their destination, the better. More than enough things had gone wrong today. He didn't need anything else.

He scanned the heliport as they walked toward the building. The place looked almost deserted. There was a single chopper way over on the other side of the tarmac in front of another building, but other than that all he could see were some float planes at a dock out on the water. Either business was booming and everybody was out or they were shutting down for the season. He pushed open the door and entered the office. It consisted of one large open space that, like the runway and aprons outside, was mostly empty except for a single agent working behind the counter. The man looked up at them briefly and then returned to what he had been doing.

A stainless steel brewing machine with a confusing array of lights and spigots sat against the back wall. On the counter next to it was a basket of fresh fruit and a plate of muffins and cookies wrapped in plastic. The three men moved toward it in unison. None of them had eaten since the night before, and the prospect of coffee and food was irresistible.

The faint click of the door closing behind them was almost indistinguishable from the sound of their footsteps as they crossed the tiled floor. Fernandez glanced back, thinking perhaps the pilot had followed them in, but there was no one. Must have been the wind. It was only after he had made himself a cup of coffee that he noticed the desk clerk had disappeared. That must have been what he'd heard.

The other two took their drinks over to a cluster of armchairs grouped around a low table in the center of the room, but Fernandez moved back to the wide glass windows that overlooked the terminal. His mind would not let him relax. He had to figure out what was going on. They were so close to their deadline. He could not let something get in the way now. Everything had been going perfectly and then, suddenly, they had been sabotaged. And it had to have been sabotage. Nothing else made sense. But by whom? Harry? Not likely. He had been a willing party in the plan almost from the beginning and would have stood to lose a great deal of money. Besides, he couldn't have called in the coast guard. He was already dead.

The captain? Possibly, but he had no reason to sink his own ship and he had been with Fernandez from the time the propellers had been fouled until the men left in the dinghy. The coast guard had to have been called after that. That left his own men, and they would have already been over in Shoal Bay and wouldn't have known there was a problem on *Snow Queen*. Besides, only Alex and Gunter had had access to a radio. It didn't make sense. There was something he was missing and he needed to figure it out fast.

Movement caught his eye. A tanker truck was moving slowly across the tarmac in the direction of the helicopter, but there was no other sign of life. He scanned the view again, then came back and sat down. Another hour or so and they would be at the warehouse, preparing the weapons.

He was just reaching for his coffee when he heard another soft click, and the room was suddenly filled with the pounding of heavy boots and screaming voices yelling instructions to get down on the floor. It happened so fast, he had no chance to react. Within seconds the three men were surrounded by an emergency response team in full combat gear and heavily armed with MP5 submachine guns, all of which were trained on their targets. Fernandez closed his eyes as handcuffs were snapped around his wrists. The pain of failure was almost physical, but it was nothing compared to what he knew would happen when his boss found out.

▶ "We got them."

Mike's voice, distorted by distance and the speakers, still conveyed both relief and pride. "Picked them up at the heliport in Campbell River. Pilot said they were headed for Vancouver."

"That's great news." Dan was staring out the windshield, watching the marine-police catamaran nose carefully into the cove.

"Yeah," said Mike. "Now I just have to figure out what the hell they were planning."

"Gonna be hard for them to do anything now, without their people or their equipment."

"I don't know. Still doesn't feel right. None of it makes any sense. Only two of the guys on the crew boat were armed, and that was just handguns. Nothing with any range or power. And one of the guys from the helicopter—the one with the ponytail—had a gun, but there isn't much else and most of it is not operational. There has to be something else. It was way too big an operation, way too much planning, for what we've got here. They wouldn't have had a chance of getting through security."

"Maybe they weren't aiming for the conference."

"Maybe." Mike wasn't convinced. "But everything points to that and the timing's right. Shit! I'm not going to be able to sleep till the whole bloody thing is over. There're some pretty big targets there tomorrow."

"Yeah. It does seem weird. Wish I could help you more, but I think we're done up here. Only thing left is I've got to go with Hargreaves and show him where we left Robbie."

"Right. Poor bastard—Robbie, not you. You taking Walker with you?"

Dan laughed. "Thanks. And no, I think I'm going to try to keep Walker as far away from Hargreaves as I can. Don't think the two of them would be a good mix."

"Sounds like an interesting guy."

"Yeah," said Dan, realizing as he said it the truth of that statement. "He is."

▶ Mike remained at his desk for a while after Dan had hung up, thinking, allowing his mind to wander, letting all the pieces float. It was something he had learned from Dan and he needed it to work now. Needed to get Dan back on the force too, but that was a whole other story, and he could deal with it later. Right now there was a piece of this puzzle he was missing. Had to be. But what the hell was it?

He got up and wandered onto the concourse. The lights were coming on in the buildings that lined Burrard and West Cordova Streets, and he could feel the mood of the city changing as night descended. The last cruise ship of the season had departed a couple of weeks ago, and the restaurants and bars around the walkway there were filled with the end-of-workday rush. They would all be closed tomorrow morning and the walkway would be shut down with solid barricades to prevent access.

He turned away and walked back toward the ocean. The ferries that connected the north and south shores threw dancing shards of yellow light on the water as they moved across the inlet. They were too far away to be a serious concern, and each one would have its own security detail anyway. Closer in, there were a few pleasure boats out on the water, stragglers heading back into Coal Harbour marina after a day out on the water, but by tomorrow morning the marina would be closed off, all the would-be sailors kept at the dock by a flotilla of police boats.

To the west, Harbour Green Park was dark, only the leaves of the trees along the pathways visible in the yellow light of the lamp standards. It too would be sealed off in the morning, and although the traffic on Lions Gate Bridge would continue to thunder across the narrow span that linked the cities of the north and south shores, there could be no threat from there. Not only was the distance wrong, but pedestrian access would be closed and the traffic moving too fast. If there was any interruption there, helicopter patrols would be there in an instant.

That left the streets and buildings, and the streets would all be sealed off, traffic diverted well before it reached the area. So what was left? Only the buildings, and except for the cruise-ship terminal, which was closed down, the rest were five-star hotels, and few were positioned in such a way that windows overlooked the entrance to the conference center. Those that were had either locked off the rooms or were hosting the VIPs themselves, and all were subject to intense security. What did that leave?

Damn it! He was missing something. He had to be. He tried to picture the street as it would look the following day. There would be crowds of onlookers clustered behind the barricades that had been set up. Some would be protesters: loud, restless, quick to react, and easy to provoke. It would be easy to get something going there, but why? Some kind of diversion? That would mean something happening somewhere else. A kidnap attempt? That would need a car, and it couldn't get in. A marksman? But where would a sniper set up?

Mike ran through the drill again as he circled the convention center for a third time. He was walking south toward the emergency exit when his eyes drifted over to the Fairmont Pacific Rim, one of those five-star hotels surrounding the convention center. It had no windows overlooking the entrance, but it was the only one that had a direct view to the east side and the emergency exit. His gaze drifted upward. Twelve stories of luxury suites, all thoroughly checked and the guests cleared, and all the rooms with heavy, sealed glass windows. Above them, the offices of the top financial firm in the city. He had thought about closing it down for the day, but pressure from the local politicos and the big-money boys had finally convinced him to let it stay open. He opted instead to scrutinize the appointments list and implement security screening.

The windows of the building faced west, and the lights had been turned off. As night fell, row upon row of dark glass reflected the glittering lights of the North Shore and the traffic on Lions Gate Bridge, each row a perfect replica of the one below it. Except for the top floor. Three of the windows there showed a sharp break in the pattern that created a distortion. Mike stared at them, his heart picking up speed as adrenalin surged into his bloodstream. Those would be the partner's suites, large and impressive and with a stunning view overlooking the water. Each had a tracery of ornate wrought iron in front of it where the occupant could step out onto a miniscule balcony and take in that view, maybe impress his clients with it. And that meant that the windows opened. That was why there was break in the reflections. It was caused by the frame. Shit!

Mike pulled out his phone and pressed a button, his eyes still fixed on those high windows. "Get a team together and meet me over at the Fairmont Pacific Rim. And get one of the partners of that financial firm down here, I don't care which one. We need to go in now."

► THIRTY-FOUR ◄

► Dan and Walker sat together in the cockpit, watching the police boat approach. It rode high in the water, its twin hulls carving identical wakes that streamed out behind in a ribbon of foam.

"You want to come along and help show them where Robbie is?"

It was the last thing Dan wanted, but he thought he was right in assuming Walker's answer would be the one he hoped for. In any case, he had to ask. Walker had become both a friend and a partner, and Dan had learned that it was never wise to make any assumptions about his choices. Walker would make his own decisions.

"Nope." Walker glanced toward the stern, where Claire was standing. "Don't think she should be alone. Too many memories."

Dan nodded. He too had noticed Claire grow quiet and withdraw into herself as Hargreaves and his team approached. She knew why they were coming.

"Yeah. Probably a good idea. It only needs one of us anyway."

He was more than happy to have Walker and Hargreaves stay as far away from each other as possible. He couldn't imagine two more different personalities and he figured they would be a bad mix, each of them reacting and pushing the other into more and more antagonistic behavior. Hargreaves's prejudice ran just beneath the surface. Dan had heard it and Walker would recognize it in an instant. In different circumstances, their meeting might end in either a shouting match or a fist fight, but not here. Here, Hargreaves was in charge, and that could only end badly for Walker.

And if he was honest, there was a selfish piece too. It wasn't just about Hargreaves and Walker. Dan thought that any meeting between the two men would inevitably end up in some very uncomfortable questions being directed at him, and considering Hargreaves's authority, he would be required to answer them. And he didn't feel like doing that. Hell, he wasn't even sure that he could answer them if he wanted to. He didn't really know the answers himself.

As it turned out, Hargreaves was perfectly happy to leave both Walker and Claire behind. In fact, Dan was pretty sure that if the man hadn't needed to have someone point out the exact location of Robbie's body, he would have been happy to leave Dan behind too. Inviting a civilian onto his ship—and Hargreaves made it very clear that he thought of Dan as a civilian—was not in the rule book, and that made it something Hargreaves was far from happy about.

The recovery was both quicker and easier than Dan had expected. He joined three of Hargreaves's team in one of the big inflatables and they slid the boat down a ramp and into the water. Dan had already shown them the general location on a chart in the wheelhouse, so they knew where they were going and didn't waste any time. The trip was both fast and rough. The boat could travel at nearly forty knots and the hull bounced off the top of each wave, jolting every bone in his body. In less than half an hour they were flying past the now familiar cove where Tom had his shack, and bare seconds after that they were slowing, settling down in the water, bringing the blur of the shoreline into focus so that he could identify the exact place on the bank where he and Walker had left Robbie's body.

"There!"

He pointed to the jumbled pile of rocks he and Walker had put in place to protect Robbie. They were just as they had left them, the exposed limestone pale in the weak sunlight and out of place on the darker shale of the ledge.

Dan wasn't asked to take part in the retrieval itself. He was not part of the recovery team, and he hadn't expected to be involved. He was content to stay in the boat and simply sit and watch. His job was over.

It was quiet on the water except for the occasional murmur of voices drifting down, and the silence lulled him, pulled his mind back over the events of the past few days. So much had happened. So many lives had been lost or changed forever. He thought—hoped—that it was finished, the bad guys caught, their plans defused, but he really didn't know. Didn't even know what their plans had been. A few months ago, he would have been crazy with adrenalin, his mind racing to sort it all out, tie everything together. Now it didn't bother him. He had done what he could do and it was okay.

He thought he heard a whisper of sound flow through the air and he turned his head to catch it, but it was his heart, not his ear, that had heard. He felt his spirit lift as it once again responded to the remembered rhythm of Walker's chant, echoing it back to the land and the sea and the wide sky. It was finished. The circle was closed. Even when Robbie's remains had been removed, Walker's one simple, primeval act of grace and generosity would ensure that this lonely burial site remained a spiritual place where memories of a life would linger.

The return trip was a slower and more somber affair, with a black body bag occupying most of the floor space in the dinghy and all of their thoughts.

▶   Walker left shortly after Dan's return. He and Claire were standing out on the grid, leaning against the transom as they watched him approach. Walker had worked his magic again. The two of them were both relaxed and laughing, completely at ease. He raised an eyebrow as he caught Dan's eye, seeking an answer but not wanting to ask the question out loud. Dan nodded. It was done. Robbie was on his way home.

"You going to head south?" Walker asked as he leaned forward and peered down at the water running past the swim grid.

"Yeah," Dan answered. "Probably leave tomorrow. We'll head over to Half Moon Cove first. Have a look at Claire's boat."

"Huh." Walker nodded. "Think you can find your way? Don't want to have to send the boys out looking for you."

He grinned and Dan couldn't help laughing.

"Yeah, Walker, I can find my way. And thank those boys for me. They did a helluva job."

Walker shook his head. "No thanks required. They didn't do it for you." He was still smiling, but his eyes, fixed steadily on Dan, carried a message.

"Yeah, I know. But thank them anyway."

Walker nodded as he untied the line holding his canoe and pulled it up to the grid. The currents that he used to carry him around the islands like a private highway were already running hard.

"*Halakas'la.*"

"Goodbye, Walker. Be safe." Claire stepped forward and wrapped her arms around him. He straightened, his body stiffening in surprise, and his eyes sought Dan's as fear and pleasure warred on his face. Dan grinned at his discomfort but said nothing, and slowly Walker's arms raised to enfold Claire's slight body and his chin settled on the top of her head.

They stood there for a moment and then Claire raised her head to look up at him.

"I'll be back, you know. I don't know how or when, but I'm coming back up here. And I plan on finding you again so we can spend some more time together. Talk some more."

It was Walker's turn to smile. "Sounds good. I'd like that."

He looked at Dan. "You planning on coming back too?"

"Yes," said Dan. It was a spontaneous response. He hadn't even thought about it, but he knew as he said it that it was true. He would be back. And soon. "Yes, I will. Maybe next year."

"Make sure you bring some of those chocolate-chip cookies for Annie."

Dan laughed. "I'll bring her a whole case of them."

Dan and Claire stood and watched as Walker lowered himself awkwardly from the swim grid using his powerful arms, twisting his body into the waiting canoe. He lifted his hand in a brief wave, then pushed off and let himself drift out into the fast-flowing current. The last they saw of him was the stern of his canoe as it disappeared around the point, heading east.

Dan hauled anchor early the following morning and pointed *Dreamspeaker* north. Claire stood beside him at the wheel as they motored back past a silent and empty Shoal Bay. He felt her tense as the wharf came into view, a faint tremor that pulled her body taut, and he reached out and pulled her to his side.

She looked up at him and smiled. "It's okay. I'm fine. It's just hard to believe it all happened. *Island Girl* and Robbie . . ."

"I know. But it's over. They've caught them."

She nodded, but she didn't pull away and gradually her body curved against him, fitting itself to his side.

In Half Moon Cove, winds and tides had dragged *Island Girl* into deeper water, but part of her port-side deck and the upper side of her cabin were still exposed. Dan and Claire climbed into the dinghy and spent a few hours checking out what they could see, peering through the water and in through the portholes. There wasn't much: a few cushions were floating and the tops of a row of books were barely visible, misshapen and swollen but still in place on their shelf. Everything else was hidden beneath a scum of debris that covered the surface, riding on the waves that lapped against the roof. There was nothing that could be salvaged, and by late afternoon Claire had had enough. She sat back in the dinghy, stretched her shoulders, and looked up at him.

"Well, at least I learned a lot. Should make it easier the next time around—if there is a next time."

Dan smiled. "Oh, there'll be a next time. You're way too good to lose."

She frowned at him, searching for a double meaning, but he kept his face bland as he reached for the motor.

"How about we go over and get your kayak? We can anchor in that little cove and get an early start tomorrow morning."

She nodded in agreement. "Sounds good."

▶ She called her insurance company on the radiophone as soon as they got back on board *Dreamspeaker* and asked if it would pay to refloat the vessel. The agent told her it was a possibility, but they couldn't make any promises: it was going to take time for them to verify the condition of the boat and make their decision. They asked her to call them again when she reached Victoria. She signed off, put the microphone back in its bracket, and stood quietly, staring out the window to where the waves lapped against the coaming of her boat.

"You okay?" Dan moved up behind her and pulled her back against him, letting his chin rest gently on her head.

"Yes," she said, her voice soft. "I was just saying goodbye."

▶ They made love that night as they motored slowly south. A following breeze added an easy swell to their passage and a canopy of stars lit their way, pulsing and brilliant against the black infinity of the universe above. There was a rightness, a sense of shared experience, even an inevitability that pulled them naturally toward each other. A gentle coming together of two people who had been drawn close by circumstance and bonded by loss. Whether it would become anything more than that was uncertain, but for now, it was perfect.

Claire left three days later, the morning after they arrived in Victoria. She said she was going to go up to Nanaimo and report to the Marine Institute. She told him that she needed to explain the loss of her research. She said she needed to tell them what had happened to Robbie. She said she wanted to talk face-to-face with the people who knew him. She said she had to see if there was any possibility of getting another contract. She said she needed to check in with the insurance people. She didn't say she was coming back. She didn't promise to return. He didn't ask her. But they both knew the invitation was open.

▶ A few hours after Claire had left, Mike arrived, exhausted but exhilarated, his face pale and etched with fatigue but a broad smile lighting up the pallor. He had flown back from Vancouver earlier that morning and had come straight down to the wharf.

Dan stood up and reached out his hand. "Congratulations."

"Wouldn't have got him without you. And even after we picked them up, I still figured we had everything covered—till you started rambling on about 'there's gotta be more' and 'something else.'"

"Hey! Anyway, it wasn't me. Walker's the one you gotta thank."

"Yes, I'd like to meet him sometime. Sounds like quite a guy."

"He is, but I'm not sure about the meeting part. He's hard to find. Keeps pretty much to himself."

"Yeah, well, if you run into him again, tell him thanks. Could have been very nasty if we hadn't caught the guy."

"Who was he? Anyone I know?"

"Could be. We think he's Nasiri."

Dan inhaled a sharp breath. Nasiri had been at the top of their Red List for years, possibly one of the most wanted terrorists in the world and responsible for at least seven assassinations.

"Jesus!"

Mike grinned. "Yep. Mohammed ibn Saleh ibn Tariq al-Nasiri himself. He's got passports from Italy and Spain and Colombia, even Mexico, in every name you can think of—except Mohammed, of course—but we've got a guy from Interpol on his way here now and they're pretty sure it's him."

"That's great. How the hell did you find him?"

"Like I said, I thought we had it all figured out, then you got me thinking. If they were planning to create a diversion, the real threat had to be somewhere else. The only thing that made sense was a sniper set up somewhere, but we had all the rooftops closed off, everything shut down—and then I saw those fucking opening windows up there on the top floor of the Fairmont, and they looked right out over the emergency exit. Exactly where we would be evacuating the VIPs. I still can't believe I hadn't noticed them before. Henshaw's gonna kick my ass when I get back to the office. And the goddamned thing is, I deserve it."

"Mike, you're the one who figured it out. And you caught a bad guy that even Interpol hasn't been able to catch. Hell, half the forces in the world have been trying to catch him for years. Don't think you have too much to worry about. They'll probably give you a commendation."

They spent a few more minutes bullshitting and then Mike brought Dan up to speed on exactly what had happened. He had called in a team to search the financial firm, and it had discovered a briefcase that had been left there the day before. Mike called in the crime-scene boys to check it out, and they found a rifle, carefully broken down and hidden under a stack of bearer bonds. There had been enough prints on it to fill an album. He figured those alone should be enough to nail Nasiri.

"I called Henshaw. Got him out of bed. He wanted me to take everything and shut the building down. Asshole! We never would have got the guy." Mike shook his head. "Maybe sitting at a desk turns your brain to mush. Anyway, I told him I was going to have the boys remove the rifle and put everything else back in. Put a whole SWAT team into the offices on either side and have Henderson stand in for Bainbridge. Henshaw wasn't too happy about it, but he finally came round. The partners weren't too happy about it either, but they agreed. We had them tell the receptionist that Bainbridge was ill, but to keep it to herself. Not to say anything about it to Nasiri. The rest was easy. The son of a bitch just walked right in, exactly on schedule. The girl did real good. She knew our guys were there, but she just gave him his briefcase and the team took him down. They had him out of there in less than ten minutes."

Mike's face had been lit up with animation as he relived the story, but as he came to the end, the pallor reappeared. The stress of the last few days was catching up with him and Dan cut him short.

"You're out on your feet, Mike. Go home. Get some sleep. I'm here for the winter. Come on over in a couple of days and we'll have a few beers."

"Sounds good." Mike stood up to go, then turned back. "That really was good work you did out there. You should think about coming back."

Dan smiled and shook his head. "Like I told you, that wasn't me."

"Yeah, well, I'm looking forward to hearing about Walker, but you think about it anyway. You're good. We need guys like you."

Dan smiled and watched him stumble up the ramp to his car, then went back into the cabin. It was good to be talking to Mike again. Good to be back at the marina and good to have friends around. Certainly better than he would have believed possible a year ago. But it wasn't perfect—at least, not yet. There was still something missing.

▶ That something arrived a week later. He was sitting out on the stern deck, watching the constant movement of boats and people, letting the noise and bustle of the city wash over him. There had been a pretty constant stream of visitors since his return and he hadn't had much time to relax. People on the dock had dropped in to welcome him. Mike had been back several times, and most of the guys from the squad had dropped by to say hello. They had all made it clear they would love to have him come back, but he still wasn't ready to think about that. Didn't know if he ever would be.

The docks were crowded, and for the first time in a week, the clouds lifted and sunlight gilded the water. It reflected off the rigging and shone along the railings, bringing the marina to life. It warmed the flowers that filled the planter boxes on the houseboat moored in front of him and danced across the lawns that edged the waterfront. It shone on Claire's hair as she walked down the ramp, and as he watched her walk along the float toward him he felt a smile growing from somewhere deep inside.

"Hi," she said, looking up at him. "Any openings for a deckhand?"

"Nope," he answered, the smile now encompassing his whole being. "But I do happen to have another position open if you're interested, and I think you might be perfect for it."

She laughed. "Oh yes, I'm interested," she said as she reached out her hand and let him help her aboard.

ACKNOWLEDGMENTS

Special thanks to Bruce, Vivien, Michael, Pearl, Barb, and the wonderful people of Alert Bay, Klemtu, and Bella Coola, all of whom have taught me more than they could ever imagine.

Thanks also to Lynne, Virginia, Gale, Margie, Marci, and Ada for their gentle prodding.

And to all my relations: *gilakas'la*.

R.J. MCMILLEN has written for various publications, including *Pacific Yachting*, *Greyzine*, and *Season Magazine*. She is a traveler: a nomad of sorts. Born in England and raised in Australia, she spent three years working in Greece before meeting her Irish Canadian husband and moving to Canada. Three children and seven grandchildren later, she now divides her time between British Columbia and Mexico, where she shares a house with four dogs, several noisy parakeets, and an ever-increasing number of fish.